The Kiss Off

Stephen Larkin

For Mom and Dad

1

The heat bore down on the city in relentless waves. Young boys, enjoying the summer as only young boys can, ran, played stickball, and swam in the river. Men and women moved about wrapped in the oppressive heat and humidity that was the summer of 1930. Their emotion drained, as they walked the city hoping in vain for a cool breeze.

Away from the city, cars had begun pulling up to a pier, where a party boat would soon depart for the coolness of the open sea. People arriving grew more animated as they walked up the gangplank, onto the deck of the *Robert Forster*. The breeze off the water was refreshing and steady, the people began to drink and chat among themselves. A quartet began to play the popular songs of the day.

A taxi pulled up to the dock. As the doors opened, two young women stepped out, eyeing the sleek vessel moored at the dock. The attractive women, dressed in their most elegant attire, gazed about, then looked at each other and smiled.

"I told you this would be a time, Leeny."

The other girl nodded, turning to her friend, "We're still in port, Geri."

"I know. Just wait 'til we're on the water; you'll like it."

A few of the young men, standing on the deck eyed the young women with interest, as they moved quickly towards the ship.

A black sedan pulled up behind the now-departing taxi in which the two women had arrived. The sedan parked off to the side, amongst other vehicles. The door opened, and a tall, physically impressive, man dressed in a business suit stepped out onto the pavement. Pulling the brim of his hat down over his eyes, he glanced about at the revelers, his eyes stopping at the two women as they made their way onto the ship. His face portraying a momentary look of annoyance, he started towards the ship, walking with a noticeable limp. The other people, noting the approach of the large man, cleared a path for him.

Walking up onto the ship, the man paid his fare and then moved towards a vacant area of deck. Moving casually, his eyes were everywhere as he searched for the young women. Noticing that they were engaged in conversation with some young men, laughing and at ease, he relaxed.

The deck lights dimmed as the ship's whistle gave a long call. The deck hands began to remove the gangplank, preparing for departure, while the people on board began to cheer. The man, standing a good head above all the others, kept to the shadows. The young people looking forward to a good time were soon oblivious to the tall stranger.

He edged closer towards the young women, sipping a drink and listening to their conversation.

"Brian and I work for Chase Manhattan Bank. We're loan officers."

The other woman laughed. "I'm Geri and this is my friend Eileen."

Eileen, with her fair complexion, engaging smile and her long blond hair, could only be described as beautiful. Her smile could melt any man's heart, while her dark green eyes caught and held their attention. The other woman had set her sights on the shorter of the two men, moving in closer to him. His friend, noting this development, focused his attention on Eileen, although she seemed distracted, and her efforts at conversation were slightly strained.

The ship, having pulled away from the pier, was quickly making its way out to the open sea.

The tall man positioned himself in a quiet corner, continuing to observe the young women. He was pleased to note that Eileen's friend seemed to be growing more preoccupied with her companion, Eileen seeming marginally interested in her young man.

The tall man turned, staring out the window at the darkening ocean. As a young man he had spent some time at sea. Looking to the south, he noted the darkening sky, thinking perhaps that a turn of the weather might suit his purpose. As he stared out the window, his senses were keenly attuned to the four young people under his watch. Catching snippets of conversation, he grew annoyed that the young woman had now begun to drink.

This would make her unpredictable.

He had taken pains to ensure that no one would recall the older man with the slight limp, counting on his ability to blend into a crowd. On the boat, among the younger crowd were a few older couples. With Prohibition having been in place for many years, older couples took advantage of opportunities to have a drink, too. Sipping his drink, he casually smiled at a woman walking past him. Turning to glance at his quarry, he observed the other woman and man were quite entwined and the object of his attention was speaking with the man's friend, who now appeared to be growing intoxicated.

Relaxing, the tall man recalled hunting with his father, and the lesson of patience when tracking prey that he was told repeatedly by that stern, demanding man. He had learned to forget the beatings and the cruel discipline, trying like a good son to remember the rare happy times of his youth.

On the bridge of the *Robert Forster*, the captain scanned the water, navigating his vessel out to sea. His instructions were explicit: only an existing severe storm could prevent him from leaving port. Taking note of the cloudy sky, he addressed his first mate, "Mr. Vetter, steer south by southwest; maintain speed." The slim man at the wheel replied, "South by southwest, aye sir." Hearing the music from below, the captain hoped these people wouldn't be in for a rough night.

On the deck below, people stood at the rail, taking advantage of the cool breeze. Some stared at the city lights receding in the distance, happy to be away from the heat, even if just for a short time.

Soon after, a steady mist began to fall. The swells of the ocean rose higher, forcing the revelers to make their way inside.

Eileen O'Sullivan stared at her friend, in conversation with her companion, ignoring her. Looking back at the young man with whom she had been speaking, she saw that he was now engaged in conversation with a group of men about sports, hearing references to the New York Yankees. Standing alone, feeling the movement of the ship, her thoughts turned to her childhood in Ireland.

Her father had been a fishing captain in Galway. It was a hard life but she had loved it. Her mother had died shortly after giving birth to her; while her father, brokenhearted, never remarried. Without sons, he had taken her aboard his craft, seeking to teach her of life on the sea. She tried, but lacking the physical strength, he decided to put her ashore and hire a mate. This had stretched their already meager finances.

She tried to help out by getting work in Brady's Pub on the Claddagh Quay. An unexpected storm, which had sunk five vessels including her fathers, was what started her on her journey to America. Big Jack Brady, the pub owner, had sponsored her ticket to America, arranging for her to have employment with a friend. Eileen had left Ireland with grand hopes for her future, which had been cruelly dashed when Brady's friend had tried to rape her. Fleeing his house, she had spent time on the streets, hungry and cold, until another woman, taking note of her beauty, had suggested she seek out Virginia Maitland.

Virginia "Ginny" Maitland was one of the most influential women in New York. Prior to her marriage to local businessman Charles Maitland, it seemed people knew very little of her. A woman of undeniable intellect, she had helped build her husband's already sizable fortune into an array of vast holdings, stretching into every aspect of American industry. A woman of average height, she was elegantly beautiful; her face a delicate visage with slightly high cheekbones and an endearing smile. Possessed of a wicked sense of humor, she could hold her own with any man. She was true to her friends and she suffered fools lightly.

A cornerstone of her operation was a bordello, situated at a posh Fifth Avenue address. It wasn't the typical whorehouse. Ginny had never forced or coerced a woman to work in the bordello. Recognizing the limited opportunities open to women, her single instruction to those who chose to work in the house was to gain information. Experience had shown her that most men were prone to bragging. The women were charged with telling their tales to Ginny's assistant, and she would then transcribe them into a summary for Ginny's review. Ginny would then take action based upon their reports, with any financial gain incurred being shared with the woman who had gained the information.

Ahead of her time, Ginny had established "retirement funds" for her girls, as she liked to call them.

She had also arranged for a physician to make regular visits to ensure their health. The women, when they chose to leave her, always retired in comfort and security.

She was loyal to them and they were fiercely loyal to her.

Ginny also had another enterprise of which she was justifiably proud. Her agents throughout the city helped young women gain honorable employment. Given their limited educations, the positions were often as domestic help; but it was honest work and they were grateful for it.

It was in such a situation that Eileen O'Sullivan had met Ginny Maitland.

Eileen had made her way to the address that the woman had provided, arriving she had doubted her ability to gain entrance to the grand house. Shortly after knocking, the door opened, with a seriously large man staring down at her.

"Yes? What is it you want, lass?"

She sighed, inwardly grateful, hearing his Irish accent.

"I would like to speak with Mrs. Maitland."

Expecting rejection, she was relieved.

His voice higher than expected, he bid her "Come in then, I'll see if she is available." Ushering her in, he pointed at a richly upholstered chair. Leaving her, he moved through a nearby doorway.

Sitting, she felt her body collapse into the comfortable chair.

She gazed about the small waiting room, feeling a comfort she hadn't known since Ireland.

After a few moments, a, stylishly dressed woman entered, looked at her, and smiled.

Eileen was quickly to her feet, her voice anxious "Mrs. Maitland, I'm an honest woman looking for work; I was told you might help me."

The woman gazed at her, and Eileen saw compassion in her eyes.

"That's fine, dear. I'm Claire, Mrs. Maitland's assistant. Would you follow me, please?" Taking her by the elbow, she directed her into the house. "I was about to have a cup of tea, would you join me?"

Eileen gave her a weary smile. "Yes, that would be grand, thanks."

They walked into a larger sitting room and Claire directed her to a chair. As they sat, Claire casually asked, "What's your name?"

Embarrassed by her lack of introduction, Eileen flushed. "Eileen O'Sullivan, miss, I apologize for not."

Claire held up her hand, silencing her. "There's no need to apologize. Please, tell me, how long have you been in America?"

A maid entered the room carrying a tea service, setting it by Claire. "Thank you Bertie," Claire said. "That will be all." Smiling at the women, the maid quickly departed.

Pouring the tea, Claire gave a quick look at Eileen. "Do you take cream and sugar?"

"Yes, miss, please."

"Call me Claire, please."

Taking a sip of her tea, Eileen savored the hot liquid as it slid down her throat.

Claire watched her a moment, then proceeded with more questions. "Now, tell me, how long have you been in America?"

Relaxing, Eileen opened up to Claire, telling her of her arrival just a few short weeks ago, of her promised employment, and finally of Big Jack Brady's friend's betrayal. Claire listened intently as the girl spoke, sipping her tea. When she had finished, Claire's face had a hard look about it.

Her voice cold, "The miserable bastard, what is it about men always thinking like that?"

Eileen smiled at the comment. Claire made a note to have someone pay the man a visit. Claire continued to ask her questions about her schooling, and if she had any professional training or experience.

Finishing their discussion, Claire stood up. Eileen rose as well, with a hopeful look in her eyes.

"Eileen, I will speak to Mrs. Maitland about you."

Eileen flushed. "Oh thank you, miss, I..."

Claire held up her hand again, a small smile on her face. "No thanks are necessary. You'll need a room for the night." She held a card out to Eileen. With the card was a ten dollar bill. "Go to this address, and mention my name at the door. They will be expecting you. The money will cover your cab fare and allow you to have some dinner."

Eileen asked. "What is your last name, Claire?"

Claire looked at her for a moment and gave a deep, throaty laugh. "Porter. Claire Porter."

Her eyes full of appreciation, she replied softly. "Thank you, Claire Porter."

Claire smiled back, naturally liking the young woman. "After a bath and a good night's sleep, you'll feel like yourself again," and then "tomorrow, you will meet Mrs. Maitland."

After giving her directions to the address on the card, Claire ushered her out.

Walking back into the house, she went upstairs and knocked on a door at the end of the hall.

From the room, a woman's voice answered, "Come."

She entered; behind a desk sat Ginny Maitland, Claire waited patiently while Ginny finished writing. Placing the pen down, Ginny met her gaze.

Interested, Ginny asked "Well, what did you think?"

"A good woman, I'm thinking more for the domestic side, not the castle." The "castle" was their name for the bordello.

Ginny nodded. Experience had taught her to trust Claire's instinct in such matters.

"All right then, why don't you bring her around about ten and I'll speak with her. Thank you, Claire."

Claire nodded, recalling the rape, "I'd like to send Frank to see the bastard who attacked her."

Ginny thought for a second and agreed. "Yes, I think a visit by Frank is merited here, please speak with him." Aware of the story, having listened on the intercom

The next morning, a car was waiting to drive Eileen back to the house to meet with Mrs. Maitland. As the prior day, she was met at the door, this time by Claire. Exchanging pleasantries, Eileen thanked Claire for the new dress which was sent to the rooming house.

Turning inward, Claire said "Follow me,"

Eileen followed Claire up the elegant, wide staircase; she took note of the décor of the house. It was as grand as any fine manor in Ireland. She felt that Mrs. Maitland must indeed be a woman of influence. They came to a door, on which Claire knocked.

A woman's voice answered "Come."

Opening the door, Claire guided her into the office.

Sitting behind an ornate desk was a woman, stylishly dressed, Eileen thought her quite attractive. She put her pen down; she rose, and came around to meet the two women.

Offering a smile that put Eileen at ease, she held out her hand. "I'm Ginny Maitland. You must be Eileen."

Eileen found herself instantly liking the woman. "Yes, I am, Mrs. Maitland."

Ginny held up a hand to stop her. "Ginny, please, we're friends here."

Eileen was struck by the honest sincerity of the woman. Ginny gestured towards the chairs, and the two sat.

Claire spoke, "Ginny, if you'll excuse me, I do have other matters to attend with."

Ginny nodded. "Thank you, Claire."

She turned back to Eileen. "Claire has told me of your situation. I have some enterprises around the city; I think I might be able to assist you in obtaining employment."

"I would be eternally in your debt."

Ginny noted the honesty. The gratitude in her eyes raised feelings she had not felt for some time. They both sat silently for a few seconds.

Ginny considered her words for a moment, "I have a very dear friend whose wife has recently passed, due to illness. I would like to help him during this tragic time. He has no family in the city, and it would I think help him to have someone to keep his house, until his grief lessens. If this is a position that might appeal to you, we would arrange for you to stay at your current lodging while you work for my friend during the day."

Eileen stared, sensing the woman's pain. "Ah, the poor man; of course I accept. Is he an older gentleman?"

Ginny shook her head. "No, he's about ten years older than you."

Eileen nodded. "What is it the gentleman does for a living, if I might ask?"

Ginny gave her a half-sad smile. "He is a police detective."

Surprised, Eileen smiled, and the deal was struck.

Eileen's thoughts returned to the present as the swells continued to rise. She easily stood the deck, having grown up around fishing vessels. Amused, she watched the others having trouble navigating the dance floor, especially after a few drinks.

Alone with her thoughts, she ventured outside.

Confronted by the pitch black of the ocean, and being far offshore, she made her way to the rail. The soft rain on her face felt good, returning her to her childhood and her father's boat. When thoughts of her current situation intruded, she pushed them aside.

It was just a night to enjoy the elements.

Watching her, the large man had made his way out onto the deck a distance away from her. Staying in the darkness, he moved slowly towards the young woman, senses alert, observing all about him. It was the opportunity for which he had been waiting.

Once he got close to her, he drew a stiletto. Keeping it near his body, avoiding any telltale reflection, he was soon next to her.

Turning, she gave a slight cry as he startled her. Her emotions quickly turned to fear as she recognized the man.

"Quiet, fraulein," he whispered as he held the knife to her chest.

"Please, don't hurt me…I'm sorry."

The large man pushed the knife into her chest, covering her mouth to stifle any cry. As she stared into his eyes in shock, he spoke gently to her, "You should have been happy." He easily lifted her, tossing her over the side into the dark water. As she sank into the cold dark water, her life gently flowing from the wound in her side, her last thoughts were of her revenge.

2

The first sensation that crept into his waking mind was the sound of the ocean. He lay comfortably in bed, his eyes slowly opening, as he turned his head to see the woman sleeping next to him. He took a deep breath, stretching in the comfortable bed. Feeling contented, he enjoyed the luxury of the bed, along with the gentle breeze coming through the window. His smile grew, recalling the passionate lovemaking last night with the woman sharing his bed.

Slowly disengaging from her, he turned, and sat up. Looking at the clock, he was surprised at the early hour. His immediate thought was to turn and lay back in bed, but, annoyingly, he had to go to the bathroom. Rising, he walked to the door and into the hallway.

Returning, he pulled on a pair of shorts and a T-shirt. Sitting on the bed, putting on his sneakers, the woman stirred.

Sleepily, the woman asked "What time is it?"

"Six thirty."

"Aren't we on vacation, Nick? Why are you up so early?"

He smiled. "You know me, sweetheart. I can't sleep late. I think I'll take a short walk on the beach."

The woman gave him a "suit yourself" look, speaking sarcastically, "Have fun."

"Thanks."

Walking towards the front door, he grabbed his pack of Lucky Strike cigarettes.

Walking out of his bungalow, he stared out onto the ocean. As he took a deep breath, he surveyed the beach, taking in the early morning and the fishermen standing in the surf of the Rockaways.

Lighting up a cigarette, he walked down to the water. Reaching the surf line, he turned and walked along the water line, the early sun and the breeze off the water invigorating him. His thoughts were focused on a number of stories, but the most important issue today being was where he and the woman would eat lunch. He had a car, so he thought she would enjoy a trip to Coney Island.

Ahead of him, a young man was casting his rod into the water. As Nick approached, the young man was reeling in his line, lurching at the strain.

Nick, now a short distance away, called out "Got a big one?"

Glancing over at him, the young man gave him a "what do you think" look.

Walking up to the young man, Nick stood nearby watching him. He reeled in, gave some line, and then reeled in again. Curious as to the size of the fish on the line, Nick waited, smoking his cigarette. A bulge appeared in the water as the young man continued to reel in his line. Staring at the bulge, Nick noticed colors definitely not associated with marine life. He began to move into the water.

"Aw, shit," he moaned, when he saw what appeared to be an arm being lifted out of the water. Turning to the fisherman, he said, "Keep reeling."

Quickly moving into the surf, he was up to his waist when he reached the object on the fisherman's line. Reaching into the water, Nick grabbed the floating mass. It was a body.

A floater, shit, he thought. *He hated floaters.*

Yelling back to the fisherman, Nick said, "Drop your damn rod and give me a hand."

The fisherman quickly complied, moving towards Nick. Together, they grabbed the body in the surf and pulled it towards the shore. Nick, noticing the fisherman's obvious distress, continued to encourage him. Reaching the water line, they pulled the body onto the beach.

Breathing hard, Nick asked "You okay" as he looked at the fisherman.

He didn't reply as he quickly crawled away to vomit on the beach.

Nick felt a twinge of sympathy for the guy.

Looking back at the body, he began to remove some of the seaweed from the face. Once the face was clear, Nick muttered, "What happened to you, Jane? Do you have a story I can tell?" Noting a red stain on the clothing covering the upper torso, he examined what appeared to be a wound. She had been stabbed.

He turned to the fisherman, asking him "Hey, you all right? You have to keep people away from here. I have to call this in."

The fisherman, still on his knees, looked at Nick, giving him a weak nod.

Nick turned to some bystanders who were moving in to see what was happening, and addressed them, "Everyone stay back, please. A young woman has drowned. I need to call this in so we can get an ambulance out here."

An elderly couple gazed at the body, a look of sadness in the woman's eyes. The small crowd appeared to be obeying and standing back; Nick took off at a good sprint towards his bungalow. Arriving, he threw open the door, moving quickly inside. The woman sat up in bed, startled.

"Nick? Is everything all right?" He went to the phone. The woman, asking again, got out of bed and walked into the kitchen. "Nick?"

He held up a hand to silence her.

"Operator, can you get me the copy desk at the Daily News? Thanks. I'll wait."

The woman was staring at him, a look of concern on her face.

He looked over to her. "There is a dead girl on the beach."

His companion gave a hushed sigh. "Did she drown?"

Nick shook his head. "I think she was murdered."

The woman looked down, slowly shaking her head.

Nick had the phone to his ear, "Hello, this is Nick Parsons. Beatrice, is that you?" He paused for a moment. "Yeah, I'm on vacation, something came up. I got a story I need to call in. A dead woman washed up on the beach in the Rockaways. I'll be calling back in a minute with the details, so have someone ready. Thanks."

Parsons ran to his overnight bag. Rummaging through it, he pulled out his Moleskine notebook and quickly found his pen. Throwing the bag on the floor, he called back to her as he ran for the door. "Call the cops and tell them we need an ambulance."

As he approached the gathering crowd, he scanned the people. Noticing an elderly man with a camera around his neck, he went over to him.

Pointing at the camera, He spoke to the man "Is there film in that?"

The man nodded.

"Good. Let me use that film and I'll give you five bucks."

The man seemed unsure.

"It's Okay; I'm a reporter. We'll need a photo for the story."

Seeming to relax, the man handed the camera to Nick.

Checking the camera settings on the camera, Nick moved towards the corpse.

"All right, can everyone get back, please? We need to take some photos here, for evidence."

The crowd drew back to a respectful distance.

Nick began to take photos of the dead woman from a number of different angles. He was struck by the woman's appearance. Even after her time in the ocean it was easy to see that she had been beautiful. He noticed a ring on her left hand. Taking a photo of it, he recalled that it was one of those Irish rings, with the two hands holding a heart. There was also a locket around her neck. Reaching over, he opened the locket, which contained pictures of an older man and a woman.

Immersed in his work, he thought, *Parents?*

He took a photo of the open locket.

Finishing the roll of film, he rewound it, removed it from the camera and put it in his pocket. Looking about, he saw the owner of the camera and held it out for him. The man took it and Nick pointed in the direction of his cottage.

"After we're done here, you and I will finish up."

Opening his notebook, he began to write down his observations: the time, the surf, the sky, the people on the beach, and he meticulously commented on the dead young woman.

In the distance, he heard a siren approaching. Satisfied, he was finished; he stood with the others waiting for the ambulance to arrive.

He saw two white-jacketed men walking onto the beach, obviously looking for the woman.

Yelling and waving, he caught their attention.

In short order, they were on the scene, ordering everyone further back.

Nick approached the older of the two men.

"Hi, I'm with the Daily News. Can I ask where you're going to take her?"

The man rolled his eyes, as he and his associate lifted the woman, placing her on the stretcher.

The younger man replied, "The morgue at Brooklyn Hospital."

"Thanks." Turning, Nick grabbed the camera owner by the arm, gently directing him towards his cottage.

Opening the door, he called out, "Mabel, you decent? We have company."

He heard the bedroom door slam shut.

"Wait here," he instructed the man

He went into the bedroom.

The camera owner could hear raised voices, and in a few minutes Nick reappeared holding out a five dollar bill. Thanking the man again, Nick quickly went to the telephone.

Calling the copy desk back he dictated his story, of the dead woman found, washed ashore on a beach in Rockaway.

When he had finished his call, he told Mabel they were leaving. He had to get the pictures to the paper to accompany the story.

On their drive back to the city, Nick considered the writing of the story.

The day had started slowly at the Thirteenth Precinct.

A tall, muscular man, moving with an easy athletic grace, walked into the building. He had a ruggedly handsome face with too many lines, given his age. Walking to his desk, he acknowledged the greetings of a couple of officers. Standing by his desk, he turned as he heard his name called.

"Kroon wants to see you, Mike" said another detective.

"Thanks."

Working his way back towards Kroon's office, he knocked on the half-open door.

"You wanna see me, lieutenant?"

Kroon looked up from paperwork. "Yeah, come on in. Sit," he gestured towards the chair.

Mike sat, staring at Kroon.

Mike Callahan raised his eyebrows slightly.

Kroon nodded, looking uncomfortable.

"I need a favor, Mike." Callahan waited. "It's about Shaw, he needs a partner."

Callahan sat shaking his head. "Don't do this to me, Jack."

Kroon looked desperate. "Hear me out. Doc is going to be in the hospital for another couple of weeks.

Bert "Doc" Holiday was Mike's regular partner, who was currently in the hospital having suffered appendicitis.

"You know what a piece of shit that kid is and you want me to babysit him?"

Kroon gave Mike his pained smile again. "I know, and if his dad wasn't Thomas Shaw, senior senator for the great state of New York, we wouldn't be having this conversation. I need you to help me out here, Mike, at least until Doc gets back."

"God damn you, Jack. All right, I'll do it for you."

Kroon visibly relaxed. "I knew you wouldn't let me down, thanks. I owe you a beer."

Callahan gave him an annoyed look. "You owe me many beers."

Kroon looked past Callahan into the squad room, calling to a nearby detective "Jimmy, find Shaw; tell him I want to see him." The detective looked up from his paperwork got up, walking away.

Turning back to Callahan, "Mike, I know we've juggled this kid around, but the mayor has been on my ass constantly about him getting street experience, and we both know who has been on the mayors' ass."

Callahan didn't have to answer. Daniel "Danny" Shaw was the only child of Thomas Shaw, the most powerful politician in New York. In Washington, where Shaw had been a fixture for many years, his influence ran deeply throughout the corridors of power. There had been talk of his running for president, something he did nothing to discourage, but his intent was to place his handpicked candidate into the oval office.

At the age of 66, Shaw felt the country would not elect a senator from New York to the White House. In conversations with the young governor, he found a man ideally suited for political life. He had decided to throw his considerable support behind Franklin D. Roosevelt for the presidency. Though stricken by polio for nine years, the man had a personal magnetism which wasn't to be denied. His eloquence and his ability to sway the masses more than outweighed his dependence on crutches.

Considering the current state of the nation, with the Great Depression ravaging it to the core, a man with vision was needed to bring America back. Hoover sadly seemed genuinely unable to turn the economy, and the public was growing increasingly disenchanted with his presidency. Roosevelt had spoken with Thomas Shaw about his plans to spur the recovery of the American economy. Shaw, personally disdainful of most politicians, was taken by the man. Having come to this point in his political career, he recognized his place as a power broker within New York, his influence pervasive throughout the state. As with most politicians, while having many backers, he had, over the years, developed many enemies, ruling out his thoughts of national office. Shaw, considering himself a patriot, believed Roosevelt was the right choice for the country and he would do his best to ensure his election in 1932.

He would settle for the gratitude of a president, for services rendered.

Shaw, a tall, handsome man with a full head of gray hair, had worked throughout his life to maintain his physical condition. An early marriage of political convenience had produced his only heir, a son. It had been an annoyance when his young wife had succumbed to a brain tumor, leaving him alone to raise the boy, a task quickly handed over to his servants.

Shaw, away for extended periods in Washington, often left the boy at his estate on Long Island. Known as a ladies' man, Shaw felt that the last thing he needed in Washington was a young boy to look after. During the summer congressional recess, Shaw would spend time with the boy at Long Island. Given such limited time with his father, his son constantly sought to earn his respect. It was ironic that his efforts to grow close to his father only served to push his father away. Never having been a man able to express his feelings, Shaw had counted on his wife to provide that to their son.

The son sought to understand his father's indifference, and at a young age, failing that, he began to vent his resentment on others. As he grew, it was apparent that he took after his mother, being short with a round face. His nose had a turned up effect for which other children had teased him greatly in his youth. He had grown into a presentable young man, his father deciding against a future for him in politics.

Danny had found what he considered to be an ideal career. The new director of the Federal Bureau of Investigation had energized the interest of the country in law enforcement. Shaw had spoken with J. Edgar Hoover about the possible posting of his son as an agent. Hoover had replied that Danny did not meet the physical requirements of a special agent. Shaw, furious at the rejection, knew that Hoover had learned the use of power and would not be pressured.

Turning to the only reasonable alternative, Shaw had spoken with the Commissioner of Police, of New York City. The man had been amenable to the idea of posting the boy to a political appointment within the department.

Shaw explained that the boy actually wanted to do police work, and after a conversation with the mayor, Jimmy Walker, Daniel Patrick Shaw was posted to the Thirteenth Precinct as a detective. The local brass, recognizing that it was a done deal, gave him a desk and began to search for a partner for him.

Danny Shaw quickly developed a reputation as someone to avoid.

At first he had tried to fit in, to make friends, but the constant references to his father, along with his obvious lack of any usable experience, combined to turn opinion against him. Sensing this, he had begun to take less care to hide his antagonistic nature. There had been a couple of episodes with other officers, which the brass had covered up. The effect had been for Shaw to languish at a desk waiting for a partner.

Bert "Doc" Holiday had been Mike Callahan's partner for four years. The two men had compiled an impressive arrest record, receiving numerous commendations for their efforts. Doc, with his swarthy complexion and easygoing nature was known to be popular with the ladies. A smooth talker with an easy going nature, he always seemed to have a new girl on his arm, added to this, he was well liked by his fellow officers. Callahan and Holiday had become friends, with Bert doing all he could to help Mike after the untimely death of his wife.

Doc had come into work ten days ago complaining of pains in his stomach. The other officers, Mike included, had advised him to stay away from the bootleg. He collapsed and was taken to the hospital, where he had his appendix removed. Some complications had arisen; it was touch and go for a while.

Mike had stayed at his friend's bedside and Ginny Maitland had visited, wanting to assure the best care possible for the man. Doc had recovered, but would be in the hospital for a couple of weeks. The situation had left Callahan vulnerable to Kroon's request to partner with Shaw.

Kroon and Callahan were talking when there was a knock on the door.

"You wanted to see me, Lieutenant?"

"Yeah, come in, Danny, take a seat."

Shaw sat, acknowledging Callahan. "Mike."

Callahan nodded.

Kroon cleared his throat. "Danny, as you probably know, Mike's partner Doc is going to be in the hospital for a couple of weeks. I've spoken to Mike, and he's agreed to take you on as his partner until Doc comes back."

Shaw smiled his surprise evident. "Really, that's great." He quickly added, "I mean, it's great that Doc will be able to come back and all."

Mike, you won't be sorry."

Callahan interrupted "I know, Dan. Why don't you wait at my desk, I've got something else I need to discuss with the Lieutenant."

Shaw rose, still smiling, "Sure thing, Mike."

Once he was out of the office, Callahan turned to Kroon, "I don't know why Jack, but I've got a bad feeling in my gut about that kid."

Kroon sat back in his chair, hands folded across his chest.

He raised his eyebrows and sighed, "Yeah, I know."

They both sat silent for a moment.

Callahan slowly rose. "I'll see ya later."

"OK, Mike. Hey, are you going to see Doc later?"

Callahan nodded.

"Give him my regards."

"You bet."

Callahan left the office, walking back to his desk. As he walked, he noticed the men around him watching him, thinking bad news traveled fast. Turning the corner, he saw Shaw sitting by Mike's desk, looking through his case files.

His anger quickly rose as he approached, with Shaw oblivious to his coming.

"Did I tell you to review files?"

Shaw jumped in his seat, like a child caught in the act.

"Jeez, Mike, I didn't hear you walk up."

Sitting back in the chair, Shaw had a nervous smile on his face.

Callahan sighed as he sat.

Shaw spoke, his voice enthusiastic, "Mike, I want to thank you."

Callahan raised a hand to brush away his gratitude. "Forget it."

"No, you're the first person to call me Dan. I hate Danny; I'm not a kid anymore."

Callahan was surprised. "Yeah, well, once you prove yourself, the guys will lighten up."

"Well I'm just glad to be working with you. Everyone says you and Doc are two of the best cops in the precinct." He eagerly glanced again at the files on the desk. "Which case are we going to start with?"

Callahan selected one of the files on the desk, handing it to Shaw.

"Why don't you read this? It's a case Doc and I are working on. Tell me what you think."

Taking the file, Shaw went to his desk.

Callahan went to get a cup of coffee.

A young paperboy entered the squad room, going to select desks and handing papers to the seated men. Walking back towards his desk, Callahan reached into his pocket. Seeing him, the boy smiled. "Hey detective," greeting the man.

"Got any good news there, Timmy?"

Taking his money, hustling away, he smiled "Nothing much."

Callahan sat, sipping his coffee; he scanned the paper, taking note of a story regarding a dead woman on the beach. As was his habit, he scanned the story for the details. Shaw came over with a question, distracting him. Putting the paper aside, he discussed the case with Shaw; Mike was surprised at the degree of intelligence in his questions.

3

Callahan and Shaw finished the morning having discussed a number of the open cases in the docket. Callahan, as was his nature, decided to cut the kid a break. Callahan had to admit, the kid had certainly read up on procedure. His ideas were fundamentally sound, but showed an obvious lack of experience.

"What made you want to be a cop, Mike?"

Callahan sighed. "I don't know, it just kind of happened."

"I want to do good, you know, make a difference."

Callahan stared at him, his eyes wide. "Yeah, well, that's a good thing, I suppose."

"No really, look what Hoover has done with the F.B.I."

Callahan gave him a hard look, his reply was terse. "Don't be so hot on that guy. There are stories about him and his buddy Clyde."

Shaw looked at him, confused.

Callahan softened. "Forget it. You just focus on being a good cop and forget all of that G-Man bullshit and we'll get along fine."

"You wanna get some lunch?"

Callahan stared at him for a moment. "I don't eat lunch, Dan. Why don't you go get some and I'll see you after, OK?"

"Sure, I'll see you after," Shaw replied and he left.

Checking the time to see when he was due back, Callahan got the newspaper out again. Re-reading the story about the dead woman on the beach, he sat back, staring at the words before him: *blond hair, a Claddagh ring, and a locket.*

His mind immediately seeking to reject the notion, he tried to remember the last time he had spoken with Eileen. Reaching for the telephone, he dialed the private number of another close friend.

A woman's voice answered, "Hello?"

"Ginny, it's Mike."

"Michael, what a pleasant surprise! How are you?"

"Fine thanks. How are things with you?"

"Good! I've been meaning to invite you to lunch. Are you free anytime soon?

"My social calendar isn't exactly booked. You pick a day and I'll be there."

"Tomorrow, then. Now, what can I do for you?"

"Have you had any reason to speak with Eileen O'Sullivan lately?"

"No… why do you ask?"

"Did you read the Daily News today?"

"I can't say that I have. Why?"

"There was a story about a woman's body washing up on the beach in the Rockaways."

"Oh my… is it her?"

His voice determined, "I don't know, but I intend to find out. I'm going to visit the paper and speak to the reporter who wrote the story."

Ginny's response was slightly anxious, "Good, I will call Jimmy Fields at the Baxter and ask if he has seen her recently."

"I'll call you as soon as I get back."

"Thank you, Michael; I'll be waiting for your call."

Watching the clock until he saw Shaw walking back in, Callahan got up and walked towards him, his voice betraying his annoyance at having to wait for Shaw to return. "Come on." Shaw followed as Mike walked past him.

"What…" Shaw started to ask, as he scurried to catch up. "What's up?"

Callahan signed out a car and they drove out of the precinct garage.

"Mike, where we going?"

"The Daily News. It's over on Park Place."

Shaw asked "Why are we going there?"

Callahan gave him a look, replying "I wanna check something out."

Nodding, Shaw sat back and didn't speak again.

Arriving, the pair walked into the lobby, over to the building directory. Looking about, Callahan saw two women, obviously building employees, standing by the elevator. Not waiting for Shaw, he walked over to them.

"Good morning ladies, I wonder if you could help me."

The women smiled giving Callahan a look over "Sure, are you looking for someone?"

Smiling good naturedly, Callahan said, "Exactly. I'm looking for a reporter, Nick Parsons."

"Parsons, sure, he's on fifteen," turning the woman said, as she pointed. "Take those elevators, over there."

Thanking the women, the two men made their way to the elevators, riding up in silence with others.

Arriving on fifteen, they stepped out into an office, alive with activity. Callahan stopped a man walking past, asking for Nick Parsons. The man pointed to a guy typing at a desk.

They walked over and stood before the reporter.

"Nick Parsons?"

Without looking up, Parsons asked "Who wants to know?"

Callahan took out his badge holding it closer to the reporter. "Detective Michael Callahan. I'd like to speak with you, in private."

Parsons stopped typing, looking up at the two men before him. Unsure, he stared at the men before him. "What's this about?"

Noting the activity in the room, Mike asked, "Is there an office where we can talk in private?"

Parsons spoke to a woman sitting at the next desk, "Could you tell Mr. White that I'm in the conference room with these detectives?"

He rose and they followed him, as the woman went in the other direction.

Walking into the conference room, Parsons spoke, "Take a seat. My editor will be here in a minute."

Callahan spoke, "Mr. Parsons, you're not in any trouble here. Is it necessary for your editor to sit in on our discussion?"

Nodding, Parson's voice was firm, "Policy...sorry about that."

An older man came quickly into the office, looking at the men seated around the table. "I'm Sanford White, the editor." He sat, gesturing for them to sit too.

Sizing up Callahan as the senior man, White asked, "What's this all about, detective?"

"I'd like to talk with you regarding the story you wrote about the woman whose body washed up on the beach the other day."

Parsons looked at his editor, and the man spoke, "Isn't this out of your jurisdiction?"

Callahan's face assumed a pained expression. "I'm hoping that it isn't someone I know."

Parsons was sympathetic asking. "Friend or family?"

"Friend."

"Well, she was a woman probably in her late twenties, blond hair, attractive..."

Callahan interjected, "Your story mentioned a ring, with two hands holding a heart. You didn't mention if the ring was gold or silver."

Parsons nodded. "Yeah, the police asked me to withhold that, in case they got any tips or calls."

Callahan had a sinking feeling in the bottom of his stomach. Speaking, his voice almost a whisper, "It was gold, wasn't it?"

Seeing the man's pain, Parsons replied, "Yeah...it was."

The room was deathly quiet.

Callahan continued his thoughts, "The locket contained pictures of an older man and woman. The man had grey hair."

Parsons nodded, saying nothing.

"Her parents," stated Callahan

Callahan stared out the window, lost in thought. Looking back at the reporter, he asked in a solemn voice "You didn't happen to take any pictures, did you?"

Uncomfortable, nodding slowly, Parsons replied softly, "Yeah...would you like to see them?"

"Please."

Parsons left the room and the remaining men sat, saying nothing. Shaw was curious as to what relationship the woman might have had with Callahan. In a few minutes, Parsons returned, holding a folder. Sitting, he passed the folder over the Callahan.

Opening the folder, Callahan stared silently, recalling the death of his wife, and now this. He wiped a tear from his eye.

His voice breaking, "Her name was Eileen...Eileen O'Sullivan."

Shaw, hearing the name, sat unmoving. Leaning forward, seeing the photo, his mind was racing. As soon as he was alone, he had a phone call to make.

4

Benny Fitzgibbon, sweating, was working hard, but it was work he loved. A solid, wiry man, he had always been accustomed to hard work. As the caretaker for the Long Island estate of Senator Thomas Shaw, his duties were many and demanding. He and his wife, Rita, had emigrated from Ireland a few years prior, and, by good fortune, they had landed the positions of caretaker and chambermaid at the estate.

It had been their good fortune, as they waited on one of the many lines on Ellis Island, that the senator had been touring the complex with reporters. He was posturing for the press and trolling for future voters among the immigrants in line.

Coming upon them, Shaw had stopped, staring at Rita. A comely woman with dark hair and almond shaped hazel eyes; she had returned his gaze with a smile.

Shaw stood, transfixed for a moment. Quickly, Shaw turned on the charm, for which he was renowned.

Speaking for the reporters to hear, "What is your name, my good woman?"

"Rita. Rita Fitzgibbon, sir."

He smiled. "A lovely name, and where might you be from?"

"Limerick, sir."

Shaw, smiling, nodded. "A beautiful city."

Rita, smiling back, speaking as his equal, "Aye that it is." Grabbing the arm of the man standing next to her, she continued to press her advantage, "My husband and I are looking for employment. Can you help us?"

One of the reporters spoke, "What about it, senator? Think you can help these good people share the American dream?"

Something in Shaw's eyes grew predatory, but no one noticed. "I would be pleased if you would consider working for me. I have an estate on Long Island where I'm in need of some workers."

Rita's smile grew wide. "Oh, sir, my Benny managed a great estate in County Clare. I'm certain you would be pleased with our work."

"Yes, I'm sure," Shaw responded, turning aside. "Captain, please take care of their processing, and have them taken to this address," handing the man a card.

The captain nodded, taking Rita and Benny Fitzgibbon out of line and leading them away. The reporters following Shaw applauded, while he waved off their salute with a casual smile.

Today, Benny had been working long and hard on the stone wall at the eastern perimeter of the estate. Looking around for a mortar trowel, he began to walk back towards the house. Annoyed at himself for forgetting a necessary tool, he calmed himself with the thought that he could get a cool drink from Rita at the great house. As he approached the back of the house, he could see her through the bay window standing at the sink. As he got closer, he saw another person approach her from behind and put his arms around her.

He stopped for a second, unbelieving.

He began to move quickly towards the house as he saw his wife struggling to free herself from the man's grasp. Benny thought it had to be the German bastard that worked for the senator. As he neared the window, he could hear his wife's plea's to the man. As he was about to speak, the man released her.

Peering through the window, Benny was stunned.

The man pawing at his wife was Senator Thomas Shaw.

Benny quickly recovered, calling out in a loud voice, "Rita, dear, would you have a cool drink for a hardworking man?"

Moving towards the back door, he heard steps quickly receding out of the kitchen. Entering, he had a smile on his face as he stared at his wife. "I forgot a shagging tool and thought you might take pity with a cool drink."

Rita smiled at him lovingly. "Well, it's powerful thirsty I can see you are, so it's a drink you shall have."

Benny watched her intently, trying to remain casual.

He noticed her hand shaking slightly as she poured his drink. Fighting to control his anger, he silently sat.

As she turned, her smile was radiant as ever. "Here you are, my man."

Benny smiled as convincingly as possible. "Thank you, my sweet."

Rita returned to her dishes.

Benny savored the lemonade.

"Rita, dear, who was that I saw here with you as I was coming in?"

He noticed her hesitation.

"That was himself; he'll be having a gentleman for dinner."

Benny nodded, and thought, *the miserable bastard.*

Realizing he must wait until they were alone to speak of this, he finished his drink. Rising from the table, he moved to her. Wrapping his arms around her from behind, he kissed her neck, and she relaxed in his caress.

Benny smiled at his wife. "So, who will his lordship be having for supper?"

Rita stared at him, a little uncertain. "That would be Judge Crater, himself."

Nodding, Benny recalled that the man was a fairly constant guest at the estate.

Crater, a dapper 41-year old had been tabbed in the press as "Good Time Joe." He was known for his dalliances with show girls and for ties to the corruption-ridden Tammany Hall administration.

Governor Roosevelt had recently appointed Crater to the state Supreme Court bench. The appointment was due in large part to the support of Senator Thomas Shaw. Crater had gone out of his way to court Shaw, knowing that Shaw's support was critical to his appointment. It was a major step in the career plans of Joseph Force Crater, his goal being nothing less than a seat on the Supreme Court of the United States.

Crater personally disliked the senator, suspecting that the feeling was mutual. It was just another of the countless mutually beneficial alliances which existed throughout politics. Indeed, Benny had heard the senator and the judge in heated arguments on more than one occasion.

Crater's ambition grated constantly with his patience.

Shaw, better versed in the nuances of government, continually advised patience.

Shaw had told Crater of his plans for the young governor. Crater listened, in awe of the intricate plans that Shaw was developing to assure that Franklin Roosevelt would be the next president of the United States.

Between now and that time, Crater had set about becoming a prominent man. Had evidence of Shaw's involvement with certain criminal elements come to the attention of the senate judicial committee, he would probably have been indicted. In particular, his relationship with Legs Diamond alone would have ended his political career.

Legs Diamond had developed the most notorious reputation for not dying, in the annals of organized crime. Since entering a life of crime in 1919, he had survived at least 17 bullets. Dutch Schultz, Legs' primary rival, was once heard to ask, "Ain't there nobody what can shoot this guy, so he don't bounce back?"

Legs had been the front man for Arnold Rothstein. Rothstein, having gained fame as the man who fixed the 1919 World Series, had supported Legs' bootlegging operations, until his murder in 1928. Diamond had been waging a battle to maintain his bootlegging empire since then, seeking to develop political contacts wherever possible.

Benny smiled at his wife. "Well, it's back to work for me, girl. I thank you kindly for the cool drink."

Rita smiled her best at him. "You're welcome, now off with you."

Turning to leave, Rita called after him, "Could you see if the mail has arrived yet?"

Continuing to walk, Benny glanced at a clock on the wall. "I'll run down to the box myself."

Leaving the house, Benny was again assaulted by the heat and humidity. Try as he might, he couldn't understand why the summers were so much more uncomfortable here than in his beloved Ireland.

Staying in the shade, Benny walked down towards the main gate of the estate. The road into the property was gated; the postman always hung a white cloth on the gate to signal the delivery of the mail.

Benny, seeing the tied cloth, quickened his pace.

Opening the box, he removed the large packet of mail. It was easily understood that a man as important as the senator would receive regular correspondence. Benny, as was his habit, shuffled through the envelopes to see if he or Rita had gotten any mail from friends or relatives still in Ireland.

He stopped.

Staring at a brown packet, he saw that it was addressed to him. It was the return address that gave him pause. The packet was from Eileen O'Sullivan, the young mistress of the senator.

Benny thought for a moment that he hadn't seen her about the estate lately. He recalled her laughter, her beauty, and the conversations they had shared about their journeys to America.

Benny mumbled, "What is it you've sent me, girl?"

Using his pocket knife, he opened the package.

The sole content of the package was a leather-bound book. Staring at it, he opened it and began to read. It was a diary.

Continuing to read the handwritten narrative, he was startled at the contents of the book. Stuck between pages, he noticed a paper sticking out.

Pulling out the paper, he saw it to be a handwritten note.

Looking about to see if anyone was watching, he turned back to the note.

It was written in a fine, delicate penmanship, which one might have expected from a young woman.

Dear Benny,

If you are reading this, there is a good chance that I am dead. I make no apologies for my actions, simply asking that you remember me well. As you, I sought to make my future in this great promising land. It had become my fondest hope that Thomas would return the love that I held for him.

I did not start this diary in any attempt to coerce his love but in truth to safeguard my legacy. Before God's eyes, we are all imperfect. Thomas's sin is that he seeks to be seen as perfect by the people. If you read this testament, you will see the imperfection of Thomas Clayton Shaw. I leave the final disposition of this document to you, trusting in your wisdom and judgment.

Your Friend,
Eileen Christine O'Sullivan

Benny stared at the letter, his thoughts a maelstrom. *Eileen dead...how could that be,* he thought. Scanning the diary, he saw the names of powerful and infamous men. It would seem that Thomas Shaw was anything but a man of the people. Realizing that he needed time to consider what action he should take, he stuck the diary and the letter inside his shirt.

He would share the diary with Rita. She had always been his partner in all matters. It was her common sense which had always served them well. It had been Rita, who had pressed for their immigration to the United States, which had been fortuitous to them, until today.

Closing the mailbox, he began to walk back towards the main house.

As he walked, he no longer noticed the heat. The sky was clear and birds sang in the trees. Walking along the road, his thoughts grew resolute. *If you had Eileen murdered, I will be the agent of your destruction, Thomas Shaw. I swear it to God and to that fine young woman. It matters not what happens to me or mine, I will see justice served.*

Reaching the house, he walked around back to the kitchen.

"Rita, dear, I have the mail."

"Fine Benny, please leave it on the hall table. I'm busy."

"On the hall table it is. I'll see you back at the cottage."

"Fine, I'll see you there."

Walking quickly out of the house, he held the diary tightly to his chest, beneath his shirt.

5

After Detective Callahan identified Eileen, Nick Parsons had asked that the detective share information on the investigation, saying he wouldn't print anything which could compromise the work of the police. Unsure if he could trust the reporter, Callahan had reluctantly agreed. Before leaving the newspaper, he had asked to use a telephone.

Calling Ginny Maitland, he informed her that the dead woman was Eileen.

The grief he had felt upon seeing the photos of her transformed into a cold hard anger. Ginny, too, wanted nothing more than to have the murderer of one of her girls brought to justice.

When she asked what his next step would be, he had told her he wanted to see her apartment. Agreeing, Ginny said she would call the building manager, instructing him to provide whatever they required.

Callahan and Shaw arrived at the Baxter Arms apartments, the address provided by Ginny Maitland. Pulling the car over to the curb, Callahan noticed Shaw's jerky, rodent-like movements in surveying the neighborhood.

Callahan stared at Shaw. "Let's go," he directed, nodding towards the building.

Walking slowly up the front steps, opening the heavy oak door, they entered.

The lobby was quiet. A small, lean man standing at the desk looked up from his newspaper.

"Mike, I got a call you were coming."

Callahan smiled. "Hiya, Jimmy, we're here to look at the room."

"Yeah, sure Mike, I was told to provide whatever you want. You know. Orders from Mrs. Maitland."

Noticing the racing form on the desk, Callahan grinned. "Still playing the ponies, Jimmy?"

The slight, man shrugged, replying, "Hey, a guy has to have a hobby."

"You're lucky that Avro likes you; that he doesn't want to annoy your boss." Avro, a prominent bookie knew that Jimmy Fields, never bet large with him. Once, when Jimmy got behind, Avro had asked permission from Ginny Maitland to lean on him.

Fields, having worked for Ginny Maitland for years managing the Baxter, was an excellent building manager, always careful that no problems arose at the property. The apartments that were rented showed a regular profit, the building steadily rising in value over the years. Always a business woman at heart, she understood the need for the bookie to manage his business. However, she had developed a soft spot over the years for the man, occasionally paying his mark. Learning of this from Avro, Fields had doubled his efforts managing the building.

Ginny viewed the insignificant payments as another business investment, knowing she would be hard pressed to find another manager as competent as Fields. The man had been married for many years; but after his wife's passing a few years ago, and with no children, the Baxter Arms had become his life.

Grabbing a key from behind the desk, he headed for the stairs. "Follow me," he beckoned.

Callahan and Shaw followed him to the second floor landing. Walking up to a door, Fields put the key in, and opened it. Standing aside, he allowed the two men to enter.

"Mike, I'll be downstairs watching the door. You got any questions, you let me know."

Looking about the large sitting room, Callahan waved a hand. "Thanks Jimmy."

Shaw stood quietly as Mike took in the room. It was evidently a woman's room with obvious feminine touches.

Mike walked over to a small table near a chair by the window. There was a photograph of a young girl with a handsome man; Eileen as a young girl, sitting on her father's lap.

Hearing Shaw behind him, Callahan instructed, "Don't touch a thing. Stay with me."

Replying sheepishly, disappointment in his voice, Shaw mumbled, "Whatever you say, Mike."

Callahan began to move methodically about the room, opening drawers and gently looking through the contents. Moving into the bedroom, he went to a small jewelry box, fingering through the items, which were mostly cheap cameos and some costume jewelry.

"What exactly are we looking for, Mike?"

Callahan looked at him, surprised. "Anything that might tell us something about Eileen, what she did, who she did it with, when she did it, a lead, a clue, whatever."

Shaw nodded.

Callahan went about opening drawers, embarrassed when he opened a drawer with her undergarments.

Shaw began to walk the room, his eyes darting about. There was a desk near a chair by the window and he walked over to it. Staring at the table he noted that it had a small drawer. "Hey, Mike, I think I see something."

Callahan looked over at him. "Yeah, let's take a look."

Callahan walked over to Shaw, who pointed at the drawer.

Opening the drawer, Callahan smiled. In the drawer lay a personal address book. Picking it up, Callahan began to slowly look through it.

Disappointment hit him.

Many of the entries, although in alphabetical order, were only first names. Shaw, standing behind him, tried to look at the names in the book. "There aren't too many names, we gonna call them?"

Callahan smiled, replying, "Nope, easier to have the phone company track them down."

As Callahan turned the pages, Shaw, noticing an entry, stiffened as he recognized a number. "I could take care of that for you, Mike."

Callahan turned to him, thought for a second. "Yeah, OK, here." He handed the book to Shaw. "I'll give you the phone company contact when we get back."

Shaw stuck the book in his coat pocket. They continued to search the room.

On a table, Mike found a note concerning the *Robert Forster*. Examining the date on the note, it was clear that she had been on the craft the night she was murdered.

"This is our next stop, the boat she was on when she was murdered. I've heard of it; it's one of the party boats that goes out of the Rockaways. They serve liquor and travel out far enough where they know they won't be raided. Hell, they could stay docked for all it matters; they got a sweetheart deal with the mayor's office."

Shaw looked mildly surprised. "The mayor allows it?"

Callahan smiled. "You daddy's in politics, isn't he?"

Shaw immediately stiffened, replying, "My father isn't corrupt."

Callahan waved a dismissive hand. "Hold on, that's not what I meant. I just thought you would have a better understanding of big city political machines."

Shaw looked slightly chagrined. "Dad never involved me in his business; said he wanted something better for me."

Nodding, Callahan thought that the elder Shaw saw no political promise in his son, there being something unlikeable about him. Finishing their search, finding no additional clues, they prepared to leave.

Closing the door, they walked downstairs to the lobby.

Fields looked up, "All finished?"

"Yeah, but I want you to lock the room and keep everyone out until I tell you different. If anyone tries to get into the room, you're to call me immediately. You got that?"

Nodding quickly, Jimmy replied, "Yeah sure, got it."

Callahan acknowledged Fields. "Let's go, Dan."

Outside, the heat and humidity swept over them.

Across town at the "Castle," a large black sedan pulled up to the curb. The driver got out, running around to open the rear passenger door.

A man of average height, well dressed with dark hair, emerged from the sedan. Standing, he straightened his tie, looking up and down the street.

Walking to the front door, he knocked. A bouncer opened the door, and upon recognizing him, he nodded.

"Tell Ginny, Charlie is here to see her."

The bouncer nodded again, standing aside, allowing the man to enter.

The driver, seeing that his boss was now safely in the Castle went back to his car to wait. He knew that once inside, his boss was safe from harm, as the building was a strict "safe" area. None of the mobs wanted to test the political connections of Virginia Maitland.

Charlie "Lucky" Luciano stood waiting in the private lounge.

Shortly after, the door opened and Ginny entered.

She walked over and hugged him. "Charlie, I appreciate you coming; please be seated. Can I offer you a drink?"

"Sure, the usual."

Ginny smiled, recalling his favorite drink and walking over to the bar. She poured bourbon straight up with ice and walked over, handing it to Luciano.

Sitting, she brushed her dress. Staring into his dark eyes, she spoke, "As I mentioned, I have need of a special favor, for which I would be most grateful. I need a man who can blend into crowds, who is observant, and, if necessary, is good with a gun."

Luciano took a sip of his drink, staring at her. When he spoke, his voice had a raspy quality, the result of having his throat cut during an assassination attempt. "This cop must really be something special to you."

Ginny nodded. "Yes, he is a dear friend; my instincts tell me that he might be getting into something that could be a problem. I want to know that someone is watching his back."

Luciano smirked. "I thought all cops had partners."

Ginny nodded. "They do, but I wouldn't rely on his in a pinch. He is the son of Thomas Shaw."

Luciano chuckled. "That's rich, the son of the great Tom Shaw a cop. If he's like his father, I see your point."

Ginny nonchalantly smoothed her hair. "I think we're both aware of the Shaw family traits. My friend's regular partner is in the hospital, his captain has put the son with my friend, and they are investigating the murder of one of my girls."

Surprised, Luciano questioned, "Someone hit one of your girls? It wasn't Marla, was it?"

Ginny smiled thinly. "No, another girl, not from the Castle."

"One of your charity cases, then."

"More than that, Charlie, she was a fine young woman."

Finishing his drink he held up a hand. "I know a guy who can handle the job. I'll speak with him when I get back to my office."

"Excellent, Charlie. I knew I could count on you. I truly appreciate the favor." Pausing, she added, "Also, if something happens to Mike and your man feels that Shaw's son allowed it to happen, I want him hit; he's not to live if Mike dies." She stared intently at Luciano. "Do we have an agreement?"

Luciano laughed lightly. "Hell, it would be a pleasure to hit that bastard's son; it'll be on the house, no charge."

"One final thing, Charlie. I'd like your man to call me daily, to let me know what Mike has been doing. He can use my number here. Can you ask him to do that for me?"

"Sure, no problem, I'll tell him."

"Excellent, now, why don't we see if Marla is free?"

"Yeah…that would be real nice."

They both rose and Ginny led him into the Castle's "work" area.

6

In their cottage on the estate, Benny and Rita Fitzgibbon had just finished their evening meal. Relaxing after a hard day's work, Benny sat back drinking a short glass of Irish whiskey. They always kept a bottle on hand, knowing someone in town who was able to procure such items.

Benny wasn't a heavy drinker, preferring a glass or two after dinner to relax. Rita didn't drink at all.

As he scanned the newspaper, he watched her washing their dinner dishes. Finishing, she walked over, sitting next to him at the table. Staring at him, a look of mild concern crossed her face. "What's wrong, dear?"

Taking a sip of his whiskey, "I received a package, in the mail today."

Rita sat forward. "It wasn't bad news from home, was it?"

"No…it was nothing like that."

"Tell me, Ben. I can see it has you distressed."

Putting the drink down, he rubbed his eyes wearily, "It was from Eileen O'Sullivan." The sadness in his voice easily discernable.

Rita's hand went to her mouth, "Is she ill?"

Benny smiled weakly. "No, my sweet, I fear she might be more than ill." He paused. "When was it we last saw her, do you think?"

Rita considered the question. "Ah, I'm not certain; it must be a couple of weeks now. Why?"

"She sent me her diary, with a note saying that if I've received it, she was most probably deceased."

Rita's concern grew. She stared at him recalling the nice young woman

"Why would she send you her diary, of all things, Ben?" She paused; her eyes grew wide, her voice a whisper, "You weren't involved with her, were you?"

He was shocked. "Good heavens, no! How can you even think such a thing?"

"Well, I don't know now do I? Here with you being all mysterious and such."

Rising, Benny went over to the counter. Opening the lower drawer, he reached below some linen, removing the diary. Walking back to his chair, he sat, opening the diary.

Rita sat, watching him in silence.

"The diary details her dealings with the senator. Rita, there is apparently much we don't know about the great man. Listen, I'll read a passage:

"October 5th,

Tom had been drinking again, going on about the mayor. He says that the man is a fool and that their plan is perfect. Mr. Legs Diamond agreed to move their shipments of illegal whiskey to the pier, controlled by his shipping company. Tom's trucks will then distribute the whiskey to Diamond's various speakeasies. The only problem is Diamond wanting more protection than he can pay for from the mayor. Tom went on bragging how much money he had made off illegal whiskey."

Finishing the passage, Benny looked up at Rita, who sat there, stunned.

"Himself a bootlegger, who would've thought?" She asked.

Benny nodded. "Aye, and there's more. Political payoffs and I think he has knowledge of a few murders."

Rita drew back as if physically struck. "No, not that... not that," she said weakly.

"Aye, my dear, he is not a man to trifle with."

Rita's eyes grew wide. "Oh Benny, we must get rid of this terrible book. We have a good life here; I'll not be moving to a tenement on the west side...I won't."

"I think he had Eileen murdered." Benny held up the newspaper, with the cover story of the dead woman.

Rita let out a low moan, hugging herself. "Ah no, dear Jesus, not that."

Benny nodded vigorously at her. "Aye, her note said she feared for her life. When was she last here, I ask you?"

Rita looked about, thinking. "I'm not certain; it has been a couple of weeks now, hasn't it?"

"Aye that it has. Her diary said that she was pressing himself to marry her. I feel it was her mistake to tell the great man she knew about his business."

Rita shook her head slowly. "Ah, that foolish, foolish girl." She stared intently at Benny. "What can we do? He is a man of influence; he could crush us under his boot."

Benny nodded, resolution set in his eyes. "We must first make certain that Eileen is dead. If that is so, we must then get this diary to the authorities."

"But to whom would we give it? We don't know anyone who would challenge a man like Tom Shaw."

Benny smiled thinly. "Ah, but you're wrong there my dear, we do know such a man. Judge Crater is a man of the law."

Rita thought for a second as amazement flew into her. "Are you daft, man? They're partners in many endeavors."

"Aye, but don't tell me you haven't heard their arguments."

Rita, nodding, replied "You're right, they do argue a great deal. Crater is an ambitious man, Shaw wants to control him."

Benny laughed. "Who doesn't he want to control?"

Rita sighed. "Ah, my man, what will happen to us? How can we leave this place?"

Barely audible, Benny replied, "If he had Eileen murdered, how we can stay?"

They sat in silence for a moment.

"What will you do first?" Rita asked, fearing the answer.

Benny responded, "I must go to the city. I'll see if Eileen is still at her apartment. If she hasn't been seen for some time, we'll need to see when the judge is coming to the estate, so that we might give him the diary."

Rita nodded. "Yes, when will you leave?"

"Tomorrow. I'll say that I need to pick up some supplies."

Rita suddenly sat up straight. "You must be careful, especially of that big German bastard. If anything was done to Eileen, it was surely his handiwork."

Benny thought for a moment of the man, often seen about the estate; a large, hulking man who walked with a limp. He had a hard countenance, a stare with lifeless eyes which put fear into anyone who dealt with him.

They sat in silence, considering their situation.

Benny, having always been a careful planner, coupled with Rita's attention to detail, assured that no options were left unaddressed.

Benny didn't speak it to Rita, but he was almost thankful for the current turn of events. Knowing that a man in his position could never challenge Senator Thomas Shaw, this could provide the means by which he would avenge the man's advances against his wife. It was a tragedy that a fine young woman had to die to get to this point.

"Come, lass, let's go to bed and we'll deal with this in the morning."

7

The sun having risen in a clear sky; now beat down on the sweltering city. The populace moved about their business in quiet suffering. Men carried their suit jackets over their arms, their shirts wet with perspiration. Women wearing their lightest cotton dresses fared little better.

Callahan and Shaw drove over the Brooklyn Bridge, windows open, relishing the breeze. Shaw, as was his habit, eyes darting about, seemed to feel the need to talk.

While they talked, Callahan thought Shaw was probably just a nervous type of guy thinking, *probably due to domineering father.*

Driving through Brooklyn, traffic increased, slowing their speed. Arriving by the piers in the Rockaways, they saw the party boats tied up, with the deckhands busy cleaning them after another night of revelry. The smell of fish, saltwater, and diesel permeated the air. An occasional cry from a gull could be heard, as the two men turned towards the boats.

Upon parking the car, they got out, putting on their suit jackets. Callahan tapped Shaw on the arm, "Follow me."

Shaw falling in behind Callahan, they walked towards a small shack, located in the middle of the pier. Coming up to the building, they opened the door and entered. A heavyset man and an attractive young woman in a short skirt looked up together as they entered.

Callahan walked up to the counter and grasped it with both hands, letting out a sigh. "Is the dock master here?"

Both of them looked at him, saying nothing.

"Who wants to know?" The man asked eyeing him suspiciously.

Callahan squinted, focused hard on the man. "I would say that I do."

"What's that to me?"

Callahan slowly reached into the breast pocket of his jacket and produced his badge. "Detective Callahan. We're investigating the murder of a young woman."

"I'm the dock master," the heavyset man replied.

Callahan gave the man a look which caused him to step away from the counter.

"What can I do for you, detective?"

"I need to know which boats went out last Thursday night and came back from that storm."

The heavy set man nodded. "That's easy. The *Forster* was the only boat that went out that night. She's tied up at the end of the pier, getting cleaned up."

Callahan asked, "What's the captain's name?"

"You'll only find the first mate; the captain will be home sleeping."

Callahan waited.

"Bill Erskine is the first mate, tell him I sent you."

Callahan was already turning towards the door. "Yeah, thanks. Come on, Dan."

They left, slamming the door behind them.

The young girl looked up at the man, to which he replied, "What are you looking at? Get back to work." Annoyed, he went back to his paperwork.

Walking up the gangplank of the *Forster* they saw a deckhand walking towards them.

Callahan spoke, "Could you tell me where I might find Bill Erskine?"

The deckhand, thoroughly in need of a shower, thought for a second and pointed, "Aft."

"Thanks."

They headed towards the rear of the boat. Shortly, they came upon two men repairing an inner hand rail. Coming up to them, they could hear one of the men mutter "God damn rich kids."

Callahan and Shaw stopped. "Either one of you gentlemen Bill Erskine," asked Callahan?

Startled, they looked up.

One of the men spoke, "Yeah, I'm Erskine. What do you want?"

Callahan started to go for his badge.

Erskine shook his head, "I don't need to see your badge, detective." He smiled, continuing, "I've had some experience with you *gentlemen*." He drew out the last word, for effect.

Callahan stared hard at the man. "A girl washed up on the beach last Thursday. We're investigating her murder. We'd like to know if there was anything unusual with your trip that night."

Erskine thought for a moment, responding, "Yeah, there was a woman who complained that she couldn't find her friend after we docked."

Shaw spoke, "You didn't think that was important?"

Callahan held up a hand to Shaw.

Erskine spoke, "You know how it is, they hook up with someone, go home, spend the night, we don't ask any questions."

Callahan nodded. "You wouldn't have this woman's name, by any chance?"

Erskine nodded, "Yeah, she was real persistent. I wrote her name and address down. Wait a minute, I'll go get it." He walked off.

After a couple of minutes he returned, walking up to Callahan. He held out a piece of paper. Taking the paper, Callahan read it and nodded.

"Thanks, this should help."

Erskine shrugged. "No problem."

Across town, Benny Fitzgibbon approached the Baxter Arms apartments. He had left the estate early, stating that he needed to pick up some materials to finish his repairs on the wall. The senator had half listened to him, casually waving him off with a "whatever" gesture.

Having driven Eileen home a couple of times after she had spent the night with Shaw, he recalled the route to her apartment. They had developed a friendship, after hearing that he, too, had arrived recently in the country, from Ireland.

Never having set foot inside the building, he was unsure if he would be able to check out her apartment. Walking up the steps, he took a deep breath. Upon entering, he saw a man seated behind the lobby desk, reading a paper. Walking up to him, Benny coughed.

The man reading the paper looked up. "Yeah, what do you want?"

Calmly, Benny replied "I'm here to see Miss Eileen O'Sullivan." He patted his inside jacket pocket, "I've got a letter for her. It's personal."

The desk clerk sat back slowly, staring at Benny.

"That a fact, huh, why don't you leave the letter with me and I'll see that she gets it."

Benny replied, a little nervously, "Ah, sir, that I can't be doing, as my boss charged me with seeing that I give it to her personally. You wouldn't want me to be getting in trouble now, would you?"

Jimmy Fields was stalling to study the man before him, knowing that Callahan would want to know all he could tell him.

Fields responded, "Truth is, she is out of town, went to visit her mother. So I'll take your letter until she gets back."

At that comment, Benny stiffened, knowing her mother to be long dead. He now felt that Eileen was probably dead, too.

"No...I thank you, sir, but I'll have to return when she is here. Do you know when she might return?"

"Yeah, she'll be back on Saturday. Why don't you stop by then?"

Benny, a sadness taking hold, replied, "Thank you, I shall return on Saturday." He turned, walking towards the door, his hate for Thomas Shaw growing with each step.

As soon as the visitor stepped out the door, Jimmy Fields searched for the card with Callahan's phone number. Finding it, he quickly dialed. Hearing a woman answer, he requested, "Mike Callahan, please."

The woman replied, "I'm sorry, Detective Callahan is out. Can I help you?"

Cursing to himself, Jimmy answered, "You tell him to call Jimmy Fields as soon as he can. You tell him I got something for him, about the O'Sullivan girl, Okay?"

"Yes sir, does he have your number?"

"Yeah, yeah, he's got it. You tell him to call me, Okay?"

"Yes sir, I'll tell him as soon as he returns. Is there anything else I can do for you?"

Fields had already hung up.

With the address from the first mate of the *Forster*, Callahan and Shaw went to speak with the dead woman's friend. Walking up to the apartment house they stopped, looking for the building number, it being one of the countless brownstones that dotted the landscape of the city.

"Come on," Callahan said, started up the steps, with Shaw following.

Entering the lobby, they walked over to check the hallway mailboxes.

"Three B, I got her," Shaw looked up with a smile.

They started up the stairs, the echo of their footfalls heard throughout the hallways. Arriving at the door, Callahan knocked.

Surprisingly, a young woman in a robe answered the door.

Seeing her, red eyes, and red nose, it was obvious the girl was suffering with a cold.

"I'm sorry to bother you, I'm Detective Callahan and this is Detective Shaw. We'd like to ask you a couple of questions, if you feel up to it," Callahan asked, giving her his most engaging smile.

The girl startled to attention. "Is this about Leeny? Oh my god, it is, isn't it?"

She backed away from the door, shaking her head. "She was the girl on the beach in the Rockaways. I read about it in the papers."

"You are Geraldine Costak?" Callahan asked continuing the questioning.

Staring at him, her eyes welled up with tears.

"Miss, wouldn't it be better if we spoke inside?"

She nodded. "Yes, please come in."

Stepping aside, the detectives followed her into her apartment. Callahan noticed some expensive items placed about the living room. The girl was attractive; he assumed they were obviously gifts from boyfriends. Walking over to the couch, the two men sat together. Geraldine sat in a chair, facing them. Speaking nervously, she asked, "Can I get you gentlemen anything?"

Callahan smiled. "We're fine, thanks," pausing briefly, "Could we ask you a few questions, about the night on the boat?"

"Yes, of course."

Callahan began to speak as Shaw took out his notepad.

"Whose idea was it to ride the party boat?"

"Mine. I thought she would enjoy it. She told me of her growing up in a fishing village in Ireland."

"Galway?" Callahan asked.

Nodding, she replied, "Yeah, I think that was it."

"She had been depressed, I thought she could use a good time, you know?"

Callahan nodded.

"I'm not going to get in any trouble for going on the boat, am I?"

Callahan smiled. "No, you're not. Frankly, Miss, I couldn't care less about the party boats. Detective Shaw and I have plenty more pressing matters."

"Well, Leeny had been depressed for a while at that point. She had been seeing someone; I think they were having a spat. She wasn't her usual self, so I got the tickets from a friend and I made the arrangements. On the boat I thought she might loosen up, talk about it." She stared at the men intently. "It's good to have a friend you can tell your problems to, isn't it?'

"Yes, I think it is, Miss." Callahan answered gently.

"Well, we went on the boat and it set off to sea."

"Out to sea," Shaw spoke.

Callahan silenced him with a look. "Go on."

"We started talking with some young men, bankers; we had a couple of drinks. I was watching her. She seemed to enjoy the fella she was with. You know, it was just a good time, with all young people." She seemed lost in thought for a moment. "Except for the strange guy."

Callahan spoke gently, "what about this guy?"

She spoke softly, remembering, "He looked big, strong...you know. He wore a hat which he kept down over his eyes, but I could see him watching us."

"What type of hat was he wearing?"

She bit on her thumbnail, thinking. "A fedora, you know, with the brim pulled down."

"Did he speak with you or Eileen?"

"No, after a while I think he went out on deck." Her eyes went wide; she took a sharp intake of breath. "You don't think he murdered Leeny, do you?"

Callahan answered slowly. "I can't say, Miss, but I think this is the first lead we've got on this case."

She took out her handkerchief, dabbing her eyes.

"Did you see him after he had gone outside?"

"No...I don't think so."

"When did you begin to look for Eileen?"

"After we docked, it was a little rough getting in, I looked for her. I spoke with the men on the boat; no one could remember seeing her leave. I guess I hoped some rich fella snuck her off, not wanting anyone to see."

"Did you see the big guy leave?"

Pausing, she replied, "Yeah, now that you mention it, yeah, I saw him. He was walking fast towards a car. He must have hurt his leg, he was limping pretty good."

Callahan asked. "He had a limp?"

She stared back at him. "Yeah, he limped. Is that important?"

Callahan nodded. "It could be, Geri, it could be."

Shaw quietly took notes, taking an occasional glimpse at the woman.

"That's good. She was my friend, you know."

"She was my friend too, Geri."

She stared at him with a question in her eyes. "You knew Leeny?"

Barely containing his emotion he answered, "Yes, she was my friend. I will do whatever I can to catch her killer." Looking at Callahan, Shaw could see the anger in his eyes. "One last question, did you recognize the car he had?"

She nodded slowly. "Yeah, it was a nice car, a Packard, black, with white walls."

Callahan asked. "No plate number?"

She shrugged demurely. "Sorry."

"Anything else you can recall?"

She thought for a moment, then replied "No, I don't think so."

Callahan rose, with Shaw following. "If there is anything else you can remember, I would like you to call me at the precinct." He handed her his business card.

She stared at it, and then looked into his eyes. "You catch him, that bastard. She was a good person; she didn't deserve to die on a beach."

"Miss Costak, I couldn't agree more."

8

Thanking the young woman again, they left her apartment and walked down the street, back to their car. Shaw watched Callahan, waiting for him to speak. If he was any judge of character, he recognized that the man was truly angry.

Shaw spoke, "Where we going now, Mike?"

Callahan stared straight ahead, replying, "Back to the precinct. We've got to write up our report on the dock master and Miss Costak."

"You got any ideas about who might have done this to the young lady?"

Callahan gave him a look. "Too soon, kid."

Shaw nodded. "Yeah, sure."

They drove back in silence.

Arriving back at the precinct, they parked the car. Together they walked through the parking lot, Callahan exchanging greetings with other officers, Shaw drawing quiet nods.

Walking into the precinct, the ceiling fans turning steadily overhead, Callahan grabbed a paper off a table, fanning himself as he walked. Arriving at his desk, Callahan collapsed in his chair.

A detective at the desk facing him chuckled. "Tough day, Mike?"

Callahan looked up at him. "You could say that." He began to check the messages on his desk. Loudly, he exclaimed, "Sonofabitch." Grabbing his phone, he tapped his fingers on the desk. "Come on, come on...Jimmy! You got something for me?"

"Yeah, yeah." Jimmy Fields voice came over the phone.

"An Irish guy?" Callahan said with surprise in his voice.

"Was he a big guy, with a limp?" Callahan asked hopefully.

"No...no limp, either, huh?" The disappointment obvious in voice.

"Shit, did you see what type of car he was driving Jimmy?"

"A Packard, a dark one, tell me you got me a license plate Jimmy, tell me that."

Callahan listened. "Sonofabitch," he yelled again.

All of the detectives at the desks around him stopped, looking up at him. A heavy-set detective in the corner of the room spoke, "Don't sugar coat it, Mike, tell us what you really think."

Callahan raised his hand to the fellow officers in the room. "Yeah, yeah."

Shaw stood away from the agitated Callahan.

Regaining his composure, Callahan told Shaw, "Go on, sit down. I'll fill you in."

Sitting, Shaw stared at him, expectantly.

"That was the manager at the Baxter. Some guy came in trying to drop off a letter for Eileen. When Fields pressed him, he took off. Interesting thing, he drove the same type of car as the big guy with the limp, a black Packard, although this guy was an average-sized Irishman." Callahan finished and sat quietly, thinking.

Shaw sat, staring at him. As he drew in a breath, he stiffened in his chair.

Callahan caught him. "You Okay?"

Shaw sat silently.

"Dan, are you all right?"

"Yeah, yeah, I'm Okay." He was breathing slowly, staring around.

Callahan watched him, curious.

Shaw's thoughts were overwhelming him. *A black Packard, a big guy with a limp, an Irish guy, no, no, no, it couldn't be.*

Callahan grabbed his arm. "Hey, what the heck is with you?"

Shaw composed himself. "Yeah, I'm Okay, Mike, sorry. It's just a lot to take in, in one day."

Callahan stared at him, unsure. "You wanna do homicide; you gotta be able to handle this type of stuff."

Shaw got angry. "I suppose you did from your first day, too."

Callahan sat back, thinking for a second. "No, maybe I didn't, sorry."

A few men were staring at them.

Callahan got up. "Come on," motioning to Shaw, "let's talk."

Shaw followed him out of the room.

Shaw followed Callahan into an interrogation room.

"Sit down Dan, let's talk."

Shaw, seemingly composed, now sat, staring at Callahan.

Callahan spoke, "What struck you back in the squad room? Do you have any ideas on this case? I gotta tell you, if you hold out on me, I will beat the ever-living hell out of you."

Sitting forward, his face coloring, his nostrils flaring, Shaw demanded, "Why the hell do you think I'd hold out on you?"

Callahan nodded, "I don't know, I've got a feeling here." Staring at the young man, he just thought there was something wrong here. "Dan, in case you missed something here, Eileen O'Sullivan was very special to me. I'm taking it personal. I will do whatever it takes to catch her killer, and put him in the electric chair."

"And I'll do whatever I can to help you, Mike, you gotta believe me."

Callahan stared at him, unsure of what to think of Shaw, except for one thing.

Ginny Maitland was right, he was a little shit. "All right, you stay here for a minute. I gotta talk to Kroon."

Shaw made to protest, but Callahan silenced him with a look.

Callahan turned, leaving the room, his mind running over what they had found up to this point. He considered asking Kroon to take Shaw off his back. He made a mental note to punch Doc in the head, when he got back from sick leave.

Arriving at Kroon's office, opening the door, he stuck his head in. "You have a moment, Jack?"

Kroon looked for a second at the stack of papers on his desk, then back at his friend. Sitting back, he tossed his pen onto his desk. "Sure Mike, come on in."

Callahan sighed as he sat.

Kroon allowed him a moment. "Is this about the O'Sullivan girl?"

Callahan nodded. "Yeah."

"What is it, Mike?"

Callahan related to him their findings to date. He spoke of the black Packard, the large man with the limp, the Irish guy. He spoke carefully when he mentioned Shaw's reaction to the Irish guy and the car.

Kroon stared at him intently. With a slight hint of skepticism in his voice, he asked, "You think he knows something?"

Callahan shook his head. "I dunno, either he doesn't or he's a world class liar. Either way, Jack, is there any way you can give me someone else, take the little bastard back?"

Kroon smiled sadly at his friend. "Mike, I wish I could, I truly do. You know the schedules with the politicians coming to town, I can't spare anyone. Can't you hold out till Doc gets back?"

Callahan's face grew hard for a second, though he held his fierce temper. "All right, I had to give it a shot." He got up, turning to leave, "I'm going home; it's been a long day."

"Good night, Mike."

"Walking back to Shaw, he dismissed him "Go home, I'll see you in the morning."

Callahan walked away not waiting for a response.

Shaw, looking relieved, responded, "Okay Mike, see you then."

Callahan walked out into the twilight. With the sun setting, it was slightly cooler than during the day. Walking to the curb, he hailed a cab. Getting in, he directed the driver, "Lenox Hill Hospital."

"You got it buddy," the driver replied, as the cab sped away from the curb.

Settling back into the seat, he made a note to pick up some magazines for Doc when he got to the hospital. He missed his partner; their working relationship was a perfect balance, each man always seeming able to pierce any obstacles, get to the core, and solve the case. Given his personal stake in this case, he wanted every advantage he could get.

As the taxi made its way through traffic, the driver looked at Callahan through his rear view mirror and asked, "Friend or family?"

Callahan looked at the driver, confused. "What?"

The driver, a slim fellow of average height replied, "You visiting friend or family?"

Callahan grew annoyed. "Just drive okay? Cut the chatter."

"Sure, sure, you're the boss, you got it."

"Hey, it's nothing personal; it's been a tough day. To answer your question, I'm going to see my best friend."

The driver thought for a second before asking, "He okay?"

Callahan smiled slightly. 'Yeah, he is...thanks for asking."

The taxi pulled up in front of the hospital. Callahan paid the driver, giving him a little extra in the tip.

The driver counted the money, smiling. "Thanks buddy, glad to hear about your pal." He sped off to his next fare.

Walking into the lobby, Callahan headed to the gift shop to purchase some magazines, selecting those he knew Doc enjoyed. Making his way to his room, he pushed the door open to see his friend deep in conversation with an attractive young nurse.

Seeing him, Doc smiled broadly. "Mike, hey! It's good to see you."

The nurse, startled but smiling, moved quickly past Mike and out the door.

Callahan was instantly at ease with his friend. "Oh yeah, you seem to be recovering nicely," he chuckled.

His friend smiled back. "Hey, I almost died, you know."

Callahan tossed the magazines on the bed. "You're too smooth to die; you're gonna go in old age in bed with some hot young skirt."

Doc smiled. "What can I say?"

Callahan pulled up a chair to the bedside. "I gotta few things I want to bounce off you." Doc was instantly business. "We're talking about Eileen's murder?" Kroon had told him, having spoken with Callahan.

Callahan gave him a nod. "Her friend described a guy on the boat; she thought he was eyeing them, a big guy with a limp. When they docked, he took off in a black Packard."

"No plate number huh?"

Callahan shook his head. "No, bad luck there, but it gets interesting. An average-sized guy with a brogue asked for her at her apartment, talked to Jimmy Fields. He rushed off, Fields saw him drive off, down the street."

"Let me guess, in a black Packard," Doc finished his sentence.

"Yeah," Callahan replied, annoyance evident in his voice.

"I have a feeling Fields didn't get you a plate number either."

"Nope, the Irish guy said he'd be back...I don't think we'll see him again."

"Mike, it sounds like these guys work possibly for the same guy, yet the Irish guy didn't seem to know that Eileen is dead. That doesn't add up."

"Yeah, here's where it gets more interesting. I told this to Shaw and he got strange on me."

"Strange...what do you mean?"

"I'm not sure; I had the distinct feeling that he knew something."

Doc gave him a wicked smile. "Did you take him into room 84 and smack him around a little?"

Callahan laughed, replying, "Don't think I didn't consider it. I took him into an interrogation room, pressed him. The little bastard clammed up pretty good. The bottom line is that I think he could teach lying in school."

There was a knock on the door, and an elderly nurse looked in and smiled. "I'm sorry, detective, visiting time is over. Mr. Holiday needs his rest."

Callahan smiled at her. "Certainly. We'll be through in a minute."

Nodding, she closed the door behind her.

Callahan looked at his friend, seeing the toll the illness had taken on him. "You gotta get well, you jerk," he said with a smile.

Doc lay back. "The doctors still say another week. I'm sorry, Mike."

Callahan stood, pushed the chair back to the corner and walked back over to his friend, holding out his hand. Shaking hands, Callahan could feel the weakness is his grip. "Get well buddy, I need you."

Doc smiled weakly. "I'll work on it. Goodnight, Mike." He closed his eyes.

"Goodnight Doc."

As Mike walked out, he quietly closed the door.

9

The woman held her baby tightly, trying to soothe her, to stop her crying. She knew that after a long day on the street, driving his taxi, her husband would be in no mood to hear their daughter cry. Not for the first time, she wondered how her husband would have felt if her baby had been a boy instead of a girl. He made no effort to hide his disdain for his daughter; never failing to mention the trouble *she* had getting pregnant, as if the entire burden had been hers. The stifling heat was causing her discomfort, and she responded the only way she knew, crying.

"I'm telling you, you better shut that kid up," he shouted from their living room. He was having a beer, listening to the radio.

She came out quickly, carrying her child towards the kitchen sink. "I'm gonna give her a bath in the sink. The cool water should quiet her."

Sitting, staring at the radio, he replied, "Great, whatever, a little silence would be welcome."

She quickly filled the sink with cool water, gently lowering the baby into the small bath. The silence was almost immediate, with the infant gently cooing as she stared at her mother. .

"You see, Bobby, I told you. She was just too hot."

"Hey, ain't we all…I wish I could put my ass in that sink to cool off."

She laughed nervously at his comment, hoping he would have a couple of more beers. He was one of those people who grew mellow after drinking a reasonable amount of beer. She dried her child off, holding her until she fell asleep, all the while watching her husband drink his beers.

Walking out of their bedroom, she sat across from him. "How was your day?"

He looked at her scornfully. "What do you think?"

She bit her lip, carefully replying, "They'll call you; you're a good reliable man. When they need something done, they must know how reliable you are."

He seemed to deflate a little as he sat in his chair. "I just want to be able to buy nice things for you and the kid; you know that, don't you?"

Seeing him like this, her love took hold; she asked hopefully "What about the German, have you seen him lately?"

He shook his head. He had driven the senator's man to a meeting with some shady characters, and when it seemed to go bad, he had gotten him out safely. The German had been grateful, saying he would remember, and that he would have work for him in the future.

That had been weeks ago.

Her husband had been a low-level errand boy for the mob for a couple of months, always ready to take a job that a regular mobster would reject. They often used him as they used many people throughout the city, who needed money. The bootleggers had a vast horde of cash at their disposal to use as they saw fit. Try as they might, the police were often powerless to counteract this network of operatives.

"Why don't you speak with Whistle? You said he's a friend."

He froze for a moment, thinking, and then looked at her, smiling. "Yeah, I didn't think of him, he could get me some action…that's not a bad idea."

She smiled widely; pleased that he thought her idea was good.

Leaning over she gently put her arms around him, drawing him close. "Honey, I love you; you're my man."

He wrapped his arms around her, and they embraced tightly.

Miles away, Senator Thomas Shaw sat in a dark room looking out at the Long Island Sound. Holding a drink in his hand, he had been drinking for some time. His mood was melancholy, his thoughts dwelling on the unfairness of life. His young wife had been taken away from him, he was given a disappointment for a son, and a woman who he truly cared for was causing him this unwanted pain.

His man stood silent in the shadows, watching him. The German had done and would do anything for the senator, with just a word from the man. The senator had given back him that which he held most precious, his self-respect.

Sipping his drink, staring ahead, he spoke, "I did love her, you know, she just wasn't suitable for Washington."

"Freilich, Mein Herr."

Shaw slowly turned his face towards him. "Gerhardt, we may have a problem to deal with. Can I count on you?"

The tall man stiffened, replying, "In all things, sir."

Shaw returned his gaze to the window. "Good . . . that's very good. Thank you Gerhardt."

Michael Callahan sat alone in his small apartment. Since returning from seeing Doc, he decided to have a couple of drinks. Although against the law, Ginny Maitland saw to it that he had access to her finest stock, at his request.

His phonograph played the favorite song of his wife.

A tear ran slowly down his cheek as he gazed at his wife's photograph. Carefully putting the photograph back on the table, he picked up the photo of Eileen O'Sullivan. Staring at it, his emotions turned from grief to anger. "I couldn't do anything for you, Maureen… but Eileen, I promise you if there is a god in heaven, I shall bring down the person who has done this. I swear it."

10

Benny Fitzgibbon, having risen early, was seated at their small kitchen table when Rita walked easily into the room. Gazing up at her their eyes met and, silently their thoughts turned to Eileen's diary. The entries in the book had shocked and dismayed them, as they spent the better part of the night reading it. It was fascinating to note the degree of detail in the book the dates, times, and names of both prominent politicians and known criminals were contained throughout the text. Benny had thought the senator daft for giving such information to a young woman. Rita, fearful of losing the good life they enjoyed, had at first told Benny to burn the book. She broke down in tears when Benny reminded her that Eileen had trusted them to do the right thing.

The newspapers confirmed that Eileen had been the young woman whose body had been pulled from the surf. With his easy disposition, being slow to anger, Rita grew fearful watching Benny's silent rage at their employer.

"Benny, how do we know it was Shaw who had Eileen murdered? It's possible she fell in with the wrong people, isn't it?"

"Aye, it's possible, but I don't think it probable. If the poor girl was pressing the great man to make her his wife, if she made any mention of that book, I have little doubt that he would have done her in."

"Why don't we just mail it to the police, anonymously?"

"Ah girl, can't you see what would happen? The book would never see the light of day."

She stared at her husband. "When did you grow to be so cynical?"

Staring back, sadness in his eyes, he answered, "Not cynical…practical, yes, but not cynical. The man would use all of his considerable power to assure that the book disappeared, leaving Eileen's murder unsolved." The two sat unspeaking as they considered their options. Shortly, Benny broke the silence

"We need to be certain as to how we proceed. We are agreed that I'll speak with Judge Crater when he comes for dinner on Saturday. After I pick him up, I will have more than enough time to speak with him, to seek his counsel. I believe he is a man who respects the law, who will do what is right. It would probably help him politically to play a part in this affair, too."

Looking down at the table, Rita slowly nodded.

Standing up, Benny started to leave. "It's settled then. I'm off to finish my repairs on that wall."

Rita looked up startled. "What, with no breakfast in you? Ah, sit and I'll fix something."

Looking at her affectionately, "I've been up for some time, girl. I had some oatmeal."

Returning his smile, Rita joked, "Aren't you the efficient one, soon you'll have no need for me at all."

As their mood lightened, he laughed, "Ah, sure, I could find some chores for you to do for me. I've heard you're a hard worker."

Rising, she moved towards him, giving him a playful slap on the chest.

Pulling her to him, he kissed her, holding her in a tight embrace. "It will turn out all right, you'll see."

Nodding, she looked into his eyes.

Turning to go, he stopped, looking back. "If that bastard gets fresh with you again you smack his face hard, you hear me, lass?"

"Yes…yes I will."

Benny stared at her for a moment, nodding he walked out heading towards his tool shed.

Up in the great house, Thomas Shaw awoke. Silently, he promised himself not to drink to such a degree again. It was a promise he often made, and just as often broken. It had surprised him that he seemed unable to put the young woman out of his thoughts. She was beautiful; it had appeared towards the end that she was smarter than he had anticipated.

Recalling their last argument, he thought again of her comment about keeping track of *things*. He had to admit, he enjoyed talking of his various activities to her, feeling she was impressed. The potential problem was that he was often drinking, and afterwards he couldn't recall everything he might have told her. If she had been foolish enough to keep a diary that could cause him problems.

The papers had made no mention of any diary or notes; more importantly, the police had not been out to call on him. The most positive development was that his son had been placed on the investigation with a senior officer.

He had done some investigating regarding the senior officer. He was apparently well thought of, with a reputation for solving crimes. His regular partner was laid up in the hospital for a couple of weeks. It was this stroke of luck that allowed his son to actually be of some use to him.

Danny had called to tell him of the witness from the boat, in addition to what had apparently been Benny's trip to visit Eileen's apartment. The same model car had been driven by the two different people. It was fortunate; neither of them had noted the license plate of his car. He considered it less than fortunate that Eileen had worked for the detective, and that he was taking her death personally.

Shaw decided to call in a favor at the federal level, in an effort to curtail the investigation. He had been one of the principal supporters of the new director for the Federal Bureau of Investigation, J. Edgar Hoover. Shaw had pegged Hoover as a man who understood *quid pro quo*, and the need to deal delicately with the man, knowing the intensity of his ambitions.

He didn't want Hoover looking into this incident either.

Putting on his robe, he made his way downstairs. Walking into the kitchen, he saw Rita preparing the stove. She turned, a smile on her face, and greeted him, "Good morning, sir, will you be having some breakfast?"

Noticing his red, puffy face, she immediately knew he had been drinking again.

Shaw made his way to the table, falling onto a chair. Nodding, he replied, "Coffee and some eggs, please, Rita."

"Yes, sir," she answered, smiling as she turned to her stove. She poured a cup of steaming coffee, and brought it over to the seated man. The cream and sugar had already been placed on the table, and she turned back to her stove. Shaw stared at her, not for the first time, thinking what a perfect political wife she would make. She certainly knew her place. *Why do some women just have to be so difficult?* He thought, as he sipped his coffee.

After finishing his breakfast, Shaw showered and dressed. Coming downstairs, he saw Gerhardt Yost, his man patiently awaiting him by the front door. Taking the briefcase from the senator, Yost moved to open the door.

Walking down the steps, Yost stayed ahead of the senator, opening the rear door of the car. Once the senator was in the car, Yost moved to the driver's side and got into the Packard.

Looking into the rear view mirror, he queried, "Grand Central Station, senator?"

"Yes, thank you, Gerhardt."

Sitting back, Shaw opened the newspaper; Yost had left on the seat. As the car proceeded down the driveway, Shaw noticed Benny working on the estate wall. Thinking of the man's wife, a momentary stab of jealousy struck him. He briefly wished an accident for the man, however just as quickly pushed the thought from his mind.

Returning to his paper, he took a small notebook from his briefcase and began to make some notes. His calendar once back in Washington was full; he would need to have his staff research some issues for him prior to any discussion or votes on the pressing matters. He had also cleared time for an appointment with the Director of the F.B.I., having rehearsed his discussion with the wily man. Again, he reminded himself that he certainly didn't want to trade a New York Police Department investigation for a F.B.I. investigation.

Years ago, he had established a residence in Washington, which made it easier for him to travel. The townhouse, as with his Long Island estate, functioned for him as a standalone residence. As with the estate, he maintained a limited staff to manage the property, and, unlike Rita, the housekeeper was singularly unattractive. He wanted no temptations in a town where the press was always on the prowl for a juicy story.

Arriving at the train station, Yost quickly stepped out, opening the door for him. Shaw stood, straightening his suit. Looking about at the people quickly moving past him, he thought how much he loved this city. Washington was different; it just didn't evoke the same feelings for him.

As always, the train ride to Washington passed uneventfully, and later that evening he was asleep in his townhouse.

The next morning, he rose early to meet J. Edgar Hoover. Arriving at his office, he was quickly ushered into a private waiting area. He knew from experience that Hoover made everyone wait to see him. The time you were required to wait was relative to your perceived importance or usefulness to the fortunes of the F.B.I.

After five minutes, the secretary ushered him into the Hoover's office. Hoover, a short man, sat behind a massive desk. Shaw noted that the chairs in front of the desk seemed small in comparison.

Looking up from his desk, Hoover rose, walking around to greet him. "Senator, it's been a long time. How have you been?"

They shook hands, Shaw noting the usual hard grip.

"Fine, Mr. Director. I appreciate you taking time to see me."

"Not at all; always happy to meet with an old friend." He looked questioningly at Shaw. "Can I offer you coffee?"

"I'm fine, thanks."

Hoover nodded to the secretary, who closed the door as she left. Shaw took a seat, Hoover once again sat behind his desk. Hoover stared at Shaw, waiting for him to speak.
Shaw, momentarily put off, was impressed with Hoover; the man had certainly learned the art of intimidation well. He quickly reasserted himself.

"John," he knew few people called him by his first name, "I have a situation in New York that I'd appreciate your help with."

Hoover sat, quietly listening to Shaw.

"There was a young woman with whom I had a brief dalliance."

Hoover smiled slightly, asking, "How does she present a problem? After all, you're a widower." He sat up a little straighter. "Is she pregnant?"

Shaw sighed, "No, she is dead."

The surprise was evident on Hoover's face. "How did she die?"

Playing his grief to the hilt, he explained, "We had ended our affair a short time ago. She said she had met a younger man, whom she felt she was in love with. I was disappointed, but I suppose it was to be expected. Last week her body washed up on a Long Island beach, after a storm. She had apparently been stabbed and thrown off a party boat."

Hoover watched Shaw intently, seeing only the intense grief of an old man. He was perplexed. "What is it you expect of me?"

"The senior detective on the case had a personal relationship with the woman; he is intent on solving the case. I would prefer an investigator with less of a personal interest, one who would be inclined to overlook my assignation with the woman, if it ever came to light. I've no doubt there are people in this city who would love to play over such a relationship in the press."

Silently agreeing, Hoover knew that the powerful senator had many enemies in Washington.

"I'm curious, Tom, how is it you're informed on the investigation?"

"My son is a detective; he is temporarily assigned to the senior man."

Smiling inwardly, Hoover recalled the young man, and how Shaw had wanted him posted to the F.B.I. as a special agent. It made sense that after his rejection, Shaw would use his influence to get the boy posted to the New York Police Department.

Hoover thought for a moment. "You say she was murdered on a party boat?"

Shaw nodded. "Yes."

"I might be able to do something, Tom. Let me look into it. I'll call you as soon as I know if I can assist you. Trust me, I'll do everything I can; I know how tough the press can be, especially if they get a whiff of a scandal."

Knowing the meeting was ended, Shaw slowly rose, Hoover walked around to usher him out of the office.

"Tom, I want to assure you, we'll take care of this. The poor girl obviously got mixed up with the wrong people."

Shaking hands at the door, Shaw left.

Back at his desk, Hoover picked up his phone. "Get me James Watt in New York."

In New York, James Watt, the agent in charge of the F.B.I. office sat at his desk, reviewing the report of a surveillance.

Shaking his head in disgust, he tossed the report off to the side, exhaling sharply. He was going to have to speak to Beck, the man in charge of the operation. They had allowed themselves to be made, and in doing so, blew weeks of hard work. He reached for the phone, and as he touched it, it rang.

He flinched. He hated when it did that. Picking up the phone, he answered, "Yes?"

"Mr. Watt, I have the Director on the line."

Watt quickly stiffened in his chair, *why was Hoover calling him?*

Watt calmed himself, "Please put him through."

"Good morning, Agent Watt. How are things in the New York office?"

"Fine, sir, what can I do for you this morning?"

Watt knew, as all senior personnel in the bureau did, Hoover was not one for small talk.

"I've just had a conversation with a friend from New York."

Watt thought quickly, *who might that be?*

"He's asked if we can be of assistance to him, regarding a matter he doesn't wish to be associated with."

This has got to be good, thought Watt.

"What might that be, sir?"

"Are you familiar with a recent murder, where a young woman's body was recovered from the surf on the south shore of Long Island?"

Watt thought quickly. "Yes... a young Irish woman, I believe."

"Precisely, Agent Watt."

"A New York detective, a fellow named Callahan, has been assigned to the case. Have you ever had any dealings with him?"

"Yes sir, I've dealt with Mike Callahan." *A pain in my ass*, he thought.

"Excellent. I want you to speak with him, inform him that the Bureau will assume the lead on this investigation."

Watt thought, *this isn't going to be easy.*

"Yes sir, I'll call him as soon as I hang up."

"Why don't you ask him to come to your office?"

Watt thought, *Oh shit, no, bad idea.*

"Certainly sir, I'll take care of it."

"Excellent, Agent Watt. I'll be in New York next week for a meeting. I should have some free time, perhaps we could have lunch?"

"I'd enjoy that, sir." *Of course I'll be buying,* he mused.

"Fine, then. Keep me posted on this investigation. I want to be able to keep the senator informed of our progress. I consider this investigation to be of the utmost importance. Do I make myself clear?"

"I understand perfectly, sir."

"Good." Hoover hung up the phone.

The surveillance immediately forgotten, Watt shifted his priorities.

11

Jack "Legs" Diamond was not having a good morning. The pressure on his business from the Schultz mob was beginning to concern him. He sat back in the chair at his desk, rubbing his side, the pain a result from one of the many bullets that had the bad taste to actually strike him.

Two of his enforcers stood off to the side, watching him. Diamond glanced up at them, annoyed. "You took care of the sonabitch?"

The men nodded together; the tall one spoke, "Yeah, boss, we took care of him, just like you told us."

Sitting back in his chair, Diamond smiled. He was a handsome man, known for his stylish dress, and a manner that put his men at ease. "That's great, just great. Let the Dutchman see that we're not ready to roll over for him just yet."

"You need anything else, boss?"

Diamond thought for a moment. "Yeah, go down to the south warehouse, tell the boys to keep a sharp eye out for any trouble. Shultz won't take this lying down."

"You got it, boss." They left together.

Alone, Diamond considered his options.

Since Rothstein's death, it seemed as though it was a constant battle to maintain the necessary political support for his operation. His recent dealings with the man from the senior senator from New York were paying off almost as well as anything Rothstein had ever managed. Having police protection, under the auspices of the mayor of New York, would take a lot of the pressure off his organization. Additionally, having a judge in his pocket would assure that if any of his boys were picked up, they would be taken care of.

He hoped to meet with the man again tonight at the Chateau. Legs enjoyed the Chateau greatly.

The three Frenchmen, who had opened the establishment in 1906, had modeled it after the casino in Monte Carlo. It was said the main floor was able to accommodate a thousand guests. Diamond was a regular patron of the Chateau which boasted bathhouses, elaborate gardens, and a pier with ferry service to New York, and Stamford.

He thought briefly of the senator's man. Considering himself to be without fear, he felt uncomfortable in the presence of the man. Diamond always kept two men in the immediate area whenever he met with the German. He had demanded assurances that the man was not an associate of the Dutch Schultz, early in their dealings. He had been assured that the senator was more comfortable dealing with him than Schultz, with his known reputation for violence.

Diamond's bravado had earned him a special place in the hearts of the public. The press had long relished printing the activities of the criminal elements of the city, and Diamond had taken pains over the years to divorce himself from the more violent aspects of the mobs in New York. He looked forward to tonight, enjoying rubbing shoulders with the upper class from the city, those who frequented the casino. The so called "captains of industry" who Diamond felt were little better than the people he dealt with.

Everyone was in it for the money.

Diamond was fairly comfortable with the current mayor. He and others felt he was a man they could do business with, not that he was on the take; it was just that he had an appreciation for the problems of *businessmen*. Walker, a prominent man about town simply wanted his electorate to be happy, and Diamond was doing his best to see to their needs. After all, it was only a matter of time before the country repealed prohibition; after which, all of this would become more difficult. Once the government regulated their businesses, profits would drop well below their current untaxed levels.

Focusing on the business at hand, looking about, "Tom, come here."

Tom Regan, a handsome man with chiseled features turned towards Diamond. "Yeah, boss." He walked into the inner office and stood before Diamond.

Diamond gathered together the papers on his desk, folded them, and passed them over to the man before him.

"Tom, I want you to handle this delivery." Diamond stared at the man, seeming to want to offer an explanation. "Tommy, it's not that I don't trust Ike or Leo, it's just that I trust you more."

The man seemed to consider the comment for a moment, smiling slightly. "Sure Legs, you can trust me. The Dutchman gets any ideas; we'll take care of him good."

Diamond smiled. "Good, yeah, I'd pay extra to see that."

Turning as he went towards the door, Diamond called him back. "You doing anything later?'

Stopping, he looked back, he thought for a moment. "Just gonna see Verna later. Nothing I couldn't put off. You need me for something, Legs?"

Diamond smiled, thinking about Verna. "Yeah, I'll be going to the Chateau tonight. I want you and Pete to go with me."

The man seemed pleased. "Sure, boss, what time you figure to go?"

"I wanna be there by seven."

"No problem, I'll be back well before that. Pete should be here in a couple of hours." Tom paused for a moment. "That big kraut bastard going to be there?"

"Yeah...probably. You got a problem with that?" Legs asked.

Tom Regan smiled. "Hell no, I'll just bring my big gun."

Both men laughed.

"See you later, Tom."

Across town, Lucky Luciano sat at his desk with one of his men standing before him. "Vito, I got a job for you."

The stout man stood silently before his boss.

"It's a favor to a close friend. You gotta keep an eye on someone."

The large man simply nodded.

Luciano smiled. "This job is a little different than usual."

The standing man slightly cocked an eyebrow.

"The guy you gotta watch is a cop"

The large man raised both eyebrows.

Luciano gestured to the man. "Sit, Vito, please."

The man sat in one of the chairs before the desk.

"The guy I want you to keep an eye on is a friend of a good friend of mine. You ever hear of Ginny Maitland?"

The man nodded.

Luciano chuckled. "As I said, he's a cop. He's also a close friend of hers." Noting the confusion in the man's eyes, he continued, "He's involved in the murder of that dame that floated up on the south shore of Long Island." Luciano didn't bother to ask if the man had read about the dead girl in the newspapers. "The dead broad was one of Ginny's girls; she worked for this cop, as his maid. She wasn't a hooker. The cop is taking it personal, so is Maitland. The best part of this is that this cop is teamed up with the son of Thomas Shaw, the senator. Your job is to watch him and make sure nothing bad happens. If Shaw's son, that little shit, allows anything to happen to the cop, you take him out. You got that?"

The man nodded. "Yes sir."

"I want you to call me at the end of each day, let me know what is going on."

Vito spoke, "Who is this cop I gotta keep an eye on, boss?"

Luciano sat back in his chair. "His name is Callahan. Mike Callahan."

"He works out of the Thirteenth Precinct. I'll have someone who can point him out to you available tomorrow. Once you've made him, it'll be pretty easy. You be here early tomorrow, I'll have Sal go with you downtown to the precinct."

Vito nodded. "OK boss, you got anything else for me?"

Thinking for a moment, Luciano shook his head. "Nah, you can take off. Thanks."

Rising, the man left the office.

Luciano sat back in his chair; gazing straight ahead, he considered the possibilities of the situation. Ginny Maitland had her fingers into every piece of action in New York. If this cop was able to catch the guy that hit this girl, he had to parley that into a closer relationship with her. With her connections, he could take some major steps against the other gangs. It had long been a thought of his to consolidate the gangs into a larger organization, with him of course at the helm.

Distracted for a second, he looked at his watch. It was time he got back to work, he had to finish up here; he was going to the Chateau later. Luciano enjoyed the atmosphere greatly, and it was a safe place to discuss business. A number of politicians regularly gambled there; it was understood that the local cops had been instructed to take care of the joint. He often wondered how much the Frenchman paid for protection. It had to be quite a sum. He wished they were in his territory.

12

As the sun set, the temperature dropped slightly, the humidity lessened. The guests had begun to arrive and the owners, Louis, Andre, and Jacques were busy seeing to the many details that would assure their guests had a pleasant experience at their establishment.

Approaching the main entrance, Andre saw Senator Thomas Shaw walk casually into the foyer. He hastened over to him. "Senator, it's always a pleasure to have you as a guest at the Chateau des Beaux Arts."

Flashing his best political smile, Shaw held out his hand. "Andre, it's good to see you. I hope my luck has somewhat improved since last time." Smiling, he continued, "We shall see, eh?"

Andre recalled Shaw's last visit. The man had lost a sizable amount of cash, at the poker table. Speaking with the dealer afterwards, he was informed that the man was simply a poor player. He and his brothers ran an honest establishment, but he recognized the need for men with inflated egos to recover some of their losses. Occasionally, such men were directed to a table, where an accomplished dealer would allow them to recover some of their losses over time. He had no plans to offer Shaw such an accommodation, as he knew the man was quite wealthy. Gazing over at the other guests entering, he excused himself.

Shaw saw his man enter the foyer, having parked their car. With a motion of his head, he ordered Yost to follow him into the casino.

Working the room like the polished politician he was, he made note of a couple of people he would speak with at greater length before the evening ended. Yost stayed a discreet distance from the senator at all times.

Out of the corner of his eye, he noted a man moving towards him. He turned as the man approached; he was already wishing he would leave.

Legs Diamond stopped within speaking distance. Smiling, he faced the senator. "Say, aren't you Senator Thomas Shaw?"

Hiding his annoyance, Shaw replied, "I don't believe I've had the pleasure."

"Jack Diamond," he stuck out his hand.

Shaw gave him a perfunctory handshake. "Mr. Diamond."

Shaw was at ease due to the policy of the Chateau, that no photographers were allowed in the establishment. Recognizing the need for its patrons to have an enjoyable night out without having to worry about the tabloids was a major reason for its success.

Yost moved slowly up to Diamond, staring down at him with dispassionate eyes. Just as quickly, Diamond's men were at his side.

"Why don't you tell your large friend to get a drink and I'll do the same?"

Shaw stared at him for a moment then nodded. "Gerhardt, why don't you have a drink? Bring me my usual." The large man stood, quickly moving away towards the bar.

Staring at Shaw, Diamond instructed his men, "Boys, have a drink, and bring me a bourbon, straight up."

"You got it, boss."

They moved away towards the bar.

Standing alone, Shaw noticed an unoccupied table off in a corner. Gesturing, he suggested, "Why don't we have a seat?"

Smiling, Diamond moved towards the table, with the smallest nod of acknowledgement.

As they sat, Shaw asked, "What do you want, Mr. Diamond?"

"I've suffered some losses lately; I've had to respond."

"Yes, I know, I read the papers."

"I want what was promised. I want protection."

Shaw smiled slightly. "Why do you think the police haven't been around to speak with you?"

"Don't play dumb, I can't afford a war with Schultz. You need to have your people tell him to back off."

Realizing the weakness of Diamonds position, Shaw began to enjoy himself. "I'm sorry if you can't protect your people, but I can't begin to understand how that becomes my problem."

Diamond sat back, wanting to rip the man's throat out. He spoke calmly, "You piece of shit. We had a deal. I haven't heard you complaining while you've been getting your cut of my action."

Shaw leaned forward, his voice a whisper "Let's discuss this like gentlemen; there's no need for vulgarity."

"You politicians are all the same. Take what you can get, hope the public don't get wise to your action. Maybe I'll have a pal talk to Winchell. Yeah, that might cause you to feel my pain." Ever the astute judge of people, Diamond caught a fleeting note of concern in Shaw's eyes. Pressing his advantage, he continued, "A call to our mutual friend in City Hall would certainly ease my pain. His concern for the widows and orphans is commendable, and I'm happy to contribute to that. I would hate to have to take actions I might otherwise regret." He smiled. "How's that estate working for you on Long Island?"

Shaw hesitated for a moment. Knowing Diamond's reputation for avoiding violence, he was unsure of where the conversation was going.

"Maybe a delivery or two could be made on your beach, and it would be something if a couple of boys from the papers happened to be tipped off."

Shaw moved closer "You've made your point, Mr. Diamond. I'll make the necessary calls to alleviate your problem."

Sipping his drink, Diamond replied, "Yeah, fine. You do that and everyone is happy."

Rising, Shaw said, "You'll excuse me; I have other people I need to speak with. "Good evening." As he walked away, the German fell in behind him. As he passed, the German stared at Diamond with his cold, lifeless eyes, a slight smile on his lips.

Never one to show weakness, Diamond raised his glass to the man, smiling back. Watching from across the room, Lucky Luciano wondered what Legs Diamond and Senator Tom Shaw were talking about.

Mike Callahan walked casually into Floods Tavern, heading towards the bar. "Hey, Billy. I'm supposed to meet a guy."

The bartender looked up. "Hey, Mike." He pointed to a table in the corner where Special Agent James Watt sat nursing a soft drink.

"Thanks, Billy."

Callahan walked over to a man seated at a table, pulling out a chair he sat down.

"It's been a while, Callahan, how've you been doing?"

"You mean other than my wife dying?"

Watt silently cursed to himself. "I'm sorry for your loss Mike, really."

"Forget it. What can the New York Police Department do for the F.B.I?"

Watt took a sip of his drink. "We'd like to help you out on a case."

"Oh yeah, why is that?"

"The director has taken a personal interest in the case of the young woman whose body washed up on the south shore. He feels our crime lab is better equipped to examine the forensics, and we have the manpower to thoroughly investigate the murder."

Callahan stared intently at him.

Noting his demeanor, Watt proceeded carefully. "Also, the director feels that the case falls under our jurisdiction."

A waiter placed a drink in front of Callahan. Slowly, he picked up the glass. Taking a sip, he considered what the agent had just told him.

"No."

Watt blinked. "No...what?"

"I'm not going to hand this case over to you."

"Just like that? Mike, consider your position."

"What about my position?"

"Well, for one thing, Hoover has a lot of influence in Washington. If he wants the case, why not just give it to him? I'm sure you probably have a backlog of cases, with your partner being out on a medical."

Callahan took another sip of his drink and nodded. "Did your homework, know about Doc being laid up. That's very good."

"What's the big deal? It's not like she was related to you."

Callahan placed his drink on the table. "Jim, to answer your question, I did know this girl."

Oh shit, thought Watt.

"After Maureen died, she was my housekeeper. I'm going to find who killed her. You can make book on that."

"How about you let us have the case, I keep you informed every step of the way, and you can have the arrest?"

A thought struck Callahan. "Did Hoover say why he wanted this case?"

"Come on, Mike, if he's got a reason, he isn't telling me."

"Why don't you tell *the director,* if he wants to discuss this further to give me a call?"

Watt shook his head. "Mike, you're a good cop. You don't need the pressure that Hoover can bring down on you."

Callahan's temper grew. "Are you threatening me?"

"No... I'm not, but it will go above me, then it's out of my hands."

"You tell Hoover I've already got some leads; I don't need the goddamn F.B.I. to help me finish. Am I being perfectly clear?"

Watt sighed, "Yeah, you're clear, Mike. I'll tell Hoover what you said. I hope it doesn't get ugly for you."

"You let me worry about that Jim. Good night."

Standing up, Callahan headed for the door. He waved to the bartender, "Night, Billy."

"Night, Mike."

Watt sat there quietly for some time considering what he was going to tell Hoover. He was a man who didn't take disappointment well. A situation like this could present an obstacle for his career within the bureau.

As soon as Hoover mentioned Callahan's name, he knew this wasn't going to be an easy one. *Well, so be it,* he thought. He had offered Callahan the opportunity to step away from the case; everyone would have benefited.

Now he was going to have to take more drastic steps to deal with Callahan. He didn't want this, but he had no choice. Watt recalled Ed Cook, and what had happened to him after he had disappointed Hoover. Cook had been the agent in charge of the St. Louis field office. After the incident, which really hadn't been his fault, Cook was transferred to an office in Idaho. Watt shivered at the thought of such an outcome for him.

It was regrettable that it had to end this way. He would need to be certain that Callahan didn't suffer any permanent injuries. Grabbing his hat he rose, making his way quickly to the door.

13

Benny and Rita, after reading the diary, agreed that Shaw had Eileen murdered. He had bristled while reading her telling of the day Shaw had threatened her, if she didn't drop the subject of marriage. Having drunk his fill he had mocked the girl and her dreams of fitting into Washington high society. Benny's heart had broken as he read the tear stained pages.

Having no illusions regarding the senator, he knew him to be a ruthless man. If he ever laid his hands on Rita again, Benny would beat him senseless. A look of concern crossing his face, thinking that he'd need to make certain the German wasn't present.

Walking into the kitchen, he could smell the enticing aroma of Rita's cooking. After breakfast he would finish the work on the south wall, after which he had a short list of other chores requiring his attention.

Moving to Rita's side near the stove, he spoke softly to his wife. "Good morning, my sweet."

Rita turned, smiling. "Well, here I thought you'd be sleeping the day away."

Benny stretched, rubbing his hands against his chest. "Not when I smell your delicious cooking on the stove. Now, enough of your lip, girl, I'll be having my breakfast."

Playfully, she slapped him in the arm. "Sit then and let's eat."

He buttered a piece of toast. She took a sip of her coffee.

"Rita, we will obtain positions at another estate."

Quietly, she replied, "I know, Ben...I know."

"Friday, when the judge comes to dinner, I'll be the one to fetch him in town. I can mention the existence of the diary, asking his opinion on what to do. He'll know if the law can charge the senator with Eileen's murder. If he feels that can't be done, perhaps we can give the diary to the newspapers. It could destroy his career; an inadequate price to pay for Eileen's murder. We'll have to listen to what he says."

They finished their breakfast in silence.

Vito and Sal, Luciano's men, sat in their car a short distance down the street from the police precinct.

Sal, a short, thin man watched the main entrance to the station intensely. He had instructions from their boss to point out Mike Callahan to his partner. Luciano had been emphatic that Vito begin tailing the cop as soon as possible.

Leaning forward, he spoke softly, "There's your boy, Vito."

"Which one, Sal?"

"Tall guy, grey suit, easy walk, just passing the news stand, no hat."

"Got him." Vito watched, picking up whatever mannerisms he could.

Callahan stopped, looking across the street. For a second, the men froze thinking he would stare their way. A shorter, younger man was trotting across the street to him.
He ran up to Callahan, spoke to him.

Callahan shook his head at the younger man, waving his hand at him in a dismissive gesture. The younger man held up both hands in a placating manner. Nodding, Callahan pointed at the entrance to the precinct, and they proceeded to walk in together.

Sal spoke again, "That kid was Shaw's son."

"Yeah, I know. Lucky had a photo of him."

"Lucky really say you were to hit the kid if anything bad happens to the cop?"

Nodding, Vito replied, "Yeah, that's my orders."

Whistling, "Lucky you, given his old man there's guys who would line up for that hit." Sal seeming envious chuckled.

Laughing, Vito replied "Yeah, I guess so."

"OK, I'm gonna take off. You don't need me anymore. I can catch a cab to the ferry and tell Lucky you're on the job. Remember, stay off them, and don't let the cop make you. You got any problems, you can call me. You also gotta check in with Lucky at the end of each day." Finishing his instructions, Sal opened the door, stepping out he walked away from the car.

Vito didn't need to wait long before Callahan got behind the wheel of a car with another man in the front seat. Their car merged with traffic and Vito waited a second before he moved out to follow them.

Tom Shaw sat in his study sipping his coffee, his mind focused on the call he had received from his son. It appeared that Gerhardt had been less discreet than he had hoped. A female witness, a friend of Eileen's, had been able to identify him. Thankfully, she had failed to get the license plate number from his car.

Of somewhat greater concern was the question of why his man Fitzgibbon had paid a visit to Eileen's apartment.

Why would he do that?

Fortunately, they had not turned up any sort of diary. Eileen's off-hand remark about a diary had concerned him greatly. Under the influence, he couldn't recall the number of times he had told her of his plans or activities.

Reflecting on the situation, he forced himself to believe that she wasn't able of keeping any sort of detailed notes regarding his dealings with the likes of Legs Diamond or other members of the criminal element of the city.

It annoyed him that he hadn't heard anything from Hoover, accepting that he couldn't force the issue further there.

He could rely on his son to keep him informed of any progress the detective was making. Danny had spoken highly of the detective, saying he was one of the top homicide investigators in the precinct. It would be regrettable if he had to take action against an officer of the law. Hopefully, it wouldn't reach that point.

"Good morning, agent Watt."

Watt kept his voice calm and casual, having dreaded this phone call, "Good morning, sir."

"Well, were you able to speak with the detective regarding the case we spoke of?"

"Briefly, sir. He's been difficult to pin down."

"You've told him that this matter should be under our jurisdiction?"

"Oh yes, sir. He was skeptical, but he agreed to meet with me later today to resolve the issue."

"Excellent, Agent Watt. When can I expect word that you've assumed control of this case?"

"I would say first thing tomorrow morning."

"Good, I look forward to hearing from you"

Hoover hung up.

"Good bye…" Realizing he was speaking into a dead line, he hung up.

Grabbing his hat, Watt strode out of his office.

"I'll be back later, Mrs. Pender."

His secretary looked up as her boss walked quickly past her. "Yes sir," she said but he was already out the door.

Watt went to a coffee shop down the street from his office. He walked in, grabbed a paper, and as he paid he told the hostess that he would be meeting two friends for breakfast.

As he was seated, a waitress came over. "Coffee please, I'm waiting for two friends."

The waitress nodded, and walked away. She returned with his coffee and was gone again.

A few minutes later, two men entered the shop. They made eye contact with Watt, waved and walked over to his table.

Watt didn't get up, inviting them to sit. "Smitty, Bobby, thanks for coming."

"No problem Jimmy, what's the problem you need help with?"

He placed the newspaper aside. The waitress was quickly at their table.

Watt looked up, and spoke quickly. "Two more coffees and three specials."

"You got it."

The men got back to business. Watt leaned slightly forward. "The director has charged me with a special project."

The two young men sat forward, waiting to hear more.

"There's a murder case currently being handled by the New York Police, which he feels should be under Bureau control."

"What case are you talking about?" Smitty asked.

"That young woman whose body washed up on the south shore of Long Island last week."

"So what's the problem, Jimmy?"

"There's a homicide detective who has a special interest in the case, he won't listen to reason."

"So, why doesn't Hoover just call his boss?"

Watt smiled slyly. "There are other considerations."

The men sat back in the chairs considering the possibilities. The waitress arrived with their food, and they sat back as she placed it on the table. They all began to eat.

"So, what do you want us for, Jimmy?" Bobby asked.

Watt thought for a moment, actually feeling badly about what he was going to say. "I need you guys to put this cop out of commission for a couple of days, so I can move in and take the case." Watt studied both men intently. Young agents just up from the academy, they were undoubtedly eager for advancement. "I would of course, mention your assistance to the director."

He could see the ambition in their faces. It was common knowledge in the Bureau that any agent who earned the favor of the director, was quick to rise in the ranks.

The two men looked at each other, silently reaching agreement.

Smitty spoke, "Yeah, we can do that. Nothing permanent, right?"

Watt reacted quickly, "No, just a roughing up, put him in the hospital for a couple of days."

"You got his address?"

Watt took a piece of paper out of his pocket, passing it over to them.

Bobby took the paper, opened it, and nodded. Looking at his partner, he said, "I know where this is; we're okay."

"You'll let me know when you've *spoken* with him."

"Sure thing, Jimmy, just one question."

Watt looked a little puzzled.

"What's his name?"

Embarrassed, he replied, "Callahan. Mike Callahan."

Both men stood, pushing their chairs out, having finished their breakfasts.

"We'll *talk to him* later today. We'll call you"

"Thanks for breakfast, Jimmy. See ya later."

Watt watched the men depart, his sense of foreboding increasing. Callahan had a formidable reputation among the cops. He needed to consider his options, should these men fail in their task. The director did not suffer failure lightly.

He would need to place the blame appropriately, to limit the damage to his career. He smiled ruefully, thinking, *I can handle that.*

14

Breaking and entering had been easy. They had been instructed in the techniques used by criminals at the academy. Many of the young agents practiced the craft, thinking they might need the expertise at some point. The men had easily entered Callahan's apartment.

They froze, as they heard someone approaching the apartment door.

Callahan walked slowly towards his apartment. As he approached his door he casually looked down at the floor and stopped. The thin piece of folded paper that he kept wedged in the lower portion of the closed door frame was lying on the floor. He drew his revolver, considering his options, thinking where an assailant might be hiding within his room.

Approaching the door, he put his key into the lock, turning the knob. Upon opening the door he immediately noticed that the curtain from the far window was the closed. Moving quickly, bringing his weapon around, he side stepped into the room.

"Don't you move, goddamn it!" Mike shouted

One of the agents taken completely by surprise, his weapon holstered, he held up his hands. Before he could speak again, out of the corner of his eye he saw another figure move, reflected in the mirror on the far wall. Turning as he fell towards the floor, he fired.

Callahan tried to bring his weapon around, but the other man was on him, punching him hard in the head and the face. Finally, able to free his hand with his weapon he quickly swung it against his assailant's head again and again. The man fell over onto the floor.

Quickly sitting up, Callahan held his weapon on the fallen man. Seeing that he was unconscious, he turned his attention to the other man. He was lying immobile, his breaths coming in short rasps.

He rose, turning on the light on the table near the radio.

Walking back to the unconscious man, he moved his arms, patting him down. Feeling a weapon he removed it, tossing it on the couch. Checking for identification, he pulled out a billfold, and opened it.

He was stunned to see the identification of an agent of the Federal Bureau of Investigation. Furious, he knew immediately who had sent these men against him. Wondering what their instructions had been, he went over to the second man, where he found similar identification. Seeing that the second man was in distress, he went to his phone.

"Send an ambulance to 410 Varcy Street. This is a police matter; a man is shot."

Realizing he had a few moments, he went back to the unconscious man, slapping him. Slowly, the man regained consciousness. Callahan put the barrel of his gun between the man's eyes. "Who sent you? And please realize I could pull this trigger and get away with it, Agent Daley."

The man seemed to quickly assess his situation. Sneering, he replied, "You're gonna have more trouble than you can handle, cop."

"Really? I doubt that. You and your partner entered my apartment without a warrant, failing to identify yourselves as federal officers when I entered. Once I make my report, you'll be lucky if Hoover lets you clean his toilet."

Realizing the truth in his words, the agent looked away.

"My partner?"

Surprised, "I called an ambulance, what the hell did you think?"

"Now, while we are waiting, what the hell are you doing in my apartment?"

"Forget it, Callahan; we'll be out on the street before you know it."

Callahan smiled. "Yes, but what are you and stupid over there going to do for jobs, once I speak with the papers? I'll do my best to see that Hoover either transfers you to the smallest office he has, or we can have a nice chat." He saw a note of fear in the man's eyes.

"You wouldn't do that," he retorted, uncertainty in his voice.

"Wanna bet?"

"You'll take care of me and my partner, your word on it?"

"If you know anything about me, you know my word is good, and you have it."

Shaking his head, "Okay, Okay, it was Jim Watt. He wanted us to put you in the hospital for a couple of days so he could move in and take some murder case away from you."

"Did he tell you the case?"

"Some murdered girl, washed up on the beach. Don't know more than that. He did say Hoover wants the case for the Bureau."

Anger welled up in Callahan. The question which he now needed to answer was why the Director of the Federal Bureau of Investigation was so interested in Eileen's murder.

He heard the siren of an approaching ambulance. "Wait here, I'll bring the medics up. I'm going to tell them you, me, and stupid came back to my apartment after dinner, and an unknown assailant was waiting for me. Your partner stepped in front of a bullet meant for me."

"Okay, thanks Callahan."

Standing up, Callahan walked to his door.

"Oh, and if I see you or stupid again…you'll wish I didn't."

Sitting alone in his apartment after everyone had departed; Mike considered the developments in the case. He thought of the two men, the large guy on the boat, and the Irish guy at the apartment. In two of the three cases there was the black Packard.

Hoover's involvement could only mean one thing: *Eileen was involved with an influential man.*

Murders happened in the city every day. Eileen wasn't a celebrity whom the director could milk for publicity for his agency. Therefore, it was most probable that whoever was involved in the murder had approached Hoover.

Sighing, he ran his fingers through his hair.

How many men of influence lived in or near New York City?

He reminded himself to check with Danny tomorrow; he wanted to see how he was coming with the list of Packard owners in the area. As he was falling asleep, he wondered what make of car Shaw's father owned.

Across town, James Watt hung up his phone, anger and disappointment gnawing at him. He would deal with the two men later. His immediate problem was Hoover.

What was he going to tell him?

He wondered if Callahan would come after him. Daley said the cop had seemed furious when he had told him of their purpose for being in his room. Anger rose within him as he thought, *let him come; I'll handle a dumb cop.*

15

Awakened by the ringing alarm, Callahan was annoyed as he blindly groped for it and knocked off his night table. "All right, you pain in my ass," he grumbled, as he threw his blanket off, swung his legs around, and rose to a sitting position. The alarm continued to ring.

After his wife's death, he purchased the alarm to ensure he wouldn't oversleep. When Maureen was alive, she had always woken him for work. She had a natural instinct for waking up when necessary. In their years together, she had never let him oversleep or miss any time at the job. Whenever Mike would ask her how she was always able to wake at the proper time, she would just smile, saying it was her job to take care of her man.

God, I miss her, he thought.

Reaching down quickly, he snatched up the alarm from the floor and in one movement he shut it off. Shaking off the remaining haze of sleep, he suddenly recalled the importance of today.

Eileen was to be buried today.

He had made all of the arrangements, with Ginny Maitland insisting on taking care of any of the financial costs. Grabbing his watch off the nightstand, he looked at the time and let out a sigh of relief, seeing that he had more than enough time to get to the church.

Ginny had insisted that he ride with her to the funeral mass. Knowing Eileen to be a devout Catholic, they had agreed that she receive a full funeral mass.

After showering and dressing quickly, he was standing on the street when he saw Ginny's car turn the corner. Smiling, looking at his watch, he saw that, as always, she was precisely on time. The car pulled to the curb by him, and stopped.

Acknowledging the driver, he opened the rear door. Ginny and Claire sat together. He smiled, greeting them, "Good morning, Ginny, Claire."

"Good morning, Michael. Sit between us," Ginny said as they separated, allowing him to sit.

Glancing at Claire, Callahan said, "The notice was in the papers." It was more a statement than a question.

Nodding, "Yes Mike." Claire answered.

He had arranged with Ginny to have the funeral notice posted in the papers, hoping that the mysterious Irishman might show up, to pay his last respects. It was, he realized, a bit of a reach, but in speaking with the apartment manager, Fields, he was certain that the man had not been aware of her death. The man was most probably a friend, who, if they were lucky, might offer a clue as to her murder.

Mike held no illusion that the tall, limping man would be there. That one had accomplished his task and sunk back into the darkness. It would be up to him to draw this man back into the light, and to bring him to justice.

Ginny spoke, "I hear you had a little commotion at your place last night."

He looked at her, surprised. "You don't miss much, do you?"

Calmly, she continued, "Why were federal agents taken away from your apartment in an ambulance?"

"Have you put a tail on me Ginny?"

She smiled her famous smile, saying, "I wouldn't dream of it, but I do hear things."

"It was a mistake on the part of an agent named Watt. I intend to speak with him about it."

Calmly Ginny added, "One of the agents had been shot."

She stared intently at him. "Michael, please, what happened?"

"You're right, I apologize. I had a meeting with Watt who told me that Hoover wants the Bureau to take over the case."

Claire spoke, "Hoover, what could be his interest?"

Ginny sat silent, while Callahan replied, "I honestly don't know, but I intend to find out. My feeling is that Eileen had involved herself with a man of influence, who went to Hoover to be certain that the case is forgotten."

Staring thoughtfully out the window, Ginny spoke. "Eileen a mistress, I can't picture that, Mike."

"It's what seems to make sense. I'm open to suggestions."

They rode in silence for a moment.

"Is Jimmy going to be at the church?" Mike asked.

"Of course, I agreed that was a good idea. If Eileen's Irish friend makes an appearance, we'll be able to speak with him." Ginny replied.

"Danny Shaw will be outside watching for him." Mike added.

Knowing her feelings, "I told him, he's not to come into the church, unless he sees the car, then he's to let me know immediately"

"Thank you Michael."

A couple of blocks from the church, Benny found a parking space. Stepping out of the Packard, scanning the block, he felt comfortable that the car couldn't be seen from the church. Not wishing to raise any notice, he felt the police might be watching the funeral.

After breakfast, he had a short, heated discussion with Rita. She had not wanted him to attend the mass, being concerned with Shaw's possible involvement. Walking up towards the cross street, he headed for the church.

On the street outside of the church, Danny Shaw sat in a car, watching the main doors. He was pleased that he also had a view of the doors on the side of the church. It had annoyed him when Callahan told him he wasn't to enter the church, but had understood when he was told who Mike would be attending the mass with.

Jimmy Fields, dressed in the suit he had worn to his wife's funeral, made a point of arriving early and selecting a seat which offered him the widest view of the inside of the church. He had been instructed by Ginny to watch for the Irishman, who had visited the apartment house looking for Eileen. Knowing her personal involvement with the death, he had sworn he would finger the guy, if he showed up.

Watching the doors, Jimmy saw Ginny Maitland, her assistant Claire, and Callahan enter the church. Moving towards the altar, Callahan scanned the church, caught Field's eye and nodded. He spoke quietly to Ginny; she gently grabbed his arm, spoke back to him, and released him as she entered the pew.

Casually walking towards the church, Benny continued scanning the street looking for anything suspicious. Across the street, Danny Shaw was jolted in his seat, seeing his father's handyman. Benny was already inside when Shaw acted, getting out of his car.

Jimmy Fields sat watching the few people inside the church. Upon seeing a man enter, he sat upright.

It was the Irishman. Fields watched the man, obviously nervous, take a seat towards the rear. Fields got up and moved towards Callahan. Benny failed to notice the apartment manager, as he sat next to Callahan.

Speaking in a whisper, Jimmy said, "He's here, Mike. The Irishman."

Looking straight ahead, Callahan replied, "Where is he sitting?"

"Near the back. Towards the side door."

Nodding, Callahan said, "Thanks, Jimmy. Good work." Callahan informed Ginny that the man was in the church.

The priest came on to the altar, and they all rose. Eileen's coffin had been brought to the church by the funeral home. Mike rose from his pew, walking towards the wall; he caught a glimpse of the man. Moving towards the side aisle, his eyes on the man, he began to move faster.

Noticing the tall man walking towards him, Benny instinctively rose, quickly making for the side door.

"Police, stop!"

"Bollocks!"

He was out the side door, where he ran directly into Danny Shaw.

Shaw was visceral. "You stupid Mick! Go that way," pointing down the alley. Benny took off at a run. Watching him run, Shaw fell to the ground.

The door quickly burst open, Callahan running over to Shaw. "Which way did he go?" Shaw played at being woozy. "Dammit, did you see which way he went?" Shaw pointed in the opposite direction. Callahan took off quickly in pursuit.

Getting up, Shaw smiled at Callahan's retreating figure. "Not so smart, are we."

Dusting himself off, he walked back to his car.

A few minutes later, Callahan returned. Walking over to the car, he asked angrily, "What happened?"

Confused, Shaw replied, "What do you mean?"

"How did he get by you?"

"I must have been too close to the door."

He stared at Shaw with an astonished look. "That was probably our last chance to get that guy."

"You think he's the killer?"

"No, no I don't, but he might have led us to the big guy with the limp."

"I'm sorry, Mike."

"Yeah, I wouldn't have had this problem with Doc."

Shaw replied, the anger in his voice evident. "Yeah, well, too bad I ain't Doc."

Callahan got in his face. "Too damn bad is right. You wanna be smart? Shut up. I'm going back inside. You can leave." Without waiting for a response, Callahan walked back into the church.

The priest was finishing the service, as Callahan returned to the service. Claire made eye contact with him, gesturing inquiringly. Shaking his head, he looked down for a moment.

Outside, Shaw sat in the car, considering how best to inform his father that Benny had gone to the funeral service. He had also begun to develop anger towards Mike Callahan.

He would show him.

He would show them all.

Across town, two of Diamond's men waited on a street corner. A brown Ford coupe pulled up to the curb and they walked over to the car.

The German sat in the car. Tom Regan leaning over, looked in the side window, he spoke to the German, "Legs says the delivery is going to happen at Hemlocks beach at 11 tomorrow night."

The German nodded; his face unreadable.

Regan stared at him, "You got that, Heinrich?"

"Jes, I undestaend," looking at Regan with dead eyes.

Taken aback momentarily, Regan asked, "What?"

"Don't worry little man; we will take care of you."

"Why, you...," he began, as his partner grabbed his arm.

"Tommy, the hell with him. Let's get back to the boss." Regan stepped away from the car.

"Yeah," jerking his thumb down the street, "run back to your big shot boss." The German spoke, disdain in his voice.

The two men turned, walking away from the car. Laughing deeply, the German pulled away from the curb.

As the German drove away, a small, wiry man watched from across the street. He was one of the men watching Diamond's men, at the direction of Lucky Luciano. After the night at the Chateau, Luciano had been very interested in the relationship between Legs Diamond and Senator Thomas Shaw. The watcher knew the German, and as the German drove away, he hurriedly ran back to his car. He drove away quickly, knowing that his boss would reward him for the information he was bringing.

In his car, the man thought, *Life is good.*

16

After rushing home quickly, Benny parked the car and burst into their cottage, yelling, "Rita... ah where are you, girl?"

He was greeted by silence for a moment.

"Benny, is that you?"

Benny quickly bounded up the stairs. Rita was putting linens in their closet, her back to him. He came before her, breathing hard. She turned and stared at him, unsure. Placing the linens on a table, she gently wiped her hands on her apron. Looking up into his eyes, she asked "Is everything all right, dear?"

"Ah, where do I start?"

Moving to him, she took his hands in hers. "At the beginning, love." She guided him over to the bed and they sat. "Did you go to her funeral?"

"Yes, and he was there."

Concerned, she asked, "Who was there?"

"The young master, Daniel."

Rita looked away, confused. "Why was he there? The little bastard."

"He's a shagging policeman."

Remembering, Rita stared speechless for a second. "Did he see you?"

Benny laughed. "See me? I nearly bowled the little bastard over running into him."

Concerned, Rita asked "Who were you running away from, Ben?"

Benny answered unsure, "I don't know, a big man, a police officer."

"*Ach*, if Daniel Shaw can be a police officer, you were wise to run. They are all a corrupt bunch of hoodlums"

Skeptical, Benny replied, "I don't know... but Danny was angry, he helped me get away from the man who was after me."

Looking sharply at him, she said, "He did, did he?"

Getting up, she began to pace. "We must throw the diary away; it's bringing evil down on us," wringing her hands as she spoke.

 Benny asked "Ah love, you know we can't abandon Eileen."

Turning on him furiously, almost shouting "What about me, your wife? Answer me that, you noble bastard. You'd ruin our life here because of a dead girl who we barely knew."

Lowering his head, his eyes began to water. "What would you have me do, girl? I did think of her as the daughter we never had."

Her rage grew, her eyes alight with emotion "Don't you blame me, Benny Fitzgibbon. I wanted children, I did… I did."

He rushed to embrace her, holding her tightly in his arms. "Ah, lass, you're the love of my life, but we must do the right thing here."

"I know…I know."

Slowly they separated.

"You said the Judge comes to dinner on Friday?"

"Yes…you know it."

"We must give him Eileen's diary. He'll know what to do with it." Rita stared uncertainly into his eyes.

"You're certain of that, are you?"

Glancing away, unsure, she spoke hesitantly "I don't know. What else can we do?"

Smiling sadly, Benny answered. "I am open to suggestions."

She punched him gently on the shoulder. "Ah, how could all of this turn so bad?"

Before he could answer, there was a knock on the door. They looked at each other unsure. He held a finger to his lips, silencing her. Turning he walked to the door, opening it slowly.

The German stood there. "The senator wants to see you."

Forcing himself to be calm, Benny replied, "Of course. Tell him I'll be along shortly."

"Now."

"All right, then." turning, speaking calmly, "Rita, I'm going up to the main house to see the senator. I'll be back in a bit."

"All right, Ben," her voice barely above a whisper.

Benny followed the man out, closing the door behind him. They walked up the gravel path, towards the main house.

"How are you, Gerhardt?"

The German kept on walking looking straight ahead.

"*Gut.*"

They approached the main house. Entering the main house, the German pointed to the sitting room. Staring at him, Benny proceeded slowly into the room.

The senator was seated in the corner, reading. Looking up, he smiled, gesturing to a chair "Ah Benny, take a seat. I'll be a moment."

Walking over, Benny took a seat across from the man. Sinking into the comfortable chair, he noticed that the senator's seat was higher than his. Trying to sit forward, he waited. The senator appeared to take no notice of him. The senator was purposefully having Benny wait to heighten his anxiety.

Finally, looking up, the senator spoke "Ah, Benny, thank you for coming so quickly."

"Not at all sir; the German, ah...Gerhardt said you wanted to see me."

Sitting back in his chair, the senator seemed lost in thought "Yes, I received a call from my son; he said he saw you at a funeral today. The funeral for Eileen O'Sullivan. Is that correct?"

Benny stared at the man, appalled at his nerve. "Yes sir, she drowned off the south shore of Long Island."

Shaw seemed actually surprised. "My god, that's terrible…just terrible."

"You hadn't heard about it sir?"

"No, I've been so busy in Washington. I have wondered, though, how she was faring after we stopped seeing each other."

There was a moment of silence between them.

"Did you speak with any of her friends, at the service?"

"Ah sir, I did not, I had to leave suddenly. Some large fellow wanted to speak with me and I wanted no part of him, all things considered."

"Of course… I understand. That will be all; thank you, Benny." Picking up his papers, he began to read again.

Realizing he was dismissed, Benny rose. "I'll be about my duties, then."

Without looking up, Shaw waved his hand dismissively, saying nothing.

Walking from the room, he passed into the foyer, thinking, *"Oh yes… you knew nothing…you lying bastard. Your day will come."*

Opening the door to leave, out of the corner of his eye, he saw the German watching him.

In another house, Luciano's man stood before his boss, Lucky Luciano. Unlike Benny, he wasn't nervous, or afraid of losing his job. On the contrary, he knew that his information would yield him a reward.

Luciano sat back comfortably, behind his antique oak desk. He had been told by a politician that he had "bought" that appearances were important, and underlings should never feel comfortable when they were in your presence.

"Tell me again, Antonio, what you saw."

"Well it's like I said, Mr. Luciano. I watched Diamond's boys, like you told me; they met with the big kraut that works for the senator."

"How close were you?"

Uncomfortable, he tried to keep his voice calm, "I was across the street; a lot of their guys know me."

Nodding, his face impassive, "Go on."

"I saw Regan, and another guy."

Luciano sat up straight. "You sure it was Regan?"

Nodding furiously, seeing Luciano's interest "Yes sir, it was that Mick sonofabitch."

Luciano considered what he was hearing. Regan was Diamond's second in command. If he was speaking with the German, Diamond's dealings with the senator were on a serious level.

He needed more information before he would act. His good friend Meyer Lansky had always said, "You can't never have enough information about an opponent." He was investigating the source of Diamond's support and would soon have an answer.

Smiling, Luciano spoke "Antonio, you did good. On your way out see Carlo, tell him I said so. He'll take care of you.

Antonio quickly came around the desk, grasping Luciano's outstretched hand. Reverently, he kissed the hand. Backing away slowly, bowing "Thank you, thank you."

Luciano waved him away, gently.

I gotta find a way to make this work for me, he thought. Sitting alone for a while, he contemplated his options.

17

"Mayor, you've got to come down hard on the rackets, otherwise people are gonna think you're in their pockets."

James J. Walker sat, staring at his chief advisor.

Mike Farrell, his chief advisor, stared back at the mayor, waiting for some kind of response. Having been with the mayor since 1926, he felt more than a reasonable pride in the measure of success that Walker had attained.

"Mayor... Are you listening to me?

"Yes Mike, despite what you might feel, I do listen to you more than you think."

Emboldened, Farrell pressed "Great sir, great. You've got to come down on the rackets. The press is starting to eat you alive."

Walker considered how his involvement with the undesirables of the city had increased, much to his chagrin. In his efforts to accomplish good for the poor of the city, he had left himself open to criticism. *No. let's be honest,* he thought, *he had left himself open to criminal investigation. How had this happened? It had always been his goal to improve the lot of the oppressed in this great metropolis. How had this gone wrong?*

"What do you suggest we do, Mike?"

"Well sir, its common knowledge that there are a number of speakeasies around the city, ones that a lot of big shots frequent."

Walker looked at his aide sharply. "Sure, that's a grand idea; get all of the important people angry at me."

"Let me finish, sir. Don't you see, the people would look at such a move positively."

Skeptical, Walker raised his eyebrows, "Really? Why exactly would they view it that way?"

"It would reinforce their opinion of you as a champion of the people."

"I don't know, Mike. I really don't think that's a good idea. Besides, I believe that Prohibition will be repealed in the near future. There is a growing movement against the amendment."

He wasn't really concerned with the feelings of the elites who might frequent such establishments; his arrangements having allowed some of those establishments to flourish in his city. He viewed it as a harmless crime, which really didn't hurt anyone. People would find a way to drink, having always done so. It also allowed him to fund some activities that aided those out of work and the homeless.

"No, I'm sorry Mike. I just don't think we should do anything at this time."

Farrell sighed, "Sir, I..."

Holding up his hand, Walker silenced him. "Let me think about it some more. Perhaps we can do something, but not just now, okay?"

Realizing he was beaten, Farrell nodded. "Yes, sir."

"Good." Walker looked at his wristwatch. "We have that budget meeting in a half hour, don't we?" Farrell nodded. "Yes, sir." Farrell got up, realizing their meeting was over, "I'll round everyone up."

Walker smiled. "Thanks Mike."

The day passed uneventfully for Callahan, after the fiasco at the funeral. He had been furious with Shaw for allowing the suspect to escape; and, recalling the kid's attitude afterwards, his anger grew. A question that had bothered him all day was why the Irishman ran from him after he had identified himself as a police officer. He didn't believe that the man had anything to do with Eileen's murder. Fields had said he expected her to be at the apartment.

He had sent Shaw home, choosing to pursue what was probably his only other potential lead in the case, Special Agent James Watt. Going to the federal Building, he watched as people exited the building at five o'clock. Thankfully, he hadn't seen Watt in the mass outpouring of people. Moving closer to the building entrance, he waited. With the sunset, the heat of the day had cooled, and as evening came, the activity in the area began to quiet.

Callahan looked at his watch. Fifteen more minutes, and he would call it a night.

Looking back up, he saw Watt exit the building. Seeing he was alone, he smiled. There was a parking garage two blocks away. If Watt had driven to work, it was probable that he would leave his car there.

Watt began to walk towards the garage. Callahan followed at a discreet distance. As Watt entered the parking lot, he waved to the attendant. Callahan noticed that the man didn't return the wave. He was sleeping.

Callahan quickened his pace.

Watt had stopped to tie his shoe; Callahan, quietly moving, was almost within striking distance.

Stopping to look at the rear bumper of a car, Watt bent down, appearing to inspect some damage.

Callahan moved quickly up, grabbed him by the back, and slammed his face into the car. Groaning, he fell to the ground. Looking about to make sure there were no witnesses, Callahan dragged the semi-conscious agent into a darker area of the garage. Callahan reached into his jacket and took his weapon. Slapping him, his voice impatient, "Come on, Jimmy, wake up."

"What..." focusing on the detective, "Callahan, you're in serious shit my friend, assaulting a federal agent."

Callahan smiled. "You got any witnesses? I got five guys who will swear I was with them tonight." He punched Watt in the face. "That was for sending those clowns to my apartment."

Grimacing, Watt felt his lip.

Callahan drew back his fist again.

Holding up his hand, Watt spoke quickly "Wait, come on. I'm sorry, Okay?"

Callahan hit him again. "Sorry ain't gonna do it, Jimmy. I want information."

Watt held up both hands surrendering. "What...what do you want?"

His voice hard, "Come on, you know, the case. Why does Hoover want it?"

"I swear to God, I told you everything I know."

Callahan punched him in the face again.

"I didn't get any names, I swear it! Hoover only said he wanted to help out a friend. Probably some big shot who had something to do with the dead broad."

Callahan punched him in the face again.

"What the hell was that for?"

His voice full of menace. "Her name was Eileen."

"Right...sorry."

"Tell you what, Jimmy boy, you're going to get the name of the guy that spoke to Hoover, and give it to me."

Incredulous, his eyes wide "And how exactly am I to get him to tell me?"

"That's your problem. If you don't, I'm going to see you again, and really give you a beating."

Watt stared at him, saying nothing, and Callahan punched him in the face again, knocking him out.

Standing, Callahan dusted himself off and straightened his tie. Looking around, he saw that the garage was quiet. Staring down at the unconscious man, he quickly walked towards the exit, past the sleeping attendant, and into the night.

18

Judge Joseph Crater had finished his day at the courts, went home, and prepared for his evening at Senator Shaw's estate on Long Island. He greatly enjoyed his visits to the estate. The senator's man Benny was to pick him up and drive him out to Long Island. Given the amount of drinking that usually took place during such visits, he would spend the night and return to New York tomorrow. He had cleared his schedule in anticipation of the evening.

Crater, being known to be fastidious regarding his appearance carefully examined himself in a full length mirror. He prided himself on his reputation as "Good Time Joe" and for the ladies he had spent time with. Upon checking his watch, he grabbed his hat and coat, and left his apartment. Stepping out the door, he saw Shaw's car waiting at the curb.

He smiled. The Irishman, Benny, was nothing if not extremely punctual. Benny quickly jumped out of the car to get the door for the judge as he approached the vehicle.

"Good evening, Judge."

Crater nodded "Good evening, Benny. How are you this fine evening?'

"Fine, sir, and yourself?"

Crater seemingly in a good mood, "Just grand, thank you."

Opening the door, Crater seated himself in the rear as Benny closed the door. Moving quickly to the driver's side door, Benny got in and started the car. Crater sat back, relaxing.

After traveling for a few minutes, Benny spoke, "Can I ask a question sir, about the law, that is?"

Curious, Crater responded "Of course, Benny. What might your question be?"

"Well, the law, it's supposed to be equal for all, is it not?

Crater's interest growing "Why, of course. No person is above the law."

Hesitant, Benny asked "What of someone of influence, could they skirt the law?"

Interested, Crater gave a classroom answer "There are many complexities involved in the law, Benny. If a person of influence was charged with a crime, they would be entitled to legal representation. The state would need to prove their case against such a person. If successful, that person would then be punished according to the statutes of the law."

"But if they had better lawyers than the state, they could get away with a crime."

"Yes, sometimes that is the case. That is why we strive to be diligent when preparing a case against an accused individual. The law is not perfect, so it is up to those of us who uphold the legal system to look beyond all other considerations, and to adhere to the law." The car moved smoothly through the evening traffic.

"What type of proof would assure the best chance for a conviction of a criminal?"

Crater was actually enjoying the conversation. "Oh, a number of things, the most important being an eyewitness to a crime. Others could be an accomplice who turns states evidence, or a deathbed statement."

Watching Benny, Crater couldn't help but notice his intensity. His curiosity aroused, he was interested in where this conversation was headed.

"That last one sir, what would be involved with something such as that?"

"Well, that would involve a person taking the statement of someone who was dying, regarding a crime. That person would then testify in court as to the veracity of the statement."

"Would a document sent by someone to a friend accusing another person of a crime be considered evidence against that person?"

"Yes, but the writer of the document would be called to testify, to substantiate the contents of the document."

"What if that person was dead?"

Crater stared intently at Benny from the darkness of the rear seat.

"What precisely are we talking about here, Benny?"

Having discussed it with Rita, Benny felt he now had to take the judge into their confidence. "I have such a document in my possession."

Very interested, Crater kept his tone even "Can you elaborate?"

"Can we speak in confidence, sir?"

"Of course, Benny. Consider our conversation to be confidential."

Taking a few deep breaths, Benny spoke. "It's about himself, sir."

Confused, Crater shook his head slightly "Who?"

"The senator."

Crater sat upright. "Senator Shaw?"

"Yes, sir."

Crater couldn't believe the conversation. "You have a written document accusing the senator of a crime?"

"Yes sir, a number of crimes, including the murder of a fine young woman."

Crater was almost unable to speak.

Watching him in the mirror, Benny couldn't help but notice the intense look in his eyes.

Crater spoke deliberately, "Are we talking about the young woman who the senator had been seeing for a while?"

"Yes sir, her name was Eileen O'Sullivan."

"I can't believe it."

"Ah, but you can, sir, she kept a diary."

Crater's mind was racing; such a document would give him complete control over Shaw. Forcing himself to be calm, he realized he had to get the diary from this man, knowing only then would he have control over the powerful senator.

"You mentioned other crimes. Are these crimes are mentioned in the diary?"

Benny was committed. "Bootlegging, sir. He has an arrangement with a fellow named Diamond."

Incredulous, Crater asked "Legs Diamond?"

"Yes, sir, I believe that is his name."

"Benny, I want to congratulate you for bringing this to my attention, but I do have a question."

"Yes, sir."

"Why do you believe the senator was involved in the murder of Miss O'Sullivan?"

Sadly, slowly, emotion in his voice "The German most probably killed her on that boat, at the direction of the senator."

"Yes...of course." Crater considered the German, silently agreeing that he was most probably capable of murder. Calming himself, he spoke in an even voice, "You say you have this document in your possession. May I ask how you acquired it?"

Nodding, Benny answered "I received it in the mail, shortly after Eileen was murdered."

"So the diary is at the estate."

Noting the intensity on the face of the judge, Benny lied, "No it's not, sir. We gave it to a friend for safe keeping. We thought it best not to have it at the estate."

The disappointment on Crater's face was all too evident.

"I see, I see. How long would it take to retrieve it from your friend?"

"Well sir, I'll be going into the city on Friday to purchase materials and supplies for some of the tasks I'm in the midst of at the estate."

Speaking calmly and not wanting to shout at the man, Crater asked "Do you have a telephone in your cottage?"

Nodding, "Aye, we do." Benny answered.

"Good. Once we get to the estate, I want you to write down your number for me. I will telephone you; we'll arrange a meeting."

"Wouldn't I just bring it to you at the courts?"

"Good heavens, no. Tom Shaw is a powerful man. If he found out that the diary existed, it would disappear without a trace. I will examine the document, and if I feel that the diary presents credible evidence on which the state can establish a case against him, I will indict him."

"I guess that would be sufficient. Can you promise that if convicted, he would receive the death penalty?"

"That would depend on a number of factors. I would, of course, need to speak with the detectives investigating the murder. If they can establish that Gerhardt was on the boat the night Eileen was murdered, that would weigh heavily against the senator."

Benny considered his comments. "I can accept that."

Crater spoke in a soothing voice, "Yes we must allow the justice system to work. While it's not perfect, it's all we have." Crater's last thought was that the diary would never see the inside of a courtroom, and that when he told Thomas Shaw who provided him with the diary, Shaw would probably have the German deal with him.

Benny turned the car into the estate. Pulling up to the main house, he got out, quickly moving to open the rear door. Exiting the car, Crater followed Benny up the steps to the front door, and they entered.

Gesturing, Benny turned heading for the senator's office "Please wait in the salon. I'll tell the senator you're here."

"Thank you, Benny."

Upon knocking on the door, the senator replied, "Come."

"The Judge is here, sir."

"Thank you, Benny. Tell him I'll be there shortly."

"Yes, sir."

Returning to the salon, Crater stood looking out the window towards the ocean, a drink in his hand. "The senator will be with you shortly."

Turning, the judge smiled. "Thank you, Benny. I'll see you in the morning."

"Good evening, sir."

Sipping his drink, he gathered his thoughts, as the senator strode into the room.

"Good evening, Joseph. How are you?"

Crater's smile was broad. "Quite well, thanks. I just received some wonderful news."

Curious, Shaw stared at him "Anything you'd care to share?"

Shrugging, "In time, Thomas, in time."

19

Callahan awoke in a positive frame of mind, being especially pleased with his conversation with Jim Watt. His right hand bothered him, having struck the man a number of times in the head. The results had been what he hoped; he felt that Watt would find some way to get him the name of the man who had gone to Hoover.

He dressed quickly and headed for the precinct. As he entered the building, he waved to a couple of friends and moved towards his desk. He was surprised to see that Shaw wasn't already sitting there waiting for him. He sat down and began to read his messages. Some of them related to other cases he was working on, the others minor matters he could ask Shaw to take care of. He smiled at the thought of letting him experience the basics of police work. Despite what the movies and the dime store novels portrayed, the job was often just tedious work.

Out of the corner of his eye, he noticed Shaw entering the room. Glancing up at the clock, he noted that the kid was late. As he approached, he also noticed that he didn't look well at all; in fact, he looked hung over. Sitting at Mike's desk, he let out a long sigh.

Callahan stared at him. "You look like you drank some coffin varnish."

"I've got a bad cold coming on, Mike. That's all."

Smirking, "That's a bunch of hooey kid. If you're not hung over, I'm not worthy of the rank of detective. What gives?"

Shaw thought for a second, considering his words "I got together with a couple of friends last night."

"Yeah, well you make a point to do that when you have off the next day. I want a man with a clear head watching my back on the street. Am I clear on that?"

Mike actually felt for the kid, until he replied, "Yeah, well, I heard Doc likes to hoist a few pretty regularly."

The men around the desk stared over, surprised that the kid would speak up.

Controlling his anger, Callahan spoke in an even voice. "Yes, you're right, *Danny,* he does, but I've never seen him in the state you appear to be in this fine morning. Doc is an experienced man, who I have trusted my back to many times. He's not an unproven kid like you, one who had to use his daddy's influence to obtain his position. Now go get a cup of joe, and get out of my sight for a while. I'll let you know when I need you."

Slowly getting up, Shaw could see the look in Callahan's eyes; he spoke, "I'm sorry, I was out of line."

Nodding still annoyed at the kid "Yeah..." His phone rang then, interrupting him before he could finish his reply.

"Callahan." He paused as he listened. "Yes, Miss Costak, yes I'm fine. Are you over your cold? I'm glad to hear you're feeling better. If you're calling to check on the status of the case I have to... what? I'm sorry; go ahead, really... a diary? Why didn't you mention this when we spoke?"

Standing next to the desk, Shaw was, transfixed.

Geri Costak spoke enthusiastically into the phone, "I'm so sorry, detective. When we spoke, I was taking medication for my cold; I guess I was a little foggy. I was speaking with my friend Peggy yesterday when she mentioned writing something in her diary, and I remembered that Eileen mentioned to me once that she kept a diary. I recalled asking her if she kept any scandalous secrets in it, you know, teasing her.

Callahan, with an edge to his voice "What did she reply?"

"You have no idea."

Slowly, his voice hopeful "Do you any idea where the diary might be, Geri?"

"No, sir, just that she said if anything happened to her, she would give it to a friend. I'm sorry… she didn't say who that might be."

"Geri, I want to thank you for calling me with this information. Yes, it's helpful; all information in a case is potentially useful. What I need to do now is find that diary, to see what it says. If we can do that, it could possibly answer a lot of our questions."

"If I can remember anything else, detective, I will call you again."

Callahan, hopefully "You do that, Miss Costak. I would certainly appreciate it, and I'm certain that Eileen would, too."

Geri; her voice a sad whisper, "OK. If you find anything, do you think you could let me know?"

"Miss Costak, if we find this diary, I will let you know. I promise."

"Thank you, detective. Now, I gotta get back to work."

"Thanks again, Geri. I'll be in touch."

Hanging up the phone, he sat back in his chair, his mind racing. They would have to search her apartment again.

Looking up, he saw Shaw standing next to his desk. The kid looked like he was ready to upchuck. "Go to the men's room; throw some cold water on your face," Callahan instructed. "We're going to pay a visit to Eileen's apartment again, to search for her diary. We might need to tear the place apart, so if you're going to pull a sick act, do it here. We'll leave in a few minutes; I gotta make a call first."

He watched Shaw move quickly towards the men's room. Grabbing his phone, he dialed Ginny's private number. "Good morning, Ginny… I'm fine thanks, how are you doing? Listen, I received an interesting call this morning, from the girl who was on the boat with Eileen. She said that Eileen kept a diary, yeah…imagine that. The girl also said that Eileen joked that it contained scandalous secrets."

"Do you have any idea where this diary might be, Michael?"

"No, that's the rub. The girl said that if anything happened to her she would send the diary to a friend."

Ginny, thoughtfully "Well, if she had placed it with a lawyer, it certainly would have been sent to this friend by now, and there would be no way to track it down. However, if she feared for her safety, she might have mailed it herself, a short time before her murder. You could check with the post offices near her apartment."

Mike smiled. "You've missed your calling; you would have made a terrific detective. That's exactly what I intend to do, after I give her apartment a more thorough going over."

"Very well, Michael. I'll call Jimmy, tell him to let you tear the place apart if need be. You call me and let me know what you find."

"Count on it, thanks Ginny."

"I'll speak with you soon. Take care, Michael."

Annoyed, Callahan went to the men's room, looking for Shaw. He scanned the room, but upon seeing no one, he called out, "Dan, you here?"

Silence answered him.

Walking back to his desk, thinking he missed Shaw in the hallway, he was surprised to still find nothing. After a few minutes, Shaw entered the room, making his way over to Callahan.

"Where the hell were you?"

Embarrassed, rubbing his stomach "Upchucking, sorry. I do feel better though. Let's go.

Callahan stared at him intensely. "So, you were in the men's room the whole time?"

"Yeah, why?" His voice slightly angry.

"I went into the men's room looking for you."

Seeming to remember, "Oh, I forgot. I went down to cafeteria, got a candy bar. I needed something for my stomach."

"Where is it?"

Confused, Danny stared at him. "Where is it?"

Annoyed, realizing the question "I ate it."

The feeling that Callahan had after the incident at the church returned. Staring at Shaw, he hooked his thumb at the door and said, "Let's go."

A couple of the men near his desk watched them leave, glad that they weren't Shaw's partner.

The drive over to Eileen's apartment went quickly and silently. Walking into the lobby the detectives saw Fields behind his desk. Hearing them, Jimmy looked up. "Hey, Mike. Mrs. Maitland called; I got my toolbox behind the desk here, if you need to crack anything open."

"Great, Jimmy, let me have it." Fields handed it over. Callahan passed it to Shaw, and the three men headed for the stairs. Coming to the apartment, Fields opened the door and stood back.

Callahan and Shaw entered the apartment. As Mike expected, not a thing had been touched.

"All right, watch and learn Dan. I'm going to take this place apart."

On Long Island, Senator Thomas Shaw still hadn't calmed himself. He couldn't believe the call he had received from his son, telling him that the stupid little bitch had kept a diary. On top of that, hearing that the book contained scandalous secrets unnerved him greatly. It didn't help that he was nursing a rather large hangover, the remnant of his evening with Judge Crater. Shaw shook his head slowly, thinking, *that crazy bastard could certainly drink.*

Recalling the evening, he remembered how pleased Crater seemed with everything. Whatever Shaw said, Crater had smiled and agreed with him. That was most unlike the good judge. Shaw had pressed him for the news that so pleased him, with Crater simply saying he would be able to tell him soon.

Lightheaded, he thought, *No, it couldn't be. How would he have gotten his hands on the diary? Eileen never seemed too friendly with him; in fact he was convinced that she didn't care for him. Would she have had the foresight to arrange for Crater to get the diary in the event that anything happened to her?*

Standing quickly, he gripped the edges of his desk, shouting, "GERHARDT!"

Within seconds, the German ran into the room, looking about for the source of the distress to his employer. Finding nothing, he turned to him. "What is wrong, sir?"

Shaw slumped back into his chair. "Please sit, Gerhardt. We must talk. There has been an unexpected development related to Eileen O'Sullivan."

He gestured towards the chair. "Sit... please."

The German sat, while Shaw proceeded to tell him of the diary and his fear that Crater might already have the document. Silently he cursed himself for being so open, so boastful, in front of the beautiful young woman.

"You'll need to arrange for someone to follow the judge. Someone you can trust completely, someone who will obey you without question, in the event we need to take action against the judge."

The German nodded slowly. "I think I know such a man; he is one who will do anything for money."

"Yes, but can you trust him to keep silent?"

Smiling wickedly, Gerhardt answered "Yes, he is not stupid. He knows what would happen if he speaks to anyone."

With a sigh of relief, he replied, "Excellent. I knew I could count on you. Call him immediately and keep me informed. If we must act, I want to be able to move quickly."

The German rose, coming briefly to attention "I will take care of it at once, sir." He walked quickly from the room.

Sitting alone in his study, Shaw wondered how things could get to this point. It was so unfair, he thought, he had dedicated his life to the people of New York. He wasn't going to let her ruin his life.

20

The taxi driver listened intently to the German. His ship had finally come in; he would be looking at some serious money, and he would finally garner the respect he deserved. The thought pleased him greatly. The German had said that this was a major concern to his boss. Bobby dismissed the German's comment about what would happen if he spoke about any of his activities.

Like he would do that.

He would be paid a daily retainer that would cover his receipts at the cab company, allowing him to follow the judge. He had silently laughed at the thought of tailing "Good Time Joe," figuring he'd be going to a lot of speakeasies.

Sitting on the couch listening to him, his wife felt proud and relieved that he had finally gotten a call from someone offering him work.

"You see, babe? I told you they would call me. The German says he needs a guy like me who can do the job and keep his mouth shut. Like I'd ever blab about a job, especially for someone like the senator."

Priding himself on his ability to blend into a crowd, he knew he'd be spending some time in the judge's courtroom, and he didn't want anyone taking notice.

He had taken note when the German was explaining the job to him, saying it might be necessary to take action against the judge; and, if it happened, he could expect something extra. It excited him to be able to buy something nice for his wife and kid.

"I gotta get dressed; I don't wanna be late for work. I'm gonna be working some extra hours for a while, but when this job is finished, we'll paint the town. We can have dinner at Memmo's, what do you say to that?" he asked his wife.

She smiled broadly. "That would be swell, Bobby." She seemed lost in thought for a moment.

He stared at her, and asked, "What's the matter?"

"Well, it's just…you won't get in any trouble? After all, he is a judge."

Angry, he waved a fist at her "You think I'm some dumb sap or something? I'm just gonna watch the guy, report to the Kraut, and he pays me my money. What could be more simple?"

Mollified, she backed off "Sure, Bobby, sure…I didn't mean anything."

"All right, then. Now remember, you gotta keep your mouth shut about this. I don't want you talking to anyone about what I'm doing."

Shocked, holding her hands apart "Bobby, I'd never…"

Waving a hand at her, trying to end the discussion "Yeah, I know, I mean nobody, especially your sister. That broad couldn't keep her mouth shut if her life depended on it. If the Kraut has to do anything to the judge, I don't want anyone knowing what I was doing, Okay?"

"Sure, Bobby." She got up, holding the baby. "Let me put her in her crib, I'll make you some lunch for work, okay babe?"

"Yeah, thanks. I gotta get dressed." He rushed out of the room.

His wife went into their icebox and got what she needed to make his sandwich. She met him at the door with a brown paper bag and his thermos of coffee. The coffee was strong, the way he liked it. It wouldn't do for him to dose off and lose his tail on the judge. Giving her a quick kiss on the cheek, he was out the door. Staring around her apartment, she thought, *Yeah, I deserve better. Screw the judge, my man is gonna score on this and we'll be sitting' pretty."*

Benny was sitting at his kitchen table when the phone rang. Walking over, he calmly picked up the phone. "Hello."

He immediately recognized the voice at the other end. "Benny, can you talk?"

"Yes, sir. Rita is out in her garden."

"Good, I'd like to discuss our meeting for this Friday. I've spoken to one of the senior appellate judges regarding this matter. He is a man we can trust. Together we will determine if the diary contains sufficient material, with which we could pursue an indictment of the senator."

Benny was slightly taken aback at the comments. "You're certain we can trust this man?"

Calmly, consoling "Of course, Benny. I gave it careful consideration."

"Of course sir, I'll leave that to you."

The judge smiled, the judge knowing of course that Benny had spoken to no one regarding the diary. He had realized after the conversation in the car the other night that he might have appeared a little too intense, wanting to assure Benny that he intended to do *the honorable thing*. Once he had the document in his possession, there would be nothing Benny could do without exposing himself to the wrath of the senator.

"On Friday, I have scheduled my lunch for twelve thirty. Can you be in the city by then?"

"Yes, easily," Benny replied.

"Good. Do you know where the Federal Court building is located down at Federal Plaza?"

"Yes, I've driven the senator there once or twice."

"Excellent. There is a coffee shop located at the corner of Church and Worth streets. It's called Morgan's. I will be waiting for you there. Have the book wrapped in plain brown paper. Enter the coffee shop, and hand the package to me, at my table. I'll be seated by the window; you'll have little problem seeing me. Oh, and don't worry about being seen. I often receive materials related to the cases I'm hearing, at the coffee shop."

Silence.

He continued, "Can you do this, Benny?"

With a strong note of certainty in his voice, staring intently at the wall "I'll see you on Friday at twelve thirty. How long do you think it will take to look at the diary, to determine if you can use it against the senator?"

"I would think a few days at the very least. As soon as we arrive at our determination, you will be the first person I call. You can trust me."

"Aye, I am trusting you, judge. I'm trusting you with the legacy of a fine young woman, remember that."

Ginny Maitland listened as the caller described his surveillance of Mike Callahan. She smiled ruefully as he spoke of the beating of the federal agent in the parking garage. She was glad that the agent had apparently suffered no serious harm from the beating.

It pleased her that the shadow was proficient at his task. She would dislike having Michael confront him, being unsure of his purpose. The caller finished, she thanked him, sitting back in her chair. Staring straight ahead, she wondered aloud, "Why is J. Edgar Hoover interested in your murder, Eileen?"

It was an unexpected development, but it explained the confrontation at Mike's apartment, when the two agents were taken away in an ambulance. She rose slowly from her desk and walked to a painting on the wall. The painting frame was hinged; she pulled it away from the wall, exposing a hidden wall safe. Opening the safe, she extracted a leather bound journal. Leaving the safe open, she walked over to the bar, pouring herself a drink. Walking back to her desk, placing her drink to the side, she slowly turned the pages of a journal, searching for a name.

There was a gentle knock on her door.

"Yes."

Claire opened the door, stepping half into the room "I'm finished with those earnings reports. Do you want to look them over now or tomorrow?"

Smiling at her friend, she glanced at the wall clock "Thank you, Claire. It can wait until the morning. Why don't you call it a day and go home? I can close up here. Besides, I have Al and Jerry to watch over me. Tell Frank I'd like him to drive you home."

Smiling back, glad her day was done "All right, Ginny. I'll see you in the morning, good night."

The door closed, she was alone again. Studying the pages of the journal carefully, taking an occasional sip of her drink, a smile formed on her face. Picking up her telephone, she dialed a number for the F.B.I.

"Steven Flynn, please. Tell him it's an old friend."

"Hello?" A man answered, uncertain of his caller.

"Good evening, Steven. Ginny Maitland."

Surprise, trying to control his voice "Why are you calling me here?"

"Is this a bad time? I could come to your office."

"No, no, it's all right. What can I do for you?"

"I need a favor, Steven; I thought you might be able to help me. I would be most grateful if you're able to provide me with an answer to a question."

Silence, then cautiously "What sort of question?"

"I need to know the name of an individual who approached Hoover for a favor."

"Hoover? Why don't you have me ask the President for Christ's sake?"

Chuckling, she was enjoying herself "No, Steven; I just need to know who asked Hoover to take over a certain murder case. I want to know the person who wants this case to be forgotten. And, as I've said, I would be most grateful in fact, I'd say extremely grateful for this accommodation."

"You know he is very difficult to approach. I'd have to wait for the right moment to ask such a question. It could take some time."

Ice in her voice, there would be no negotiation here "Don't be silly, Steven. I know your little social club meets the third Thursday of each month. I also know where you meet. I will expect an answer the day after."

"What! What if he isn't there, what if I can't get him to open up?"

"That is your problem. I would hate to have some certain photos find their way to the tabloids."

"Bitch."

"It takes one to know one." She hung up the phone.

Closing the journal, she finished her drink, pleased with herself. Placing the journal back in the safe, she straightened her desk, and then grabbed her purse. Walking to her door, she shut off her light, turning to see her men waiting for her.

"Boys, let's call it a day."

They smiled in return. "Okay, Ginny."

They left the office.

21

Clothing and possessions lay strewn about the apartment, and Danny sat watching as Callahan searched. With the episode at the precinct still fresh in Callahan's mind, he was unsure as to what he should allow him to do.

Watching silently, Danny was impressed with the determination of the man; thinking, more than once, that he really must have cared for the little bitch. Standing ankle-deep in clothing Callahan stood, surveying the apartment.

"Damn, girl, I know you kept it. Tell me, where is the receipt..."

Smiling slightly, Shaw thought, *what a jerk... she was futzing my dad, stupid.*

Sweating, looking about the apartment, Callahan stopped suddenly. "What the...?"

Jumping across the room to the window, he knelt, examining the window frame. Shaw was quickly standing next to him. "You find something, Mike?"

Pulling a knife from his pocket, he began to pry the molding away from the wall. Laying the knife down, he gently began to pull a piece of paper from between the molding and the wall. Free of the wall, he opened the paper, examining it.

Smiling, as he read the paper "Ah girl, you heard my question."

"Is it the receipt, Mike?"

"Yeah...yeah it is." Staring intently at the paper in his hands, he continued, "She mailed it two days before she washed up on that beach."

He stood and walking quickly to his suit jacket. Shaw was right on his heels.

Continuing towards the door, "C'mon, we're going to the post office over by Penn. We've got a date and a number for the clerk who made the transaction."

The two men made their way out of the apartment. Callahan shut the door and locked it. Forgoing the elevator, they used the stairs. Almost running down the stairs, they cascaded into the lobby. Jimmy Fields jumped up from his desk.

"What's going on, you find something?"

Heading for the door, Callahan almost yelled "You bet, Jimmy. You tell Ginny we got what we were looking for, tell her I'll call her later," and they were out the door.

Standing in the lobby, Fields looked around, he now had to make a call "That's jake." Walking over to his desk, he called his boss.

"Mrs. Maitland, please. It's Jimmy Fields."

"Hello Jimmy, is Detective Callahan still in the apartment?"

"No ma'am, he left with his partner."

"Did he say if they found anything?"

"Yeah, he said to tell you he had found what he was looking for, and that he'll call you later."

Smiling pleased with the news "That's good news, Jimmy, very good news. Thank you for the call, I appreciate it.

"You're welcome, Mrs. Maitland."

He heard her hang up the phone. Staring at the phone for a moment, he placed it in the cradle. Snapping his fingers, he grabbed his keys and made for the stairs, knowing that Mrs. Maitland would want to be certain the apartment was secure. He wasn't going to do anything to disappoint her. Until this sad business was finished, he would make certain that the apartment was taken care of.

With Mike driving, they made quick time to the post office. Upon walking in the main entrance, they noticed the line of customers was long, and Callahan was in no mood for waiting. Taking out his badge, he went to the head of the line.

"Police business, we need to speak with a postal agent."

Staring at the badge the woman nodded the nearby customers watched, curious "If you wait a moment, I'll get my supervisor." They watched her walk quickly away.

In short order she returned, with another woman. Callahan held up his badge again.

The second woman spoke, "What can I do for you, detective?"

"Callahan, ma'am." He took the receipt out of his pocket.

Handing it to her, she scanned the receipt. "Can you tell me who handled this transaction?"

She stared at the receipt, pursuing her lips, she replied "Number twenty-seven, that would be Vivian Bell."

Callahan nodded, asking hopefully "Is she working today?"

"Yes, she is; she's in back sorting mail. Would you like to speak with her?"

"Yes; we'd like to speak with her. Is there an office where we might speak with her in private?"

"Yes, of course," she pointed, "Go over to that door, I'll let you into the secure area."

Callahan and Shaw walked over to the door. Opening the door for them, the woman beckoned them in. Following her down a narrow hallway she stopped, gesturing to a room on the right. "Wait in there; I'll go get Vivian."

She walked away without waiting for a response.

Shaw and Callahan surveyed the room. It appeared to be a spare office with an empty desk and a couple of chairs. Callahan sat behind the desk and pointed to a chair.
"Sit there," he directed Shaw, who then sat.

The supervisor returned with another woman. "Detectives, this is Vivian Bell. She handled the transaction on your receipt."

The woman seemed at ease. Callahan spoke, "Thank you for your time, miss, we'd like to know if you can recall anything regarding a transaction you handled. Please sit down," he said as he gestured at the chair. The supervisor stood off to the side.

Mike handed her the receipt, she stared at it. "Detective, I handle hundreds of transactions a day."

"Yes, of course, however this one involved this woman." He handed her a photo of Eileen.

Vivian stared at the photo for a second, she smiled slightly. "Yeah, I remember her. She was a sweet kid, an Irish girl."

Callahan smiled, putting the woman at ease "Yes, she was a fine young woman. She was my friend, and she was murdered."

Vivian looked quickly up at Mike, wanting to help "I'm sorry, detective, but how do you feel I can be of assistance in this matter?"

"Do you recall the size of the parcel she mailed that day?"

Lost in thought for a moment, she gestured with her hands. "It was about this size, about the size of a small book, or something like that."

Callahan smiled, pleased with the information "Vivian, that's very helpful. Now, you wouldn't happen to recall to where or whom she might have mailed it?"

A pained look on her face, she spoke slowly "I'm not sure." She gazed emptily about trying to recall the address. Shaking her head, she continued, "I told her the necessary postage and...," she snapped her fingers, "it was I think an Irish name, somewhere on Long Island as I recall."

Callahan and Shaw were both on the edges of their seats, for different reasons. Mike spoke gently, "Do you remember the name?"

Slowly shaking her head, "No, I'm very sorry; as I said, it was very busy day."

Callahan and Shaw both sat back. Callahan, disappointed, finished their conversation "If you happen to remember anything else about the transaction, I would greatly appreciate it if you would call me."

Shaw slowly calmed down, his face losing its flush.

Taking the card from Callahan, Vivian half smiled "Certainly, detective. If I remember anything I'll call you first thing."

Callahan rose, the others rising with him. Thanking the women again, he and Shaw walked out of the post office. Walking towards their car, Callahan turned and glared at Shaw.

Surprised, Danny asked "What... What did I do now?"

"You let that Irish guy get away at the funeral."

Sheepishly, he broke eye contact "I said I was sorry."

"Yeah, so's your old man. If that guy has Eileen's diary, we may never find it now."

They got into the car. Shaw thought, *you'll never see that diary, Mr. Big Shot Detective, I'll see to that.*

Bidding goodbye to his wife, Benny started the pickup truck. On the seat next to him was the diary. Watching him drive slowly away, she was still unsure if they were following the best path.

Turning, glancing around she couldn't quell a nagging feeling that their happy time on the great estate was coming to an end. She felt she would need to pray for a good outcome to this unhappy situation.

In the distance, she saw the German walk out of the great house towards the garage. Her thoughts turning dark, she hoped that if anyone suffered for the crime against that sweet girl, it would be that man. She was certain now that he had ended her life on that boat, on that rainy night.

Thomas Shaw sat in the anteroom of the Senate chambers reading a summary of pending legislation prepared for him by his staff. Though he was against the legislation, he had promised Senator Claflin he would support it, needing the man's support for a law he was drafting. He considered the man a fool but it was undeniable that he had a formidable political base. After all, thought Shaw, *What was the Senate if not a large horse trading parlor?*

He was roused from his thoughts, by a senate page "Excuse me, senator, you have a telephone call."

Annoyed, he glared at the young man "What... who is calling?"

"It's your son, sir."

"Oh... thank you." He rose and made his way to the phones.

The page gestured to a phone on the end. Sitting, he picked up the phone. "Daniel, why are you calling me here?"

"It's good to speak with you too, dad. I thought you might want to hear what I've got to tell you."

"And what might that be, son?"

"Do you think you might be interested in hearing who has Eileen's diary?"

"What? You know who has the diary?"

Laughing, Danny enjoyed himself "Yes, father, I believe I do."

Exasperated, he restrained himself "Daniel, why don't you tell me what you know?"

Danny explained how he and Callahan had found the receipt, and then interviewed the postal clerk. Aghast at the development, Shaw breathed a sigh of relief in that the woman didn't recall exactly to whom she had mailed the diary.

"Danny, who exactly did she mail the book to?"

Enjoying himself, Danny continued "She mailed it to your estate, dad."

Annoyed, Shaw was confused "What the hell are you talking about?"

"Father, dear father, she mailed it to your loyal retainers, the Fitzgibbons."

Shaw stood erect. "What, are you sure?"

Other senators in the room glanced over at him. He quickly sat.

"Dad, the woman said she mailed it to an "Irish" name on Long Island. I ask you, who else did Eileen know on Long Island?"

"Yes, I believe you're correct, Danny."

Angry, Danny spoke quickly "Don't call me that."

Surprised, his father responded "Don't call you what?"

"I'm not a kid anymore; I'm a detective. What would you do if Mike Callahan and his regular partner arrived at your estate with an arrest warrant?"

"I'm sorry, Dan. I do appreciate everything you've done."

"Well, you should. Callahan's a damn good cop. We've got to work together here to protect you.

"Of course, son. What do you suggest?"

"Have your German pay the Fitzgibbons a visit; let him get the diary back. Once you have it, the Kraut can scare them into keeping their mouths shut. Everything will then be jake."

"Yes, of course you're right; I'll make that call as soon as we're finished."

"All right, I gotta get back to Callahan; make sure nothing else has happened."

"Thank you, son. I'm impressed with what you've done. I appreciate it."

Surprised, Danny was pleased "It's okay. I'm glad I could help you. Goodbye, dad."

"Goodbye, son." Glancing about the room, Shaw quickly dialed his private number at the estate.

22

Following at a discreet distance, Bobby laughed, "What a sap; I might as well be sitting next to him, for all he would notice."

Judge Joseph Crater was making it easy to follow him. His cab had stopped at a couple of stores specializing in ladies' wear. Bobby smiled, knowing the reputation of "Good Time Joe" with the ladies. *Man*, he thought, *if I made the scratch this guy does, I'd have ladies stashed all over the city.*

Exiting a store, Crater glancing at his watch looked ahead, nodding he muttered something. People kept walking by, passing him with little notice of the celebrity in their midst.

Bobby jumped as his rear door opened, a man in a business suit getting into the taxi "Fifty-seventh and Lexington, and I'm in a hurry."

Turning he glared at the man "Is that so? I'm off duty; try getting another cab, buddy."

Surprised, the man shot back "What are you talking about? It's midday. You can't be off duty at this time, come on."

Menace in his voice, he wanted to end this discussion "I said get out, before I throw you out. I'm waiting for a special fare."

"All right, no need to high hat, Mack; you could have just said so when I got in." Opening the door, he quickly exited the cab.

Bobby turned his gaze back towards the Judge. "Whatta sap."

"Damn!" He threw the car into gear as he saw Crater's cab pulling away from the curb, merging into traffic. Quickly making up the distance between them, he could see Crater reading some papers in the rear seat.

Glancing at his wristwatch he noted the time, knowing the German would want a detailed report, with times, as to what Crater was doing. He was very pleased he had thought to bring the pen and the notepad. *Am I smart or what? Yes sir, Mr. Kraut,* he thought, *you're going to be very happy you got Bobby Capello working for you. I ain't no dumb broad.*

Ahead of him, Joseph Crater rode on unaware of his tail. He glanced at his watch "Driver, I need to be at the courthouse in fifteen minutes."

"Yes, sir. We're almost there."

Settling back in his seat, he relaxed "Good, thank you."

Crater was acutely aware that he had to meet Benny Fitzgibbon at the coffee shop to get the O'Sullivan diary. He couldn't recall feeling such anxiety at any time in his life. Just the thought of having that document, being able to bend Tom Shaw to his wishes, was a strangely intoxicating thought. His dream of a Supreme Court nomination finally lay within his reach.

Benny was a competent man; Crater was reasonably certain he would be on time. Once he had the document, he would take a few days off to read it, before placing it in his safe deposit box.

That arrogant bastard Shaw was in for an awakening. If he truly had that young woman murdered, Joseph Crater was going to make certain that he paid for the crime, by doing each and every thing that he wished. It comforted Crater to know that the death of the O'Sullivan girl would serve a greater purpose, that being his elevation to the highest court in the land, from which he could shape the legal future of the country.

Throughout his drive into the city, Benny had repeatedly glanced down at the brown bag on the front seat next to him, reminding himself each time that he was doing the right thing.

Yet, each time, he couldn't totally dismiss a nagging feeling that the Judge had a hidden agenda of his own. What frustrated him was that he was unable to consider an alternate approach in seeking justice for Eileen. He dismissed the thought of approaching the detective assigned to investigate Eileen's murder, due to the fact that his partner was the senator's son. He had little doubt that if he went down that avenue, the diary would disappear forever.

Proceeding slowly, now that he was enveloped in city traffic, Benny glanced at his watch. Smiling, he noted that he was right on schedule. He would meet the judge, hand over the diary, and still be able to purchase the supplies he required for the estate.

Parking the truck, he rolled up the window, leaving a slight crack to allow the heat to escape, disliking entering an extremely hot vehicle. Holding the door, he leaned in, grabbing the bag. Shutting the door, glancing about, he started walking towards the coffee shop. Glancing at his watch, he recalled the times Rita had kidded him for his punctuality.

The taxi pulled over, the judge sliding over to the curb side door, got out. Glancing at the meter, he took a couple of bills from his pocket, and paid the fare. After thanking him, the cabbie pulled away from the curb. Moving away from the cab, Crater walked into the coffee shop. The hostess at the door instantly recognizing him, smiled asking him, "You want your usual table in the rear, judge?"

Shaking his head, he countered "Not today; how about a seat by the window? I feel like getting a little sun."

"Sure, judge," looking for a waitress, raising her voice, "Carol, take the judge to table twenty-one." Carol arrived quickly, having seen the judge. "This way, judge."

In short order, Crater was seated. Taking a menu from Carol, he casually scanned it while he waited for Benny.

Parking his taxi, Bobby walked across the street, selecting a point at which he could observe the judge. Pleased as he saw him seated near the front window, chuckling, "Jeez, could you make it any easier for me, Crater?" Scanning the area, he noted a phone booth at the corner. If anything happened in the diner, he would give the Kraut a call.

Bobby failed to notice Benny as he walked into the diner, asking the hostess a question, she pointing towards Crater.

Benny walked over to Crater's table. Seeing him approach, Crater gestured towards the seat across from him. Taking note of the newcomer's common attire, Bobby figured he wasn't from the courts. The judge seemed very pleased to see the guy, who was holding a brown paper bag as though it contained something valuable.

"How long will it take you to study the diary?" Benny asked with interest.

Calmly, Crater spoke slowly "Benny, we've been through that. I will need to have another judge review the document to determine if we have a viable case against the senator. I said I will call you as soon as we make a determination as to the viability of the diary, and to the extent of any potential criminal activities contained within it."

Slowly, Benny passed the bag across the table to the judge. Containing himself, Crater casually took the bag. Opening the package, he took out the diary and stared at it. Slowly, he began to flip through the pages. His eyes widened as he saw well-known names, and they grew even wider at the mention of illegal activities. The most pleasing aspect of the notations was that they were dated, and in most cases included times. Crater smiled, thanking Heaven, that this dead girl was so meticulous.

Unbeknownst to either Benny or the judge, Bobby, having crossed the street, was a short distance away, watching them. Clearly seeing the Judges face, Bobby thought, *Boy, he sure seems happy. That book must be something real important.*

Sitting quietly while Crater scanned the book, Benny felt a growing discomfort, seeing the look in his eyes. Crater spoke slowly, "Benny, I think your friend is going to see justice. At first glance, this diary seems to have enough information to present cause for an indictment."

Benny smiled. "Are you certain?"

Crater quickly caught himself, adding cautiously "Well, remember it must be studied carefully, to determine if we can substantiate the contents. If it rises to the level of a verifiable piece of evidence, I will recommend the case be referred to the grand jury."

Unsure, Benny asked "What exactly does that mean, judge?"

"He would be arrested and brought to trial."

Bobby was moving closer when he noticed, in the reflection of the window, that a cop was taking out his book to write a ticket for his cab. Cursing, he quickly moved away from the window, running across the street.

"Hey, hey, what are you doing, officer?"

Looking at him, the cop pointed with his pen at the "No Parking" sign. Annoyed, Bobby shook his head, he hadn't seen that when he parked. "Wait, I got an explanation."

The cop nodded, voicing disbelief "I'm sure you do."

"Look, I just dropped Judge Crater off at that coffee shop. I had to help him bring some papers, for him to look at while he had lunch."

Lowering the pad, the cop turned to the coffee shop. "Judge Crater, huh? Where is he?"

"There, sitting by the window." He couldn't help but notice that the other man was gone. "Watch, I'll show you I know him," Benny started shouting and waving, "Hey, judge!"

Hearing the shouting, Crater looked up from the diary, seeing a man with a police officer standing next to him. The man was waving it appeared at him. It always stroked his ego to be recognized by the general public, so he smiled and waved back at the man.

"See, he knew me, now you ain't gonna give me a ticket for helping a judge, are you?"

The cop seemed unsure. "Well, I guess not. Try not to let it happen again."

Putting his pad back in his pocket, the cop walked away. Watching the cop walk away, Bobby was furious that he had been taken away from the stakeout. Looking up and down the street, he couldn't see any trace of the guy who had met with Crater.

The Kraut's gonna be mad, he thought.

He considered what he would tell the German regarding about his tailing of the judge. Walking over to the nearest pay phone, he dropped coins into the slot and dialed the German's number.

Furious after hearing what his son had told him about Eileen's diary, Shaw had quickly dialed his private number at the estate.

Upon hearing Gerhardt, Shaw quickly told him what his son had related to him. The anger in his voice over the betrayal of the Fitzgibbons was obvious, with the German's anger growing accordingly, as he listened.

Barely controlling his anger Shaw spoke slowly to Yost, "Listen now, you go to that damn cottage, tell whichever one you speak with that I want that damn diary, or you will kill them... you hear me, Gerhardt?"

Looking quickly about to make certain no one overheard him, Shaw spoke softly into the receiver, "You understand what I'm saying?"

Surprised at his employer's blunt language he responded, "*Ja, senator, I understand.*"

"Good, deal with it and keep me posted."

Sitting in the study, the German considered the words of his employer.

The phone rang again.

Surprised, the German answered, "Yes, sir?"

"Hey Gerhardt, its Bobby. Bobby Capello."

"What…Yes, what is it?"

"I wanted to give you a report on Crater."

Annoyed, at this distraction "Yes, what is it?

"I followed Crater like you wanted; he met a guy at a coffee shop downtown and the guy gave him a package."

Yost immediately sat up straight, "What did he give him?"

"Some kind of book. I couldn't see too clearly, but there was writing, like it was some kind of notebook or something."

Nodding to himself, Yost asked slowly "Was the man who gave the judge the book a tall, skinny guy with brown hair?"

"Yeah… how'd you know that?"

Laughing, he now knew the diary's location "I'll tell you later; thank you, Bobby." He hung up the phone.

Sitting in a chair, Yost slowly rotated his neck, enjoying the cracking feeling he got as he turned his head. Stretching his fingers slowly, he made fists as he sat. His thoughts turned to the Irish couple; his arousal grew thinking of the woman. The husband was a small, inconsequential man, not worthy of consideration.

Yost hoped that Benny would physically challenge him; it would make his attack on the wife all the more pleasing. It pleased him that the senator had placed no barriers before him, knowing that he could address any problems confronting him.

23

Steven Flynn had been on edge since receiving the call from Ginny Maitland. He had considered numerous scenarios in which he approached Hoover to get the name of the person wanting the murder of the young woman to be forgotten. What annoyed him most was that he had yet to see a situation in which Hoover would volunteer the name to him.

He wanted a drink to relax, to help him think, but after the incident, he had a strict rule against drinking on the job. Ironically, it was that situation which had brought him to Hoover's attention. A thought struck him; he sat up straight, grabbing his phone. It was well-known fact that Hoover kept a strict record of notable people who came to see him; the records also noting what was discussed.

Hoover's secretary was notorious in her defense of everything relating to her boss. Over time, Flynn had gone out of his way to cultivate a friendship with her. She wasn't a particularly attractive woman; it was accepted that she had no social life.

"Frances, hello, Steve Flynn. Yes, I know the director is in meetings all day on the Hill. Actually, I was wondering if you were free for lunch. You are? That's great. I'll be down in a few minutes." He quickly left his office, and was soon outside Hoover's office. Walking casually in, "Hi, Frances. Ready for some lunch?"

Obviously pleased to see him "Aren't you the quick one! If you'll give me a few moments, I need to freshen up. Make yourself comfortable."

Smiling as she walked past him, towards the ladies room, he waited until she turned the corner. Moving quickly, he opened the appointment record on her desk, and began to quickly scan the pages. Nothing looked remotely close to his question.

He eyed a note... to follow up with Jim Watt in New York regarding his taking over a case, but there was no mention of who he had spoken with. Hearing the secretary returning, he quickly shut the book and returned it to its place.

"Now, Steven, where would you like to dine?" It was easy to see she didn't get asked to lunch often.

"I thought we might try Alletto's."

Looking at him, she raised her eyebrows in surprise. Seeming very pleased, "That sounds wonderful. I've never been there; I hear it's very good."

Returning her smile, he echoed her pleasure "Then I'm glad that I will be the one to introduce you to the place."

Walking out of the office, she stopped and turned to lock the door.

"Does the director insist that you lock his office any time you leave?"

Rolling her eyes, she gave him a half smile "I'm glad I don't have to post an agent at the door. You know how security conscious the director can be."

Nodding, as if he understood "Yes, he's very good at keeping secrets."

As they walked towards the stairs, he was glad that they had spoken before. She had a limited range of interests, and to turn her sympathy towards him, he fabricated a marital problem. Actually, there was no problem, because neither he nor his wife cared enough about each other for either party to have a problem. It was a marriage of convenience, for their careers.

Exiting the building, they made small talk concerning Bureau affairs. He found her to be a never ending source of information about people and events at the F.B.I.

It was a short walk to the restaurant; he held the door open as she entered. The place had a relaxed atmosphere, apart from midday Washington.

Recognizing Flynn, the maître d' smiled. Flynn made a habit of tipping the man handsomely, knowing that, when necessary, it paid off. Flynn had lunched there a month ago with Hoover, and having alerted the maître d' prior to their arrival, he had fawned over Hoover, much to Hoover's delight. Afterwards, Hoover had been generous to Flynn, with perks reserved for more influential members of the government.

The waiter pulled out the chair for Frances. As she sat, she surveyed her surroundings. "Do any stars lunch here, Steven?"

Nodding, pointing at a table "I believe I saw Chaplin in here last week."

Her eyes wide, her response full of awe "Really? Did you speak with him?"

Shaking his head gently at her, he spoke softly "I think stars just want to be left alone when they're out in public."

Disappointed, hoping to see a star "I supposed they do, but wouldn't it be interesting to be a celebrity?"

Sensing his opening, he spoke knowingly "I imagine you see your share of interesting people, meeting with the director."

Smiling demurely, she agreed "Yes, I guess you could say that… but still, to be recognized for yourself, wouldn't that be something…"

The waiter interrupted them, asking if they were ready to order. After hearing the specials, they ordered a light lunch.

Flynn then directed the conversation back to his talking point. Leaning towards her slightly "You probably see more influential people than I do; you just keep it to yourself."

Sipping her glass of wine, she nodded slightly "Yes, the director sees quite a few important men."

Nodding, he spoke confidently "I know, he mentioned to me the other day about his efforts to have a murder case moved to the Bureau, for a friend."

Surprised, she placed her drink on the table "He spoke to you about that?"

Calmly, he pressed his opening "Yes, he speaks to me more than you would imagine." Acting as if he over spoke he quickly added, "I know I can trust your discretion. You know how he hates people who discuss Bureau business outside of the office."

She nodded, took another sip of wine, and leaning forward, she spoke in a low voice "I wonder why the senator has an interest in that case? That poor girl."

A mischievous look on her face, "You know how politicians are, they're fortunate to have a man like the director to watch their backs."

She tensed, whispering, "You don't think the senator had anything to do with her murder, do you?"

Reassuring, he reached over to grasp her hand, "No. senators do many distasteful things, but I certainly wouldn't number murder among their eccentricities."

Relieved, she nodded slowly "No, I don't suppose you would. Steven, this place is terrific. Thanks so much for inviting me to dine with you."

Reaching over he gently clasped her hand, smiling his best smile, he spoke emotionally "Frances, it's my pleasure. I enjoy your company, and if I may be so bold, I feel that we have a special relationship."

He enjoyed watching her cheeks flush, her eyes turning away in embarrassment. "Yes…I feel the same way."

Not wishing the conversation to proceed further down this road, he moved it towards general shop talk. It was evident that she still wanted to speak romantically. Thinking she must be desperate for romance, he felt sorry for her. She was, he thought, not an unlikable woman.

He looked at his watch, then back at her with a tilt of his head. It was understood within the Bureau that you didn't take more than an hour for lunch. The director had strict rules regarding the time allowed for activities, having no tolerance for anyone who deviated from his guidelines. They'd had a quick dessert, with Flynn making certain that he tipped heavily, and they left the restaurant.

Walking back to the office, his thoughts focused on how he would let Ginny Maitland know what he had learned from Frances. Secondarily, he thought about the next time the social club would meet. It exhilarated him more than he would ever admit, to be with those men of influence in such a relaxed atmosphere. Dismissing such thoughts, he reminded himself that he had to call Ginny Maitland as soon as he could to ensure her continued friendship.

Ginny was totally focused on the information in front of her. She smiled, pleased how well her girls had come through. The information on the railroad merger was something she would move on immediately. She would acquire her interests in the usual manner, not wishing to bring any undue attention towards her.

Her phone rang. "Yes," disliking the interruption a mild annoyance in her response.

"It's Flynn. I've got your information.

Interested, her voice more pleasant "Steven, it's so good to hear from you. I'm delighted that you've been able to assist me in this matter."

Annoyed, Flynn wasn't having any of her glib comments, "Stow it. I give you this, and you give me the photos."

Ice cold, she reasserted herself "I will be the judge of that. Don't ever presume to lecture me again, or the papers will have your photos before the end of the day. Are we clear?"

Silence, then in a defeated tone, "Yes."

"Good, it depresses me when friends argue, Steven, and we're friends, aren't we?"

Hesitation, placatingly "Yes…yes we are."

"Good, now what have you learned regarding what I needed to know?"

"Hoover's been out, totally unavailable, but I was able to reach his secretary."

Demure laughter, appreciating his approach "You're good."

"I didn't get a name, but she said that the person who wanted the murder of the woman to be forgotten was a senator."

Ginny sat up in her chair. "Really… a senator? That's interesting; it certainly reduces the field. Did she know if the man was a federal or a state senator?

Flynn hesitated. "No…she didn't." He cursed himself for not asking such an obvious question himself.

A slight pause, she spoke in a kindly tone "Steven, you've been helpful. I appreciate it."

"Can I have my photos?"

Gentle laughing, she thought him an idiot "Steven, don't be silly. It's not as if you provided me with an actual name. Come now, I'm a business woman. Give me something of truly useful value and I will respond in kind. Call me when you know more." She casually hung up the phone, smiling as she heard him yelling into it.

24

Readying himself to visit the cottage, the German felt the usual excitement at the thought of being violent with a woman.

Exiting the manor house, scanning the estate, he saw the pickup truck coming slowly up the driveway. Making eye contact with Benny as he drove past him, he gave no gesture of recognition to the man.

Parking the truck in front of the cottage, Benny began to remove the supplies from the rear bed. After a couple of trips to the shed, he went into the cottage.

"Rita dear, I'm back."

"I'm in the wash room, Ben, I'll be out shortly."

Walking into the kitchen, he went to the sink for a drink of water. Standing at the sink, he watched his wife enter the room. Walking over to him, they embraced, he kissing her on the cheek.

"Did you get everything you needed in the city?"

"Aye, I did."

Slowly, she asked in a cautious tone "How did you fare with the judge?"

Thoughtful, still not certain about Crater, "I don't know, time will tell. He said he would contact me as soon as he had completed his review of the diary."

"Did he…" she was interrupted by a knock on the door. They looked into each other eyes, unsure. Walking over, Benny opened the door to see the German.

"Yes, what can I do for you, Gerhardt?"

"May I come in?"

"Certainly." He stepped back, allowing him to enter.

Yost entered, staring at them with his dead eyes "I need to speak with you both." He gestured towards their sitting room.

Nervous, they walked ahead of him, sitting on the sofa. Upon entering the room, Yost sat in a chair, facing them.

"Why did you go to the city today, Ben?"

Unsure, he glanced quickly at his wife. "You know why, I had to get those supplies the senator wanted from Stillman's."

Smiling slightly the German nodded, leading the conversation "*Ja*, and what else did you go there for?"

Nervous, he slowly shook his head, controlling his emotions "Why do you ask?"

"A friend of mine saw you, he mentioned it to me."

"Well, he could have seen me about my responsibilities."

"*Nein*, that's not it. He saw you meet with someone, and I believe it was the judge."

Next to Benny, Rita gasped slightly.

"Now that you mention it, I did run into the judge."

A hard smile on his lips, his lip curling "Ran into him, did you?"

"Yes, we spoke for a moment. Why do you ask?"

Yost stood quickly, shouting, "WHY DID YOU GIVE HIM THE DIARY?"

Rita cried, "Dear God!"

Not backing down, Benny stood. "Because he had Eileen murdered you bastard, and I'm betting it was you who killed that poor girl."

Momentarily stunned by Benny's response, he quickly regained his composure, lunging at him. Showing surprising agility, Benny sidestepped him, landing a hard blow to the German's temple. Dropping to the floor, recovering quickly, he went at Benny. They locked in a wrestling embrace, falling, they went over the couch.

Rita had backed away to the wall, watching the unfolding events in horror. Both she and Benny had feared the German since their arrival at the estate. What neither of them expected was the intensity of Benny's response to Yost.

Years of hard work, coupled with a moderate diet, had left him tough and lean. Together with his anger, it made him a formidable opponent.

The two men rolled about on the floor grappling, each occasionally landing a blow. After a few moments, Rita could see that, despite her husband's best efforts, the size and superior strength of the German was beginning to assert itself. Looking about she sought something she could use to strike the German, to render him unconscious.

The German had gotten on top, and began choking Benny. Benny had begun to flail against the powerful arms holding him down. Yost stared into Benny's eyes, enjoying himself. "*Ja,* when I finish with you, I have some fun with your wife."

Upon hearing those words, Rita acted. Grabbing a brass statuette off the mantle, she moved towards the men. Raising it back, she brought it down hard against Yost's head. Surprised completely, he momentarily released his grip on Benny. Rita struck him again; standing over him she stood ready to hit him again. "I don't think so, you rotten bastard," she yelled in her rage.

Staring down at Benny for a second, Yost slowly fell over to the side. The husband and wife stared at each other, not knowing what to say.

Benny rasped, "Christ, woman, could you have waited any longer to hit the bastard?"

Breathing deeply, Rita responded, "How did he know, Benny, how did he know?"

Recovering still, he stared at her confused. "How did he know what?"

"The diary, how did he know you gave the diary to the judge?"

Sitting up, looking at the German he shook his head slowly, his eyes had a desperate glint "I don't know."

They stared at each other for a moment. Benny spoke slowly, "He could wake at any time. Be a good girl; get me that rope in the hallway cupboard."

Without responding, Rita moved quickly down the hall. Returning, they turned the German over, Benny tying his hands behind his back. Making certain that the rope was tight; he then tied his feet, giving no thought to the fact that he couldn't keep the man tied up indefinitely.

They sat on the couch holding hands. A thought struck Benny. "Daniel… it had to be Daniel." Rita looked at him unsure. "Think, lass, who is investigating Eileen's murder? Who could have found out that we had the diary, and that we were giving it to the judge? It has to be the little bastard. I wish we could find out the name of the detective he is working with. We could inform him that we gave the diary to Crater. Perhaps he could ensure that the judge uses the diary against the senator."

Rita stared at the floor, her mind racing on how they might find out the name of the detective investigating Eileen's murder. Her gaze snapped back, her eyes hopeful "I think I know. We can call, saying we have information. They would direct us to the man in charge."

Considering her for a second, Benny smiled, nodding. "That might work… it might at that."

Benny turned towards the unconscious man on the floor. "What about this bastard, what are we to do with him?"

A strange look came over Rita; she stared into Benny's eyes. As if struck by the same thought, he responded, "No lass, we can't kill him."

She responded quickly, "He attacked you; we could say it was self-defense."

A sad look came into Benny's eyes, "Would you lower us to his level? Not to mention that the senator obviously now knows we gave the diary to Crater. If nothing else, he'll give us the boot when he returns."

"No, he won't, he'll want to keep his eyes on us. If he fires us, we can go to the papers."

"My love, Crater has the diary."

Her smile lit up the room. "I took two pages out of it."

Stunned, he hugged her. "Is it any wonder that I love you?"

They were both distracted by a moaning from the floor. The German tried to move, and, finding his hands and feet bound, he began to struggle.

Speaking softly to his wife, he kept his eye on the German. "Follow my lead."

Walking over, Benny pushed him onto his back and sat roughly on his chest. The German stared up at him, fury in his eyes.

Smiling, Benny spoke in a calm voice, "So you were... what was it? Going to have some fun with my wife, after you finished with me? I'm sorry, but I'm going to have to kill you, Gerhardt."

Benny, reaching in his pants, quickly pulled out a knife and put it to the German's throat. The shock in the German's eyes was evident, he spoke quickly, "You can't, please, I was not serious. I was just trying to scare you."

Calmly, Benny stared into his eyes, considering. "Ah, scare me was it... I'm sorry, Gerhardt, say your prayers." Benny pressed the blade of the knife against his throat.

Staring awestruck, Rita had never seen this side of her husband before.

The German began to cry out, "No, please, don't! I swear I'll never bother you again!"

Lessening the pressure on the blade, Benny sat back. "Really... I have your word on that?"

"*Ja, ja*, I swear it."

Seeming to consider for a moment, shaking his head, Benny replied, "No, I don't believe you," and he began to draw the knife across Yost's throat.

Rushing to Benny, Rita grabbed his arm, pulling it away. Fury in her eyes, emotion in her voice. "Let the bastard live, I don't want another situation like we had back in Dublin."

Yost's eyes darted back and forth from Rita to Benny. "*Ja*, Benny, listen to your wife."

Benny paused to consider. "All right. I don't want that, either." Staring into the German's eyes, His voice hard. "You're alive because she wishes it. If I ever see you anywhere near us again, I'll kill you. Do you understand?

For the first time, Benny could see fear in the German's eyes. "*Ja*, I understand."

Slowly getting off Yost, Benny used the knife to free his feet. Helping him rise, he pushed him towards the door. At the door, grasping an arm, he cut the rope, as he pushed the German out of their cottage. The German didn't turn as he walked quickly away.

Benny shut the door. Turning towards his wife, he smiled in relief. "Well, it's a good thing you didn't wait any longer. I would've had to cut the bastard's throat." Rita smiled at him. "And that nonsense about Dublin was a nice touch."

Rita smiled broadly, pleased with herself, "I thought so."

25

The number two man in Legs Diamond's organization, Tom Regan, walked towards his apartment, his intent clear, to get drunk tonight. He had been struck by a particularly strong taste of melancholy today, being reminded about the only woman he had actually cared for in his life.

He met Diane Morris when she had visited one of Leg's speakeasies with some friends. Regan had immediately been drawn to her, asking Leo the bartender who she was. With a shrug, he had said it was the first time he had seen her in the place.

Never lacking in confidence, Tom had introduced himself, buying her group a round of drinks. They had immediately hit it off.

He was enraptured with her smile, her sense of humor, and her ability to draw him into conversations, discussing aspects of his life he had never told anyone else. They had begun to date, he thought seriously, until the end of one night when she had told him they were through. Withdrawing into his shell, he simply asked why. She explained that she knew he was a gangster and had ties with the bootleggers, and that she did not want to be involved in that life. Looking deep into her eyes, Tom was certain he had seen genuine sadness. That, however, did not alter the situation, and she was gone from his life.

Feeling bad for him, Diamond had tried to hook him up with a couple of different women, but seeing his lack of interest, he soon gave up.

Walking into his brownstone, he passed one of his neighbors. "Good evening Mrs. Gorcey," he said, tipping his hat as he passed her.

Walking up the stairs, he got to the fourth floor landing and as he stepped to his door, men emerged from the shadows. Instantly alert, he stepped back and with a turn of his head saw that there were two men on the landing below.

Staring at the men, he recognized one of them, calming himself. "Dom, what's going on here? Is this a hit?"

Dominick smiled, shaking his head "Christ no, Tom. We could have got you on the street anytime we wanted. We've been asked by Lucky to bring you around; he wants to talk with you."

The men slowly moved in around him. Dominick reached out his hand, pointing "What's in the bag, Tom?"

Regan handed the bottle over. Dominick slid the bottle out, checking the label he nodded, impressed "Good stuff. Are you expecting company tonight?"

"No, nothing like that, just gonna have a couple of drinks."

Speaking as a friend, "That's fine, Tom, you can still have a couple, with Lucky."

Realizing the futility of escaping, he nodded, shrugging "Okay, let's go see Lucky."

"Smart choice Tom. I gotta ask, you carrying?"

Smiling he nodded, "Isn't everyone?"

The men all laughed lightly at his comment. Dominick gently touched his elbow, gesturing down the stairs, directing him "Let's go."

Walking down to the cars in silence, they got in and drove off. Regan scanned the sidewalks for anyone who would know him, hoping they might alert Legs that he had been taken.

"Dom, your boss say what he wants to speak with me about?"

A quick look at him, his face a mask "Nope, you know Lucky, he keeps everything close to the vest. Relax. Like I said, if we wanted you dead, you would be dead already."

Arriving at Lucky's headquarters, Dom ushered Regan into a sitting room. "Have a seat, Tom. Lucky will be with you in a bit."

As he sat, he scanned the room, not knowing what he was looking for, but more out of nervous energy. He wasn't aware of any current problems between his organization and the mob Luciano worked with. Slowly taking a deep breath, he calmed himself.

Lucky Luciano entered the room. Walking towards Regan, he held out his hand, smiling. "Tom thanks for coming; I appreciate it."

Having shaken hands, Luciano motioned, towards a plush chair "Take a seat, Tom. I wanna have a chat." Luciano sat facing him. "You want a drink? Dom, get him a drink."

"You want your stuff, Tom?" The gunman glanced at Tom.

"Hey, I'm the host here; you get him some of my special stock. You'll like it, we get it through Cuba." Dom poured Tom a glass of a rich amber liquid.

Taking a sip of his drink, he nodded. It was good stuff. To calm himself, he knocked back the drink.

Luciano smiled, pleased with Tom's reaction. "You see, I told you it was good stuff. I'll bet you it's better than anything Diamond gets." He poured another drink and handed it to Regan. Taking the drink, Regan sat back into the chair. Luciano stared at Regan with dark eyes.

"How's business lately, Tom?"

"Not bad, can always be better."

Luciano, turning towards the gunman, "You see Dom? I told you I could talk with this man. He understands business. You ever think about your future, Tom?"

In his element, Regan smiled. "All the time."

"How's it going against Schultz?"

"Ah, you know how it is. We hit him, he hits us."

Taking a sip of his drink, Luciano nodded, watching Regan intently "I know…we gotta find a way to consolidate the organizations."

Regan sat a little straighter in his chair. "What are you proposing?"

Smiling slightly, he leaned forward in his chair "That's what I like, right to the point. Your boss, sometimes he's too smooth for his own good." Taking another sip of his drink, Luciano continued. "I hear things on the street. Everyone knows that since Rothstein got hit, Diamond's been struggling to keep things together."

Regan didn't acknowledge what was common knowledge on the street. "Are you offering your support against Schultz?"

Sitting back in his chair, Luciano held out his glass, which was quickly refilled. "I might, but I'm gonna need something in return." Slowly, Luciano made his play "You see, I know Diamond has a powerful political connection, and I'd like a piece of that."

Regan nodded, wondering where Luciano found out about Diamond's relationship with the senator. Realizing the need for a careful response, Tom spoke calmly. "Sure, I'll speak to Legs about that, it shouldn't be a problem."

"You do that, Tom. It's only good business, and if, God forbid, Diamond were to get hit, I know who I'd support to take over his organization."

Tom's ambition struggled with his loyalty, but he had to admit it was a proposal which made sense. Luciano was a man on the rise. This was not a proposal he could refuse, knowing if he did, he wouldn't make it home tonight. "I appreciate this opportunity to speak with you, Mr. Luciano. I will carry your message to Legs, and support it fully."

Luciano stared intently at him, appearing to stare through him. "Good, You see, Dom? I knew this was a man we could do business with."

"Yeah boss."

"Okay then," Luciano said as he rose, signaling the meeting was over. "Dom, you take him home, make sure nothing happens to him."

Walking over, Regan offered his hand. "Good evening, thanks for the drink."

A cold smile, with dead grey eyes "We'll talk again. Good night, Tom." Luciano left the room.

Regan glanced at Dom, who gestured to the door, saying "Let's go."

They walked to the door, where one of the men handed Regan the bag with his bottle. As they drove back, Regan slid the bottle out noting that it was one of Luciano's. Dom chuckled, "The boss wanted you to have a bottle. He didn't think you would mind the switch."

Regan laughed lightly, "Hell no, I'm never against a trade up."

Dom smiled back at him, chuckling "That's the spirit, Tom, you keep thinking like that."

The car sped along in the twilight.

Across town, Ginny Maitland sat at her desk reading a report from a private investigator, with whom she had enjoyed a long relationship. After speaking with Flynn, she had asked the detective to look at the state and federal senators from New York. She particularly wanted to know what type of car they drove and if they employed a large man and an Irishman.

Reading the report she took a sip of her drink, noting nothing surprising she continued. As she read the last page of the report she suddenly sat back in her chair muttering, "Oh my God."

Reaching for the phone, she dialed the operator asking for Michael's number. Mike's number rang many times, unanswered, until, reluctantly, she hung up the phone. Sitting at her desk with a sole light on, she stared ahead deep in thought.

Unpleasant as it might be, her immediate thought was to have young Shaw killed. In her entire career, she had not, despite the rumors, had anyone hit. This situation was unique to her experience, with her emotions running to the defense of Michael Callahan. A dear friend, she would do what was ever necessary to protect him, with her desire to avenge Eileen O'Sullivan running a close second.

She needed to confirm the information before her. If she were to act, it must be with complete certainty. Tomorrow she would have her detective begin to follow the senior senator from New York; before she had anyone killed, she needed to be sure of her reasons.

26

Sitting in his office, Luciano considered his meeting with Tom Regan. His thought was to have the man hit, as he was not really trusting of anyone who wasn't Italian. Of course, there was one exception to that rule, the financial advisor to the organization, who was a Jew. He was also a friend of Luciano's since he was a young man, and there was no one who would deny the financial ability of Myer Lansky.

It was Lansky who had put a tail on the second man in the Legs Diamond organization, telling Luciano of his ability, and more importantly of his loyalty to Diamond. Lansky had, through his many contacts, found the man to have an impressive reputation, and more importantly a lack of ambition towards running an operation. This was exactly the type of man Luciano wanted in his various operations. He wanted men who would be content in their positions, not open to suggestion or challenging him for the top spot in the organization.

Danny Shaw sat up in bed, bathed in sweat. Looking around, he slowed his breathing gradually. It had been the dream again.

He was swimming towards his father's boat, while his parents were seated in the rear, watching him. They were laughing, egging him on to them. The problem was that the boat kept slowly moving away from him. Try as he might, he couldn't close the gap.

He knew the dream had to be related to his actual childhood experiences. After his mother had passed, his father would take him out on the boat, where he would force him into the water. His father then made him swim behind the boat, which the damn German would slowly drive, maintaining the distance between them.

It was only when he appeared to be on the brink of drowning that his father would throw him a float with a rope tied to it. He would then pull the young boy to the boat and help him onto the deck.

His father had been a cruel taskmaster, sternly forbidding him to cry, telling him that it was for his own good, that it would strengthen him for life. He said he wouldn't have a weakling or a quitter for a son.

Thinking of those times, he hated his father. It bothered him that he had no memories of his mother, she having passed when he was still an infant. He couldn't understand why his mother was in the dream, believing that she would never have allowed him to do what he did.

Staring around his bedroom, he sighed. The experiences had left him with a deep fear of drowning, which was the focal point of his insecurities. He had never had a strong relationship with a woman, which wasn't due to a lack of willing women, given his position as the sole heir to his father's fortune.

Reaching for the bottle on his night table, he poured a glass of the amber-colored liquor, swallowing the glass in a gulp, savoring the taste as it went down. Slowly, he lay back down on the bed, a myriad of thoughts racing and out of his consciousness. Foremost was the need to recover the diary, and to protect his father. He would finally show his father that he was a man. He would kill whoever stood in his way of earning his father's respect. He smiled at the thought, thinking perhaps he would order the German to murder; after all, it was pretty much what the big bastard was good at. As he was dozing off, he reminded himself to call the estate and speak with the German about the diary.

Gerhardt Yost sat in the sitting room of the mansion in a silent rage, having quite unexpectedly gained a degree of respect for Benny Fitzgibbon. He wondered what the wife was referring to with the mention of the situation in Dublin, having some difficulty accepting the fact that the Irishman could take a life.

Who knew, stranger things had happened, he thought.

He had to move quickly now, to stem his losses. He would arrange to have the judge taken, they would recover the diary, and afterwards he would deal with Benny and his wife.

Grabbing the phone, he dialed the taxi driver, eager to begin "Bobby, can you talk? Good. I want you to help me with a job, a very important job. You will be well paid for it if we are successful. Are you interested?"

Yost could sense the man's greed over the phone, listening as the German outlined his plan. Once Yost had outlined his plan, Bobby spoke.

"Let me get this straight, you wanna kidnap Judge Crater, and force him to give you this book back to your boss?

Hesitation, anxiety in his voice, "You wanna use my cab to nab him, I dunno, if someone sees me I could get into a lot of trouble."

Surprise, his voice high, "You'll pay how much? All right, you got me. When do you wanna do this?"

Bobby almost laughed at the money promised to him. It would be enough to allow him to buy his own cab, or do just about anything he wanted. It was a dream come true. He would finally be able to talk care of his wife and kid like he always wanted.

"All right, I'll meet you at tomorrow at the corner of Church and Warren, yeah, sure... I'm working the evening shift. You just need to cover me for the fares I won't be bringing in."

Annoyed, the German responded "Don't worry, all of your expenses will be covered. I will see you tomorrow." He hung up the phone.

Dialing the phone Yost waited, the voice answering was slow, slightly slurred.

"Daniel, I am calling on behalf of your father. Can we speak or are you with someone?" He smiled, knowing the young man's social inadequacies.

Annoyed, Danny answered "No, I'm alone. What do you want?"

"I need your services tomorrow; we are going to get the diary back for your father."

Slowly, Danny tried to focus "What are you talking about?"

"We are going to take the judge, have him tell us where the diary is, and once we have it, this situation will be over."

"Why do you need me?"

Speaking slowly, "Because, Daniel, if we get stopped by a policeman I will want you to use your influence to make sure we don't have a problem. You'll do that for your father, won't you?"

Trying to make his voice hard, Danny answered "Yeah, I'll do it. Where do you want to meet?"

Michael Callahan walked slowly back towards his apartment, having been at his favorite speakeasy. He could run an open tab at any of Ginny's places, but he didn't want her to know when he was drinking heavily.

He made his way slowly up the stairs, but when he reached his landing, he stopped short. "Claire... what are you doing here?" Looking around, he saw they were alone.

She stared at him intently in the dim hallway light. She gave him a sad smile, "Had a few, Mike?"

He stood, weaving slowly back and forth. "What's going on, Claire?"

She walked over to him and put her arm around him. "Can we talk inside, Mike?"

Captivated by her face, he looked deep into her eyes. "You're a good woman, you know that?"

"I'll bet you say that to all the girls."

He stopped. "No, really... I mean it."

She laughed gently, punching his arm lightly "I was kidding, you jerk."

Getting his keys out with some effort, his hand swayed. He tried to put the key into the lock.

Gently grabbing his hand, Claire took the keys. "Let me do it, or we'll be here all night."

Opening the door, she walked Callahan into his apartment. Guiding him over to a chair, she gently placed him in it.

Walking back over to another chair, she sat.

Gently, affection in her voice; "Mike, Ginny asked me to stop by. She called, but you were out."

Nodding, his eyes sad "Yeah... as you can see, I was out."

"She did some investigating, you know, looking into Eileen's murder."

Callahan tried to sit up straight. "She found something?"

"Yes, she did. She found out who asked Hoover to get you off the case."

Callahan almost jerked upright. "You gotta name?"

Frowning, knowing her information incomplete, "She said only that it was a senator. But she had a private dick that she has used in the past look into it, looking for a black Packard, a big guy with a limp, and an Irish guy."

"Claire... what did she find?"

"Senator Thomas Shaw owns a black Packard, has a large guy with a limp who works for him, and has an Irish couple as housekeepers on his estate on Long Island."

Callahan stared at her in silence, for a few moments. "Well, doesn't that just change everything?"

He tried to stand up, but fell back into the chair.

Quickly on her feet, she was at his side, her voice caring "What are you doing?"

"I've gotta get some sleep. Would you call me in the morning, make sure I remember our conversation?"

Claire smiling gently at him, she spoke affectionately "Sure, I'll call you bright and early."

He smiled back, his eyes sleepy "Not too early… I'd ask you to stay the night, but I wouldn't be much company, if you know what I mean."

She stared into his eyes, gently sighing, a wistful look in her eyes "Yeah, sure, Mike. I'll let myself out; you have a good night." Leaning over, she gently kissed him.

Walking to the door, she watched him as he placed his badge and gun on the end table. A look of longing in her eyes, she smiled sadly, letting herself out.

Ecstatic was the only way to describe the attitude of Joseph Force Crater. He had finished reading the diary of the dead girl, astounded that Thomas had been such an idiot. He knew the man's ego, but even drunk, what could have possessed him to share such information with the woman?

This book would assure his nomination to the Supreme Court. It was common knowledge that a couple of the sitting judges were old, and that it was possible they could retire soon. He was certain that with the support of Thomas Shaw, that the president would nominate him.

He considered the steps he needed to take tomorrow, the most urgent being to get the diary to a safe place. Once he informed Shaw he had the document in his possession, he could be certain that the German would pay him a visit. His safe deposit box would provide adequate security. If anything happened to him, the box would be opened and Shaw would still suffer.

Yes, he thought, tomorrow was going to be a wonderful day.

27

Walking briskly into the precinct, Mike noticed Shaw's desk was empty. Waking up early, despite his hangover, he had been considering his options in dealing with Shaw, given Claire's comments to him last night.

She had called him as he was getting dressed, asking if he recalled everything she had told him. Thanking her, he had assured her he did. Looking around the office, he spotted Mabel, his voice betraying his annoyance "Hey, did Shaw come in yet?

Looking up, giving him a false smile "Morning, Mike. He ain't coming in, called in sick," smiling, her voice sarcastic "Probably too much the party boy last night."

"Yeah, probably...thanks."

Sitting at his desk, he opened the case file on Eileen's murder. It had occupied the center of his desk since that day. Scanning the file, he found the phone number for Eileen's friend, Geri. Dialing her number he listened as the phone rang, hanging up, *probably at work,* he thought.

"How's it going, Mike?"

Startled, he turned to see Kroon standing nearby.

"Not bad Jack and you?"

"Got a minute?" Kroon glanced towards his office.

"Yeah, sure." Getting up, he followed Kroon to his office.

Sitting, Kroon asked casually "How's it going on the O'Sullivan case?"

"Pretty good, I came into some information last night that could be very important."

"Oh yeah, care to share any of it?"

Smiling weakly, Mike replied "Can I see if it pans out?"

Staring intently at Mike, Kroon pressed him "Yeah, but I wanna know as soon as it develops."

Mike started to answer, Kroon held up his hand stopping him. "Look, everyone sees how you been working yourself on this, and they understand. I just don't want another of my detectives in the hospital."

"I appreciate that, Jack. I'll be okay."

Kroon held up his hand again, his voice friendly "Did you forget Doc was getting released from the hospital today?"

Moaning, he rolled his eyes "Aw shit, I did. What time was it again?"

Looking at his watch, Kroon smiled "About an hour from now. You gonna see your partner home?"

"Yeah, you know I am." He started to get up.

"Sit for a second; I'll have a squad car run you up to the hospital. I was wondering how the kid has done so far."

Callahan answered slowly, "Questionably."

Frowning, Kroon stared at his friend "What does that mean, precisely?"

"Jack, if this case develops as I'm afraid it might, I think you're going to be in for a surprise."

"Oh yeah? How big a surprise?"

"Big…very big."

"Really, I'll look forward to it. Now get out of here… tell Kelly to have one of his patrol cars take you up to the hospital."

"Thanks, Jack."

"Yeah, get outta here… and give my regards to Doc."

"You bet." Callahan was up and out the door before Kroon could say anything else.

The car had its lights and siren on all the way to the hospital. Thanking the driver, Callahan walked briskly into the hospital.

Moving quickly to Doc's room, he stopped seeing the crowd of people outside of the room, all of them women, he laughed as he walked towards the room

Sticking his head in the door, he coughed.

Doc looked up from the nurses surrounding his bed. Smiling, pleased to see his friend "Mike, hey, it's good to see you, buddy."

Smiling back, Mike almost laughed "Oh yeah, I can see how you've missed me."

Laughing, Doc replied "Hey, I almost died, you know."

Walking into the room, Mike gestured "You are going to milk this for the rest of your life."

Smiling, seeming thoughtful "Yeah, it's a possibility."

Standing next to the bed, they shook hands.

"Seriously, how are you feeling?"

Doc stared at his friend, speaking seriously "They say I can come back to restricted duty in another week. How is your investigation going on Eileen's murder?"

Thoughtful, Mike turned to his friend "Some interesting developments I'd like to throw at you."

Looking around the room, he spoke kindly "Ladies would you excuse us for a minute? Police business." Wishing him well, the nurses slowly moved out of the room.

Once they departed, Doc spoke; "Talk to me."

"Well, you know we were looking for a big guy, a gimp that drove a black Packard."

Nodding, Mike controlled his agitation "Yeah, and a little Irish guy."

"Well, Claire came to my apartment last night, told me that Ginny had done some digging. She found out that a senator had asked Hoover to take over the case and put me on the sideline."

"Yeah, you mentioned that already."

Holding up a hand, Mike interrupted "It gets better; a dick she uses found that Senator Thomas Shaw has a black Packard, a large guy with a limp that works for him, and an Irish couple that work as caretakers at his estate on Long Island."

Whistling, Doc laid back "Ain't that something. Did you speak with the kid?"

Annoyed, shaking his head, his voice harsh "No, the little bastard called in sick today."

"You send anyone to watch his place?"

"No, I left the precinct to get here…dammit."

"Well, there's the phone. Call, have a stakeout posted on the kid's apartment."

Calling, Mike arranged the stakeout.

As they were talking, the doctor, a short, balding man wearing glasses walked in, and glanced at a hanging medical chart.

"Detective Holiday, well, you gave us all a scare, but I'm happy to say you are cleared for discharge."

Leaning forward, Doc stuck out his hand. "Thank you, doctor. You saved my life, I won't forget it."

The doctor took his hand, his manner professional "Not at all, detective," smiling, mild relief on his face "It will actually be good for the hospital to have you discharged. I suspect that I'll see an increase in the production of the nursing staff on this floor."

Smiling, a sheepish look on his face "Yeah…sorry about that."

Turning, the doctor looked hopefully at Mike "You will be taking Detective Holiday home?"

Mike replied, "Yes, I'm his partner; I'll be taking him home."

"Yes, that will be fine," a questioning look in his eyes, "You don't have a daughter do you?"

Laughing, appreciating the comment "No, doctor, I don't. Thanks again. I need this guy to be back on the job."

The doctor shook Mike's hand and left.

Across town, Danny Shaw dressed, leaving his apartment about ten minutes before the stakeout was in place.

Judge Crater had awakened in a good mood with one question on his mind, *Why were there two pages missing from the diary?*

Checking his calendar, he was annoyed to note that he had a busy day, wanting very badly to get the diary into his safe deposit box. He hoped that he wouldn't need to meet with the chief justice of the courts, which would delay his placing of the diary into his safe deposit box for another day.

Smiling, he was certain that the day would turn out to his benefit. *What else could happen given that he was in possession of the diary?*

28

The German awoke with a focused sense of purpose. Today would be the day he ended this threat to the senator. It had been extremely uncomfortable for him to discuss his episode with the Fitzgibbons with the senator. He too had difficulty believing that Benny had committed murder in Dublin. After that point in their conversation, Shaw felt strongly that Yost should kill Benny. They discussed how they could take the body out to the Sound, and, with proper weighting, sink it away forever.

Callahan had seen to Doc, assuring that he was comfortably at home in his apartment. It pleased him that Ginny had agreed to have a housekeeper attend to his needs for a couple of weeks. She had dismissed his thanks with a smile, given the depth of their friendship. Callahan thought, not for the first time, how fortunate he was to have a friend like Virginia Maitland.

Danny Shaw had made his way downtown, watching constantly for anyone who might be following him. His last conversation with the German still troubled him. Kidnapping was a federal crime. If they were caught taking a federal judge, he stood to lose, big time. It had annoyed him greatly, listening to the German lecture him as to why he had to be part of the events of this day. He'd show that Kraut bastard when his dad was gone. He'd regret his lack of respect to him that was for sure.

Bobby Capello was surely the happiest of anyone involved in this affair, with the promise of his payoff at the completion of this job. He had taken his wife out to celebrate at their favorite place after speaking with the German.

Checking out his cab, he proceeded to drive to the spot where he was going to meet the German.

Stepping out of his taxi, Shaw paid his fare, walking over to the corner. Scanning the area, he noted that pedestrian traffic was light. Being the first one to arrive, he walked over to a coffee shop, sat at the counter, and ordered coffee and a muffin. His position at the counter allowed him to scan the street corner.

"You gonna want lunch, honey?" The waitress asked.

"No, this will be fine, thanks. Leave the check."

He didn't need to wait long. Seeing a taxi pull up at the corner, he watched the German get out, moving slowly with a menacing gait, as always. Looking up and down the street, his gaze turned to the coffee shop where Danny sat, seemingly for a second focusing on the window, which Danny sat behind.

Jesus, he gives me the creeps, Shaw thought, *even after all these years.* Tossing a couple of dollars on the counter, Danny rose, making his way to the door. Walking out into the sun, he felt the warm rays on his face, and for a moment wished he were somewhere else. Thinking about Mike Callahan for a second, he wished he could be that caliber of detective. It bothered him that Callahan had ridden him pretty hard, questioning his actions, but he thought, in fairness; it was only to make him a better cop.

Well, we'll just see how that works out, Shaw thought. He wondered what he would do if Mike actually confronted his father regarding the O'Sullivan girl. Walking across the street, he dodged the passing cars. Noticing him when he was about halfway across the street, Yost stared at him, offering him no acknowledgement.

Stepping onto the sidewalk, he knew better than to offer his hand. "Gerhardt, where's our ride?"

The German regarded him with disdain, glancing down the street. "Don't worry, Danny. He will be here shortly."

Bristling at the jibe, he controlled himself, responding with slight annoyance, "Good, I was afraid you'd screw this up for my father."

Looking at him, the German just smiled.

Before either man could speak again, a yellow cab pulled up. The driver leaned over to the curb side window, speaking quickly "Sorry I'm late, Gerhardt...traffic was a bitch."

Watching Danny for a second, Yost moved towards the taxi, ignoring Danny "No problem, Bobby. I knew you would be here."

Yost settled into the front seat without looking at Danny. Tempted to say something, Shaw thought better of it, getting into the back of the cab. Hearing the back door close, Capello drove the cab back into traffic.

"Okay Gerhardt, how do you want to handle Crater?" Bobby asked.

The German spoke first, "He should already be at court. We need to be ready later, if he goes out for the evening."

Capello nodded, as he drove "Yeah, all right, that's okay, but I'll need to call my dispatcher, tell him I got a fare that's running me around town, if you know what I mean."

Reaching into his suit jacket, Yost pulled out a thick envelope, handing it to Capello. Talking the envelope he quickly glanced into it and whistled, smiling "You weren't lying. You want me; you got me, for as long as you need this cab."

Yost smiled the action seeming alien to his features "I thought so."

Feeling put out, Shaw spoke up, "You mind telling me what's going on?"

Yost glanced at Capello. "Tell him."

Bobby responded, "Well, we're gonna wait until we can grab Crater, then we're gonna get him to tell us about the book that Gerhardt here wants...you got that?"

Annoyed, feeling left out "Yes, I got that. Now shut up and drive."

"What's your problem? I didn't say nothing to you."

Shaw stared out the window. In the front seat, Yost smiled.

Across town, Callahan pulled up to the bank where Eileen's friend Geri worked. Parking the car, Callahan got out, as he walked away a voice called out, "Hey, you can't park that there."

Looking around, Callahan saw a uniformed officer walking towards him. Holding up a hand, he took out his badge and showed it to the cop. "It's okay, I'm on the job."

Seeing the badge, the officer backed off. "All right. Sorry about that, detective. I'll keep an eye on your car."

Callahan nodded, liking the cop "I'd appreciate that, officer. I've got to speak with a murder witness in that bank."

"You got it, detective, take your time."

"Thanks," smiling as he nodded at the cop, Callahan walked towards the building.

Upon entering the building, he walked up to the receptionist. Pulling out his badge, he asked, "Could you tell me where I might find Geri Costak?"

Her eyes a little wide, she asked in a low voice "Is she in any trouble?"

Smiling to put her at ease, Callahan replied "No, nothing like that. I just need to speak with her," glancing over nodding at her switchboard.

She jerked slightly, embarrassed "Oh, sure, sorry."

Smiling, to keep her at ease "I appreciate your help, miss."

The receptionist dialed Geri's number and in a few minutes she came walking down the hall.

Seeing Callahan, she smiled.

Watching her approach, she made him think of Eileen. It was easy to understand how she and Eileen could be friends.

Walking up to him she held out her hand. "Detective, it's good to see you again. Do you have some news about the case?"

Looking at the receptionist, then back to her, He asked "Is there a room where we might speak privately?"

"Sure, follow me." She walked towards a nearby door.

Upon entering, they sat, she appeared anxious, possibly hoping for good news.

"We've had something of a break in the case."

Excited, she jumped up "You caught the guy!"

He shook his head "No, but we have our strongest lead yet. Do you think if you saw the big guy from the boat again, you would recognize him?"

Nodding quickly, her voice certain "Oh yeah, sure, I'd remember him. I've thought a lot about that guy since the night on the boat."

Callahan nodded, pleased at her answer "Would your company allow you time to assist the police department on a stakeout?"

Unsure, she answered slowly "I guess... I don't know."

"We have a suspect; he lives on Long Island. We'd like to establish a preliminary identification, and if you think it's him, we would then bring him in for a lineup."

"I'll do it, when do we start?"

Smiling at her, glad that Eileen had such a friend "Good, I knew I could count on you. Now, what's the name of your supervisor?"

"Mrs. Severino."

Standing up he took command of the situation "Let's go see her."

Callahan turned on the charm with the supervisor. She was an older woman, and once he had explained the situation, she readily agreed to give Geri a week off with pay.

Leaving the building, they walked down the outside steps moved towards his car. The uniformed officer noticed him coming and walked over. "You all finished here, detective?"

Holding out his hand, Callahan shook his hand. "Yep, thanks for keeping an eye on my car. My lieutenant would have been real mad if anything happened."

The officer laughed, understanding "Yeah, I'll bet. Have a good one."

Opening the door for Geri, looking at the cop "Thanks, you too."

They drove off to Geri's apartment so she could get a change of clothes. Callahan's mind raced during the drive, trying to pull the threads of this investigation together, wondering how he might get an indictment. In each case, he needed that diary. After Geri had identified the big gimp, he would get Jimmy Fields to identify the Irishman.

Benny and Rita had been on edge, since their confrontation with the German. Rita had begun to keep a large knife always within reach, while Benny kept a hammer always nearby.

Walking into their cottage, Benny sat at their kitchen table.

Rita asked with a sense of anxiety in her voice; "Have you heard anything from the judge yet?"

Troubled, he shook his head slowly "No, lass, I haven't."

Rita stared intently at her husband. "We need to protect ourselves, Benny."

Slowly nodding, resignation in his voice "I know, lass...I know."

"We need to take the pages I took from the diary to the copper investigating Eileen's murder."

"Aye that we do. I've given it some thought. I will tell the senator that some relatives of ours have arrived in the city and we want to go see them. We can take the truck and go to the police station."

She looked at him intently, asking the obvious question "How will we recognize this police officer?"

Smiling gently back at her, he answered "We'll ask the sergeant at the desk to see this Michael Callahan. Sure, he's Irish; I know we'll be able to trust him."

Having failed to hear back from the judge, Benny had begun to feel that they had perhaps made a mistake in trusting him to do the right thing. He thanked god that his wife had, as she did many times in the past, taken steps to protect their interest. Whatever the outcome, they were committed to avenging the murder of Eileen O'Sullivan.

29

Following Judge Crater after he had left the courthouse, the three men had gone to a private club, waiting while he probably got something to eat. Seeming carefree, the judge moved with a spring in his step.

Sitting in the cab parked at the end of a side street, the location allowing them to view the entrance to the club, the German broke the silence.

"He has been inside for a long time. He has to come out soon." Yost pointed to the darkened entrance to another building a short distance from the door to the club. "I'm going to wait there, for him to come out. Bobby, when you see him come out, he will want a taxi; that must be you. You understand?"

"I gotcha."

"Danny, when I get him near the car, you will help me get him quickly into the taxi. You understand?"

Annoyed at his tone "Yeah, I think I can handle that."

The German stared at him for a moment. "Good." Getting out of the taxi, he made his way across the street.

Once Yost was in place, they were all alert.

Crater walked casually out of the building. Heading to the curb, he looked up the avenue.

Reacting quickly, Bobby brought his taxi onto the street. Seeing the taxi, Crater raised his arm, hailing it. In the rear seat, Danny sunk deeply down, so as not to be seen.

As Bobby pulled smartly up to the curb, Crater walked towards the taxi, and the German moved quickly out of the shadows. Approaching the taxi, Crater thought he saw someone sitting in the rear seat and stopped for a moment.

Moving rapidly up behind him, the German grabbed his arm. Quickly reaching over, Danny flung the rear door open. Taken completely by surprise, Crater looked around trying to see who was holding him. Pushing Crater's head down, Yost forced him into the car.

"Wait, what do you want? Please don't hurt me!"

The taxi quickly pulled away from the curb. Walking towards the scene was a young couple. "Did you see that?" Asked the guy.

"Yeah, it looked like they forced that guy into that cab."

The man, a young attorney, replied, "That sure looked like Judge Crater."

His girlfriend laughed. "Be sensible, who would kidnap Judge Crater?"

He shook his head, dismissing the notion "Yeah, I guess you're right. Come on, we're already late for Billy and Kathy's."

The taxi sped down the avenue. Looking into the face of the German, Crater was afraid.

"Mr. Yost, kidnapping is a federal crime. If you release me now, I will forget this action by you."

Turning, surprise, Crater recognized Danny Shaw, immediately realizing the reason for this action. "Hello, Daniel. Doing your father's dirty work? This will go worse for you, being a police officer."

Smiling, Danny spoke with an unusual menace in his voice. "Did you honestly think you could blackmail my father? That dumb broad had it coming, for trying to make my dad marry her."

Crater's eyes widened. Turning towards Yost, nodding as he mentally put the situation together coming to an obvious conclusion. Having liked the young woman he was surprised at the anger in his voice. "Of course, it had to be you."

Shaw roughly grabbed the judge, pulling at his satchel "Let's see what you've got in the briefcase. I hope for your sake you have it, and we can end this easily." Opening the briefcase he smiled as he held up the diary. "Well, well, looks like we'll let you off and everybody can call it a night."

Yost sat there quietly, letting Danny handle the judge. Opening the diary, Shaw began to turn the pages. Stopping, he brought the diary closer to see, in the limited light.

Tapping the driver on the shoulder, Danny said "Turn on the overhead light."

Shaw ran his fingers along the edges of the pages that Rita had torn out of the diary. He stared back at the judge, his voice cold "It would seem that we have a problem. Where are the pages you tore out?"

Crater thought for a second, smiling, he tried to turn this to his advantage "Insurance."

Moving quickly, Shaw pulled his weapon and put it under the judge's chin. His voice dripping venom, "Insurance, do you think we're playing a game here?"

"You do anything to me, the press gets those pages."

"Oh yeah, we'll see about that," he quickly clubbed the judge, knocking him unconscious.

Yost looked at Shaw curious, the boy had surprised him "What do you have in mind?"

Shaw thought for a second, an idea occurring to him "We need to take him someplace quiet, where we can question him on where those pages are."

The German nodded. "Ja, I agree."

Speaking to the driver, Danny spoke with authority "Take us out of the city to some quiet beach area."

The driver watching the road. "Any place special?"

Shaw continued "Nah, use your imagination. First, I wanna put this guy in the trunk, let him think a little."

Once Crater was secure, they drove off into the night.

It was a nice night, thought Officer George Betancourt. He sat on his motorcycle, staring up at the stars. He was grateful that the captain had given him this assignment. With a short time to go until he could retire, this was the place to be. Forget about stopping crime, he was lucky if he saw a car out here. Looking forward to a nice retirement, he had already lined up a part-time job at a grocery store. He and his wife Millie would spend time together, spoiling their grandkids.

He was jarred out of his thoughts as a taxi sped quickly past him. "Where the hell is that guy going?" he muttered. Starting his motorcycle, he moved quickly out on the road turning on his lights and siren.

In the taxi, looking into his rearview mirror, Bobby spoke, "Uh oh, it looks like we got company." Shaw and the German turned to see.

Shaw spoke, "Slow down, let me do the talking."

The motorcycle cop pulled alongside them, shouting at Bobby, "Pull over!"

They pulled over to the side of the road, Betancourt slowly taking off his helmet, walked towards the taxi. Walking up to Bobby, "Where are you going in such a hurry this time of night?"

Before Bobby could speak, Shaw opened the rear door, stepping out. "Good evening, officer. I think I can answer your question." Reaching for his inside pocket, he smiled, trying to put the cop at ease "I'm Detective Dan Shaw, can I show you my badge?"

Unsure, Betancourt released the catch on his holster. He nodded at Danny.

Slowly producing his badge, Danny showed it to the cop. The demeanor of the officer immediately changed. Danny pointed to Yost. "That man is a material witness to a capital murder case. I'm taking him to a safe place until he can testify."

Betancourt nodded, accepting the story. It was at that moment that the judge acted, hearing the conversation. He began to bang on the inside of the trunk.

Startled, Betancourt drew his weapon. "What's going on? What, or who, is in the trunk?"

Danny moved towards the trunk as Yost got out of the car. The cop turned to face Yost, seeing the size of the man; he spoke again "You keep your hands where I can see them."

A shot rang out, and the cop fell to the ground.

"*Gott in himmel...* you shot him." Yost stared at Danny. "Have you lost your mind, killing a police officer?"

Bobby jumped out of the cab, nearly hysterical "Are you nuts? Shooting a cop, oh Jesus, we're in deep trouble."

Surprisingly, Shaw kept his calm. "Listen, both of you, would you have preferred it if we opened the trunk and he saw the good judge?" They were Silent. "Well?"

Shaw continued to assert himself "Gerhardt, throw the body in those bushes and get rid of the motorcycle, quickly now."

Walking over to the trunk, Shaw knocked on it. "If you make any more noise in there, I'll kill you."

Having heard the shot, Crater was quickly quiet, thinking he had heard the German say that Danny had murdered a police officer. He cursed himself for ever getting involved with the diary. He would need all of his wits about him in order to survive this night.

Callahan had followed the directions to the Shaw estate on Long Island. He and Geri had made small talk during the ride, and he saw how she had met and became friends with Eileen. They were similar people.

Passing a bend in the road, Callahan saw the red mailbox he was told to look for, pointing at it "There is the mailbox." He slowed the car down, taking in as much of his surroundings as possible. Seeing a side street slightly ahead, he turned onto the road. Parking the car, he faced it out onto the main road. Looking at his wrist watch, he settled back into his seat.

Geri spoke, "What do we do now?"

Looking at her, he smiled. "Now, Miss Costak, we wait." Turning, he grabbed a leather case off the rear seat. Opening the case, he took out a pair of binoculars, and began scanning the entrance to the Shaw estate.

Thoughtful, he observed "A driver will need to slow down, to enter that driveway." He handed the binoculars to Geri. "Take a look at the entrance. Do you think you could get a good look at someone driving a car into the driveway?"

She stared at the driveway. "It would depend on the light."

Callahan nodded. "Let's hope this big gimp shows up soon."

"Are you nearly ready, girl? We're not going to see the queen."

Annoyed, she answered sharply "Listen to himself, don't I have to look as if we're meeting our relations?"

Considering for a second, he smiled, having to admit "Aye, that would be a good idea. I'm sorry, my love."

They walked to the door of their cottage.

Benny whispered "You have the pages?"

Rita flashed him an amused look. "Is that why we're going to the city? Me, a poor girl thinking we were going to see some friends."

"Enough of your sarcasm, girl, let's be off."

Leaving the cottage, they got into the truck. Starting the truck, Benny reached over, giving her hand a squeeze. Looking at her, he smiled, she smiling back. Benny slowly moved the truck down the driveway.

Callahan heard the vehicle, snapping to attention "Look sharp, Geri, this could be it."

Staring intently at the exit from the estate, she watched as a Ford truck slowly came out of the driveway. The driver looked both ways, checking the traffic

"It's not him, Mike."

Callahan grabbed the binoculars. Looking quickly as the driver began to make his way onto the main road; he smiled and thought *it was the guy from the church, the Irish guy.*

Geri spoke, "Why are you smiling? It wasn't the big guy."

"No, Geri, it wasn't, but it was almost as good. That was a guy who went to Eileen's apartment after she was murdered, looking for her. He knew her. This is a good development."

"Okay. Do you think the big guy will show up?"

The taxi pulled up to a deserted area along the ocean. They could hear the waves breaking in the distance. Getting out of the cab, the three men walked around to the trunk. Opening the trunk, they stared down at Crater.

Danny spoke, "How you doing, judge?"

Crater had considered his answer during the ride. "Let's talk, Daniel. I want to resolve this issue to everyone's satisfaction."

Shaw laughed, enjoying the man's discomfort "Yeah, I'll bet you want to." Turning to Yost, he commanded "Gerhardt, get him out of there so we can talk. Bobby, you wait by your cab."

"You got it, boss." Bobby replied.

Crater walked with Shaw and Yost, away from the cab, into the dunes. Halting, Shaw turned the judge around to face him.

"OK, your Honor, talk to me."

Crater looked around nervously, fearing what the young man intended "All right, all right... here's the deal. I don't have those missing pages. They were out of the diary when I got it. Either Benny Fitzgibbon has the pages, or they could be anywhere. You get Benny; you'll probably get those pages."

Shaw seemed to consider it for a moment. Yost was silent, thinking what he would do to the little Irishman when they met again.

Shaw spoke, "You know, I think you're right. So we really don't need you anymore," and a shot rang out.

The judge fell to the sand, dead.

Yost stared at the body, unbelieving. "You are truly a madman. A police officer and now a judge, you are insane!"

Shaw laughed, enjoying himself. "Look, you dumb Kraut, he knows I killed the cop, and he could probably get a witness or two to say we snatched him off the street. Trust me; we're better off with him dead." Turning, he seemed at ease "Hey, Bobby, you got a shovel?"

They each took turns digging, and once they were comfortable with the depth, they dropped Crater into the hole, removing any identification or papers from his person first.

Bobby looked at Shaw, his eyes fearful "People are gonna be real interested where this guy has gone."

Shaw thought for a second, smirking "I don't think so; I think you're overrating his importance. People will forget…trust me."

Bobby shrugged. "Let's get the hell outta here."

Danny happily replied "I'm for that, let's go."

Walking back to the cab, Shaw spoke, "Gerhardt, when we get back to the estate, you pay those potato eaters a visit. You get those pages, you hear me?"

Yost nodded. "Yes, Mr. Shaw."

30

"The light is pretty much gone. We should go and plan on getting back here early in the morning." Callahan suggested.

Nodding, Geri yawned. "Anything you say, Mike."

Starting the car, turning out onto the main road, Callahan began to accelerate. A pair of headlights appeared in the distance. As the car approached them, Mike began to make out that it was a large black sedan.

A black Packard!

An idea struck him as the Packard approached. Flashing his lights, he waved his hand out the window. "Geri, follow my lead. You're my girlfriend, we're looking for the main road, we were at a party." He was waving more frantically as the black sedan slowed. The drivers came together.

Trying to appear a little tipsy "Hey, thanks for stopping, my girl and I are lost. We're trying to find the main road back to the city. We were at a party." Mike slurred his words slightly, for effect.

The German gave them an annoyed smile. "You need to go about two miles, make a left turn on Spring Hollow Road. That will take you to the main highway."

"Hey, thanks, buddy. We appreciate it."

Geri leaned forward, giggling, "Yeah, thanks, mister."

Yost drove on without acknowledging her.

Mike turned to her, his voice low and even "Did you get a good look at him?"

"It was the big guy, Mike, I'd swear to it...so help me God."

Putting his arm around her, he gave her a squeeze. "That was smart, thanking him like that."

Geri started to cry. "You get him, Mike...you get him for Eileen."

Callahan put the car in gear, they drove off.

Parking their car, Benny and Rita got out and turned to each other.

Benny nodded at the building across the street "Well, my girl, that's the police precinct where Michael Callahan works. Shall we go?"

Putting her arm through his, they stepped off the curb. Walking up the steps, they passed an officer walking down. He tipped his cap, greeting them "Evening, folks."

Returning the greeting, they walked into the police station. Looking around at the people and the activity, they were startled.

"Can I help you folks?"

Their anxiety high, they turned sharply, a large police officer stood next to them, smiling.

Benny spoke, "We'd like to see Detective Callahan, Michael Callahan."

Smiling, the man nodded "Mike? Sure, wait over there, I'll see if Mike's here."

They walked over to a bench and sat down.

After a few moments, the officer returned. "Sorry folks, Mike's out of the office. Perhaps someone else can help you."

Rita spoke, "No...it has to be Michael Callahan. We have some information we want to share with him."

The officer raised his eyebrows. "Oh...okay, would you come with me, please?" He shuffled them towards an interrogation room. "Please wait here, I'll be back shortly," he said as he closed the door.

A few moments later, a man in a suit entered. Introducing himself, "Hi, I'm Detective Penny, I work with Mike. Can I be of assistance?"

They looked at each other, obviously nervous. Benny spoke. "Do you know when Detective Callahan might return?"

"Yeah, he's supposed to be on duty in the morning."

Benny spoke, "I'll be back in the morning."

Joe Penny spoke calmly, "Can you give me an idea what this is about, so I can tell Mike when he asks me about you?"

Rita answered, "Could we leave him a letter explaining our visit and where he can find us?"

The detective thought for a second. "Yeah, I guess that will be all right. Wait here, I'll get you a pen and some paper." He got up to leave.

"And an envelope," Rita added quickly

Turning towards them, a smile on his face, he laughed. "You got it."

Benny and Rita looked at each other. "Why did you ask for an envelope?"

Rita spoke softly, grasping Benny's arm tightly "I don't want to return to the estate with those pages. We'll tell everything we know, even mentioning that shagging bastard Crater."

Nodding, he quickly agreed "You're right, aye, that's what we'll do."

Knocking, the detective entered the room "Here you go, pen, paper, and an envelope."

As Benny took the materials, Rita asked "Thank you, detective. Could we trouble you for some privacy?"

Nodding, he offered a friendly smile "Sure, you let me know when you are finished."

A short time later, Benny opened the door, looking out. Detective Penny stood a few feet away, talking to another man, and waved him over. Rita followed Benny out of the room and they walked over together. Benny held out the envelope, Penny took it, noting Mike's name, and below his name what appeared to be another name, Benjamin Fitzgibbon. The envelope was sealed.

"You'll see that Detective Callahan gets this when he comes in?"

Speaking to the couple "Yeah, I'll leave it on his desk."

Benny spoke "Thank you, sir, now we'll be leaving."

Detective Penny and the other officer watched them leave.

The other officer spoke, "What do you think is in the envelope?

Penny smiled, shrugging "How would I know...did you get a load of those two? It's probably nothing important."

"Why don't you open it and see?"

Surprised, Penny gave the officer a look of disbelief "Are you kidding? Callahan would bite my head off. I'll go leave it in his inbox. I'll catch you later."

Upon arriving back at the estate, Yost had gone to the senator's office to find him working at his desk.

Shaw looked up at Yost, expectantly. "Well, did you get the damn diary?"

"*Ja*, we got it, senator." He handed the book to the senator, who eagerly took it.

Scanning the pages, his eyes curious, yet gleeful "Excellent...excellent, Gerhardt, you will get a bonus for this. I bet that bastard Crater wasn't happy to let it go."

Uneasy, Yost spoke hesitantly "Sir...I need to tell you some things."

His mood expansive, he gestured towards a chair. "Please sit, Gerhardt."

Yost spoke slowly, "There were some...unexpected happenings last night."

Shaw grew wary, unsure of where this was going "Please explain."

"Your son...he took some...unexpected actions."

"Danny? Is he all right?"

Yost almost laughed. "As we discussed, we took Crater outside of his supper club. It went smoothly. He had the diary. As your son was looking through it, he noticed some pages were missing. He decided we should take the judge someplace quiet, where we could question him."

Shaw nodded. "Okay...a good idea. Continue, please."

"We put Crater in the trunk of the taxi we were using, and on the ride to the place of interrogation, we were stopped by a motorcycle cop."

Shaw stared at him silently.

"Danny was talking to the cop. He was ready to let us go when Crater started banging on the inside of the trunk. It was at that time that Danny shot him."

Shaw jumped out of his chair. "Danny killed a cop! That's just marvelous; now Crater knows my son is a murderer. That's worse than him having the damn diary."

Yost slowly shook his head. "I don't think the judge will give you any problems."

Caustically, Shaw glared at the man, knowing Crater as he did "Oh really...and why not? What did he promise him?"

Almost a whisper, Yost feared the words as he spoke them "Nothing... he killed him, too."

Feeling faint, Shaw grasped the desk. "I don't believe it. Danny killed two men getting this damn book back."

"Sir, if I may, your son acted as he had to, all things considered. The judge would have had the cop arrest us for kidnapping and he said that the pages were missing when he got the book from Benny Fitzgibbon. At that point, the judge, knowing that your son had shot the policeman, had to be...eliminated."

Shaw sat down, shaking his head unbelieving. "I'll be damned...you're right. Who would have thought Danny would be capable of such actions? Where is he?"

"We left him off at his apartment."

Nodding still amazed at his son's actions "What did you do with the bodies?"

"There wasn't time; the policeman will be found. The judge will never be found."

Shaw speculating on the Crater's disappearance, "The press will go crazy over his disappearance."

Yost appeared skeptical, "You think so?"

"Oh yes...they loved him. Mark my words, they'll go crazy. In a strange way, I actually like the idea of knowing what happened to the ambitious bastard. But now, we need to tie up the loose ends to this story. I want to finally be free of that little bitch."

Attentive, Yost watched the senator.

"I think you should pay the Fitzgibbons a visit, and get those missing pages. Do what you feel is necessary...but you get them."

Understanding the request, Yost nodded replying, "Yes, senator."

Shaw thought for a second, then, annoyed "They went in to the city, said they were visiting some friends or something. They took the truck."

Yost recalled not seeing it parked in the usual spot when he drove in. "I will wait for them outside."

"Very well, Gerhardt. Thank you for your assistance tonight."

"Yes, sir." Gerhardt gave the senator a curt nod, and rose leaving the room.

Walking out of the study, he headed towards the cottage. As he expected, the door was locked. Looking around, seeing an area lacking any natural light, he walked over, concealing himself, he waited.

After dropping Geri off at her apartment, Callahan proceeded to the precinct, where he dropped off the car. Leaving, he caught the subway to his apartment. Arriving at his apartment, he tossed his hat on the couch, then sitting; he grabbed the telephone, dialing Ginny Maitland's private number.

After two rings, a woman's voice answered.

"Ginny, it's Mike."

"Good evening, Michael, I've been waiting for you to call. I assume you have some developments to discuss."

"Yeah, I took Eileen's friend out to Shaw's estate on Long Island to see if we could get a look at the gimp from the boat."

Interested she asked, "How did that turn out?"

"It was getting dark, we had pulled out to leave when he came driving down the road towards us."

"Was she able to see him?"

"I flagged him down, saying we were lost. While we were speaking, she leaned forward and got a good look at him."

"And…"

"She swears he was the same guy from the party boat the night Eileen was murdered."

"Excellent."

"It gets better. Before he came back, a pickup truck pulled out, with a man and a woman in it. The guy was the Irishman, from Eileen's funeral."

"Excellent news, Michael. What are your next steps?"

"Well, what we have here is some circumstantial evidence pointing towards one of the most powerful men in our government. God, I wish we had Eileen's diary, it would make this a lot easier. I'm gonna sleep on this; we can discuss it further in the morning."

"All right, Michael, we'll talk again in the morning

"Good night, Ginny."

31

Sitting alone in his study, Senator Tom Shaw considered the events of the evening. He was astounded that his son would show the courage he did, in order to protect his interest. Picking up the phone, he dialed Danny's number.

After a couple of rings, Danny answered, "Hello?"

"Daniel, it's me."

"Hello, Dad. To what do I owe the pleasure of this call?"

Shaw couldn't tell if he was tired or if he had been drinking. Sighing, he spoke gently "Daniel...Gerhardt told me what happened tonight."

He laughed. "Surprised?"

"I'm grateful, Daniel...that you would take such extreme measures to protect me."

"Hell, you're my dad, what else would I do?"

"Precisely, Daniel, family must stick together. At the end of the day, the only people you can count on are family. I can imagine that it wasn't easy for you. Is there anything I could do for you?"

Danny sighed. "You know...I felt bad about the cop. The dumb sap shouldn't have pulled us over. On the other hand, the judge had it coming. I never liked him."

The senator laughed. "You know, neither did I."

"Dad, did you tell Gerhardt to get the missing pages from Benny?"

His voice hard, he replied coldly "Yes, I told him to take what measures he deemed necessary to get those pages."

"Good...that's good. He'll get them."

"Yes, I agree. This episode should be ended tonight. I'll finally have that little bitch out of my life."

Shaw heard his son swallow. "I'll always be there for you, dad."

"I know, Daniel. Why don't you get some sleep? I'll call you in the morning to let you know how everything goes."

"Okay...good night, dad."

Up on Broadway, the joint was jumping at Legs Diamond's Hotsy Totsy Club. The tables were all taken, and the new band had a singer that was keeping everyone entertained. Sitting at his usual table in the corner, Diamond smoked a cigarette, keeping tabs on the flow of cash for the night. Occasionally people came over to speak with him, and he was, as always, a gracious host.

It was an unspoken rule that members of opposing organizations were welcome to dine and have a few drinks at the club. Diamond was always willing to speak with the various hoods enjoying the club, trying to glean whatever useful information he could.

Outside, Tom Regan was walking up to the door of the club and he happened to glance at two men getting out of their taxi. Both men were well dressed and, as one man stumbled, his suit jacket opened revealing a shoulder holster. Quickly regaining his composure, he and his associate made their way into the club.

Diamond happened to be watching the front door when Regan walked in. Regan made his way towards Legs' table.

Arriving, he seated himself at the table. "A good night, Legs?"

A waiter quickly appeared, placing a drink in front of Regan. Regan nodded a quick glance at the man "Thanks, Andy."

The waiter quickly departed.

"So, Tommy...what have you been up to?"

"We gotta talk, Legs. There is something you need to know."

Legs looked up, curious. "Oh yeah, what's shaking, Tommy?"

"I got taken the other night, by Luciano's men."

Sitting back, Diamond stared at his friend, raising his eyebrows in surprise. Smiling, he asked "Tommy...why ain't you dead?"

Regan leaned forward, to avoid having to speak over the music "Here's the deal, Legs. Luciano wants me to double cross you. He said he would give me control of your organization."

"Bastard."

"Legs, you know I'm not a rat...right?"

Smiling, he kept eye contact with Regan "Yeah, I guess I trust you more than anyone I know."

Glancing away from Diamond, Regan noted the two men from outside seated not far from them. Regan took a moment to casually scan the club. "Legs, I think we gotta problem."

"What are you talking about?"

Smiling, Regan replied, laughing slightly, "Look around the club, you know those guys sitting at the table, three over?"

Taking a look around the club, Diamond was taken aback to notice that the patrons Regan mentioned appeared to be Italian. "Why do you ask?"

"The one on the right is packing."

Diamond was quick to act, given his uncanny instinct for survival. Catching the eye of his number one body guard, he casually he took out his comb, combing his hair. He held two fingers out on the side of his head, as he passed with his comb. The bodyguard made no movement to acknowledge his boss. Instead, he walked over to a second bodyguard, speaking into his ear. Nodding, the man disappeared into the back area, moving quickly, he went to a small room. Entering, he went to a cabinet, unlocking it; he quickly pulled out a Thompson submachine gun.

Coming out of the room, he bumped into the head waiter. "There may be action in here tonight; you let the staff know, okay?"

Nodding, the head waiter quickly moved away.

At their table, Diamond and Regan continued their conversation, keeping their eyes on the patrons. Diamond was quick to notice that the two men didn't seem to be drinking as much as the other patrons...definitely a problem.

Out on the street, a black limousine sat parked a short distance away from the club. In the rear seat of the car sat Lucky Luciano. Looking at his wristwatch, he nodded, thinking, *A few more minutes.*

Luciano had decided that he couldn't do business with Tom Regan, even though he personally liked the guy. He respected his business expertise, but the bottom line was that the guy wasn't Italian. He just couldn't place his trust in an Irishman. This really wasn't personal, this was just business. He had planned the hit, which would shortly take place. His people would finally take out that sonofabitch Diamond, who seemed to lead a charmed life when it came to being hit. He had a small degree of regret about Tom Regan. It was a shame the guy wasn't Italian; he would have been really useful to the organization.

Inside the Hotsy Totsy Club, Diamond's people were prepared. Diamond and Reagan hadn't touched their drinks for a while. Continuing to make small talk, they watched the patrons.

The two men at the table stood, exactly at the same time. Seeming to glance at each other, they stared at the corner table where Diamond sat with Tom Regan.

Diamond spoke, "Tommy, I hope you're packing, because it's happening."

At that, both men saw the standing patrons pull handguns, and turn towards the table where Diamond sat.

Diamonds people sprang into action, shouting for everyone to get down, Diamond and Regan drew their weapons, along with a number of the staff. Shots rang out, people screamed, and Diamond, as always, ran to the forefront, which upset Regan greatly.

Diamond's man emerged from the kitchen and began firing the Thompson submachine gun. One of the Italian shooters dropped, as he was hit. Diamond shot the other man, and in short order, the fire fight was over.

Patrons ran out of the club, quickly hailing taxis. There would be calls to the police over shots being fired. Although, it was certain that none of the patrons would want to spend the night in police custody answering questions.

Diamonds men began to move through the confusion towards the men who had drawn weapons.

Diamond shouted, "Get me the live one, I want answers, dammit!"

A few of the men looked at their boss. Turning towards Regan, Diamond noted that the man had stayed at his side throughout the gunfight. "Thanks, Tommy, for proving I was right to trust you."

Regan smiled. "Anytime, boss, just let Luciano try it again."

Diamond laughed, still full of emotion "Hell, the bullet hasn't been made which can kill me."

From across the room, one of his men called out "Hey, boss, we got the live one here."

"Come on, Tommy."

Quickly, the two men went across the room. The large man lay on the floor, Diamond's man pointing his Thompson at him. He stared up at Diamond with hate in his eyes.

Diamond smiled. "Bad day, huh?"

The man spit up at Diamond, the spittle landing on his pants leg. Looking down at it for a moment, Diamond took out his handkerchief, wiped it off, and, in a surprisingly quick move, kicked the man in the side. Moaning, the man's eyes rolled up into his head.

Diamond looked down, his voice venomous "Do something like that again, garlic eater, and you're a dead man."

Looking at his men he commanded "Take him to the warehouse. Quickly, before the cops get here. Get the doc; I want him taken care of. I want to know if anyone put Luciano up to this, or if that spaghetti eater thought of this on his own."

Lifting the unconscious man off the floor, the men headed for the rear door. Regan grabbed Diamond's arm.

"Yeah, what is it Tommy?"

"I didn't get a chance to finish our conversation. Luciano said he wanted to have access into the high-end protection he thinks you have."

Diamond froze. "He said that…he didn't say who that might be?"

Regan thought for a second, shaking his head "No, he didn't say."

On the street, Lucky Luciano sat in his limousine, observing the people running out of the Hotsy Totsy Club. Instinctively, he knew that something had gone wrong. If his men had done the hit, they would have been among the first people out of the club. In the distance he heard the sounds of approaching police sirens. Cursing, he knew he had to leave or risk having the cops bring him in for questioning, given his proximity to the hit. "Carlo, let's get outta here."

The driver nodded, as he put the car in drive "You got it, boss." The limousine pulled away from the curb, proceeding down Broadway.

Rita and Benny Fitzgibbon had stopped for dinner at a restaurant on the east side of Manhattan, a short distance from the police precinct. They were having an enjoyable evening, not getting out much living on the estate. Benny, an avid story teller, made her laugh, recalling memories from their younger days in Ireland. Benny had a couple of pints of beer, with Rita having a couple of glasses of wine.

They walked from the restaurant, arms around each other, Benny humming an Irish folk tune.

Driving back to the estate Benny smiled, seeing Rita asleep on the seat next to him. Although he was a thin man, Benny knew how to pace himself, driving back to the estate without any problems. Pulling up the driveway, he stopped the truck in the usual parking spot.

"Come on, my girl, we're home."

Slowly rousing herself, Rita took in her surroundings. "We're home already, Ben?"

"Aye that we are. C'mon, let's get you to bed."

Getting out of the truck, Benny moved around to her side. As he opened her door, he eased the tired woman out of the truck. Putting his arm around her, they began to walk slowly towards the door to the cottage.

Yost stood silently in the dark, watching them move towards the cottage. It pleased him that they seemed to have been drinking; it would make taking them easier. He slowly began to move from his hiding place.

Benny had left a light on near the front door, to light their way up the walk. Getting close to the door, he reached into his pocket for his key, and glancing into the window, he saw the shape of a large man coming up behind him. Realizing immediately who the man was, he shoved Rita away, turning to face the German.

Reaching into his jacket, Benny pulled out a lead pipe wrapped in tape. After the last encounter with Yost, he wanted a weapon. Not seeing the weapon in the darkness, Yost lunged at Benny. Benny quickly brought the pipe around, connecting with Yost's head. Caught off guard, Yost dropped to the ground, staggered.

Looking over to his wife quickly, Benny turned his attention back to the German. "You shagging bastard, I'm going to kill you tonight, I've had about enough."
Jumping onto the German, Benny began to beat him with his pipe. Yost tried to bring his hands up, but they were blocked by Benny's legs. Benny was relentless, with Yost dropping his hands in a losing effort. Benny raised his arm again, and as he brought it down, he felt Rita's grasp. Turning, with fire in his eyes, he glared at his wife. "What are you doing? Let me finish this tonight!"

"So you can stand trial for murder, and have me being alone for the rest of my life?"

Benny faltered, "What would you have me do, woman?"

"Ask him what the hell he was doing?"

Benny stared down at the German. "What the hell did you want, you bastard?"

His face bloodied, he spoke with difficulty "The pages you took...the senator wants them."

Realization came to Benny. "He has the diary...aw, shit, that's a bad thing."

Yost seemed to recover more, asking "Do you have the pages?"

Scornful, as he spat his response, "No, you bastard, we don't."

Yost was confused. "Where are they?"

Benny slowly smiled. "The police have them. How do you like that, you bastard?"

Yost closed his eyes, accepting his failure, he sighed.

32

"They gave them to the police!" Shaw cried out in anguish.

The senator sat back in his chair, distressed, considering his options. He stared at Yost seated before him. "Jesus, looks like the little mick gave a good accounting of himself."

Deeply stung by the criticism, Yost answered quickly "He had a weapon; he was waiting for me."

Shaw raised his eyebrows, impressed "Who would have thought? Go tell them to pack their bags and get off the estate...do it now."

Yost sat staring at his employer. "Do you really want them out of your control? Do you want them speaking to the authorities, with another reason to hate you?"

Shaw was taken aback. "What do you suggest?"

"They said they were not able to see the detective heading the investigation. You know who that is?"

Shaw thought for a moment. "Danny's partner!"

Yost smiled. "They left the pages in an envelope, with a note."

Shaw's mind worked fast. "Danny will get there early. He can swipe the pages before his partner arrives." Looking at his watch, Shaw wondered if his son wasn't already passed out on his bed. "Hell, I'll call him now," nodding slowly, "We're almost home free, Gerhardt."

Yost smiled thinly. "Yes, sir."

Across town, Legs Diamond's car pulled up in front of his warehouse on the lower east side of Manhattan. Stepping out of the car, looking about, Regan nodded to the men by the door. "Okay, Legs, it's clear."

Diamond pushed his way out of the car. "C'mon Tommy, let's talk to our new friend."

They walked past the guards, who watched Diamond with intense interest, having heard about the shootout at the club. They thought as he walked past that maybe the rumors were true, that the guy just led a charmed life.

Diamond smiled slyly at his men as he passed. "Keep a sharp eye, boys."

"Yeah, boss," they responded in unison.

Walking into the warehouse, they quickly entered the room where the Italian gunman was being held. Diamond walked over to the cot, where the man lay. Looking down at him, he turned to the doctor. "You got him on any pain killers?"

The physician for his organization, always grateful for the extra money that Diamond threw his way, shook his head. "The two wounds were flesh wounds, no serious damage. He would be more comfortable with some morphine, but I surmised you might want him with a clear head."

Diamond stared at the doctor, almost laughing. "You surmised that, did you? Well, good surmising, doc, you were right."

Diamond stared down at the man on the cot. "Hi there, remember me? I'm the guy your boss wanted hit tonight. Didn't he tell you that there ain't no bullet out there that can kill me?"

The man on the cot turned his head away, a scornful look on his face. In a flash, Diamond punched the man in his shoulder wound. Screaming, the man grabbed his shoulder.

Diamond smiled calmly. "Now that I have your attention, let's talk." The man looked at Diamond, hatred in his eyes. "What did Lucky tell you tonight, about this hit?"

Staring at Diamond, the prostrate man silently challenged him.

Watching the man, Diamond calmly held out a hand behind him, looking at the Italian, he addressed the man closest to him "Bat."

Running over to the corner, one of his men grabbed a bat and quickly handed it to Diamond. A wicked smile on his face, Diamond looked at the Italian, gently slapping the bat into his left hand.

"Now, it's just me, but I think you really oughta start talking...I mean, if you're interested in avoiding some pain."

The man on the cot considered his options. His fierce loyalty to Luciano taking hold, he turned his head. In a flash Diamond swung the bat in a wide arc, striking the man in his ribs. The man screamed, grabbing his ribs, looking at Diamond with a new emotion, fear.

Diamond turned to his men, laughing. "What do you think, was that a double or a triple?"

One of his men responded, "A triple for sure, boss."

Diamond appeared thoughtful, as though he was disappointed "That's my problem, I'm afraid to swing for the fences. Well, we can take care of that." Taking the bat, Diamond raised it in a high arc. Screaming, the man held up an arm, speaking rapidly in Italian. Lowering the bat, Diamond leaned over the man. Leaning towards the man, "I'm sorry; did you want to say something?"

The man nodded rapidly. "Yes, yes, I speak with you; please...please don't hit me again."

Diamond tossed the bat to one of his men. Laughing, he turned to the Italian, Spreading his arms with his palms open "Well, talk to me then. What have you got to say?"

Diamond's men watched, enjoying seeing their boss work over an enemy.

Diamond leaned over the man, "Talk to me, I'm all ears."

The Italian, looking furiously about, realized he didn't have a friend in the room, so he spoke. "Lucky just told us we had to hit you."

Annoyed, feeling that the man wasn't telling it all, "Tell me something I don't know,"

"He said you weren't being fair."

Dismayed, Diamond blinked, "Fair? What the hell are you talking about?"

"Lucky said you have some powerful protection, and that you weren't sharing it for everyone's benefit."

Diamond leaned in closely to the man, face to face. "Did he tell you who that might be?"

The man glanced at Regan, standing a close distance away. "He hoped that one would tell him."

Turning to Regan, Diamond smiled broadly. "Tommy, did you promise to tell Mr. Luciano who our guardian angel was?"

Tom Regan smiled thinly. "I didn't promise nothing."

Diamond turned back to the man on the cot. "You know, I think you're telling the truth. And the question now is...what do I do with you?" Diamond enjoyed watching the fear in the man's eyes. He snapped his fingers. "You gotta family?"

Confused for a moment, the Italian grew hopeful "Yes, yes, I have a wife and a small child."

Diamond stared hard at the man "You think your wife and kid would appreciate it if I sent you back to them?"

Nodding quickly, he replied "Yes, yes, they would like that very much."

Diamond seemed to think for a moment, then pulled out his handgun and pointed it at the man, who began to weep. "I dunno, my gut tells me you should be a dead man. You know, send a message back to your boss."

Weeping, he begged 'Please, Mr. Diamond, I was just following orders."

Diamond pulled the trigger, the bullet missing the man's head by inches. His men were instantly alert, wondering how this would end.

Diamond looked down at the man. "Ever since Rothstein got hit, I've had everyone looking to take over my rackets. The most persistent guy among the lot of them is that damn Dutch Schultz. I got no beef with your boss, but because he feels greedy, he sends you to hit me. I'm gonna do something that really goes against my better judgment. I'm gonna send you back to Luciano with a message."

The man on the cot listened in rapt attention. Drawing close to the man, Diamond's voice dripped venom. "You tell your boss, if he tries anything again against me or any of my people, nothing will stop me until he is a dead man."

The man nodded slowly.

Diamond's mood instantly changing his voice upbeat, "But if he leaves well enough alone, I got no further beef with him."

Diamond rose and turned to his men, jerking his thumb at the man "Get him outta here, drop him back by Luciano's place."

Moving quickly, his men hustled the man out of the warehouse. Diamond put his gun back in his holster.

Turning to Regan, he asked his friend "You think I made the smart play, Tommy?"

Regan played with his fedora, thinking. "Yeah, Legs, I think you did the right thing…but we gotta prepare for the worst."

Sighing, he gazed downwards "Yeah, Tommy, unfortunately we do."

The car carrying the Italian pulled away from the warehouse, driving off into the night.

33

Feeling surprisingly good, Danny Shaw considered the events of yesterday. It astounded him that he had killed two men. It felt great to hear his father's surprise on the phone when they had spoken in the evening. Getting ready to leave for the precinct, he chuckled, having trouble recalling where they had buried Crater. Yost had paid that cabbie so much money; he would never speak to anyone. Yost had also promised another payout in a year, if everything remained unsolved. Danny agreed that was a good idea; after all, his dad had more money than most men.

His phone rang. Looking at his watch, seeing that he was running late, he ignored it, walking out of the apartment.

At the estate, "Isn't he answering?" The senator asked.

Slowly, Yost shook his head.

Softly the senator cursed, "Dammit, why would he have to be on time today?" Looking at Yost, "Gerhardt, I need you to go to his precinct and tell him to get those damn pages. Once we have them, that little bitch won't be able to hurt us."

Yost nodded, his voice firm, "I'll leave at once, sir."

"Good...good." The senator sat back in his chair seeming satisfied.

In the city, Lucky Luciano sat with his top lieutenants and his man who had been sent back by Diamond.

Luciano spoke softly, "Okay, Mario, you tell these men what happened last night, and what Diamond said."

Staring at the men seated at the table, he was scared to death.

Luciano spoke softly, "Hey, I told you it was okay. You took two hits; I know you tried, just tell us what happened."

"Well sir, it was like you told us, go to his club in separate cars. You said sit at a table with the broads you supplied us with, then to wait until nine o'clock. It was then we were to leave the broads at the table, and go after Diamond."

"What happened then?"

"Well, it was like this, I saw his guy Regan come in, and go to his table. They seemed to talk, real serious like."

Luciano nodded thinking, *that bastard Regan had told Diamond about their conversation.* He had to admire the guy's loyalty, but if he was here now, he'd put a bullet in his head. It was obvious that once he had told Diamond, his instincts saved him again, recognizing that a hit was in progress. His other guy was dead, taken out by Diamonds guys. Diamond had taken Mario to one of his warehouses, had a doctor fix him up, and then he questioned him with a baseball bat.

Smiling, Luciano thought the baseball bat was a nice touch. You could really cause some pain, without actually killing a guy. It was obvious Mario had a few broken ribs.

"So what message did Mr. Diamond have for us?"

"He said if you end this now, he ain't got no beef with you. He said you try anything else, he ain't gonna stop until you're dead."

"And that's all?"

Mario nodded slowly trying to recall everything, "Yes sir, Mr. Luciano. That's what he told me to tell you."

Luciano sat quietly, then spoke, "Thank you, Mario. Why don't you go home, have your wife take care of you? You come back to work when you feel better."

Rising and bowing quickly, Mario replied, "Thank you, sir, thank you," as he quickly departed from the room.

Luciano waited until the door was shut.

Gazing about the room, Luciano asked "Well, any opinions on the message from Mr. Diamond?"

No one wanted to be the first to speak, as they waited for the man seated at the right hand of Luciano to speak. They were old friends, Luciano personally inviting him to this meeting. The man, a Jew, was Meyer Lansky, the financial advisor to Luciano.

Lansky spoke "May I say something?"

Luciano looked over at him. "Sure, Meyer, what do you think?"

"Diamond's organization has been barely held together for the last year or so. He lost his protection when our old friend Arnold Rothstein had the bad luck to get hit."

The men at the table shared the joke, laughing lightly.

Meyer Lansky held up a hand to silence them. "My point is that without this one influential person, Diamond would be totally exposed. We could have offered him a buyout, but we all know he's a greedy bastard, caring for nobody but himself."

Lansky continued "I've taken the initiative to find out who has been protecting Diamond, and I believe we know who that person is."

Luciano sat up straight. "You know? When were you going to tell us?"

Smiling at his friend, Lansky turned to the men at the table. "His protection is none other than Thomas Shaw, the senator from the state of New York."

There were looks of disbelief among the men at the table.

Luciano spoke, "You sure about this? We ain't never heard of any relationship between him and the rackets."

Lansky nodded. "Charlie, I paid good money for my information, I believe it to be sound."

Staring at his friend, Luciano was certain that if Lansky believed his information to be good, it was golden.

Lansky added "Now with that said, our friend the senator distances himself from any of Diamonds activities, communicating through his man Yost. The senator, on numerous committees passes along information that has allowed Legs Diamond to remain in business, since Arnold got hit." Lansky chuckled slightly. "It's long been rumored that Diamond had Arnold hit, the guy's a rat who deserves everything he gets."

One of the men at the table spoke up, "No one here disagrees with you, but he does seem to lead a charmed life." Looking around to the other men, "How many times has Diamond been hit, a dozen? The guy is just damn lucky. Dutch Schultz has gone after him a number of times with nothing to show for it, but a bunch of dead men."

Luciano silenced the men. "So what are you saying, we just roll over, leave him alone?

Lansky spoke up, "No, Charlie, I think we need to be a bit more subtle when we go after this guy, a bit more indirect."

Luciano laughed. "Subtlety, yeah that's for me, I'm a real subtle guy."

The men at the table laughed along with their leader.

Across town, as Callahan walked into the precinct greeting some friends, he noticed Shaw seated at his desk reading the paper. Walking up behind him, Callahan gently tapped him on the shoulder.

"Enjoying the seat?"

Shaw quickly got up. "Sorry, just waiting for you."

Callahan sat. "Where you been, on a toot?"

"Nah...had a bad stomach."

Callahan looked up at him. "Really? Tell it to Sweeney."

A nervous thought struck Shaw, recalling the events of yesterday.

Forcing himself to be calm, with a sheepish look on his face "Yeah, I'm feeling better, don't worry…I won't upchuck on you."

Callahan smiled. "See that you don't."

Looking about, Callahan spoke "Grab a chair and sit."

Callahan's desk was against the wall. Over time it was not unheard of for papers to fall from his inbox, into the space between the desk and the wall. Lying in that position was the sealed envelope from Benny and Rita Fitzgibbon. Detective Penny had tossed the envelope on the desk towards the inbox, turning away without seeing where it had landed.

Callahan had debated whether or not to tell Danny about the position his father was in, recalling the scene at the funeral. He being certain that Shaw had allowed the Irishman to get away. There was no way the Irishman could have outrun him that far, that quickly.

Kroon came into the squad room, looking about, he seemed upset, "Can I have everyone's attention?" Everyone stopped what they were doing, looking in his direction. "I got some bad news; a police officer was murdered last night out on Long Island. He was a motorcycle cop, just a couple of months from retirement. The report I got says he was shot at close range, the lab recovered the slug. I want everyone to keep their ears open. If you hear anything about this from any source, I want to know. We will allocate whatever resources necessary to bring this murderer to justice. That's all, thanks." Turning, he walked back into his office.

Everyone stared at each other, the anger in the room almost electric.

Shaw stared about the room, feeling nervous. If these men knew he had shot that officer, their anger would be fierce. He was glad there had been no witnesses.

Callahan stared at Shaw. "What are you thinking?"

Shaw startled slightly struggling to mask his emotions, "I…think it's a shame that the officer died so close to his retirement."

Callahan grew hard, his voice contemptuous, "He didn't die, Dan, he was murdered by some hood who better hope we don't catch him, cause if when we do, he's gonna sit in old Sparky."

Shaw was slightly taken aback; Old Sparky was the electric chair at Sing Sing Prison in Ossining.

Shaw smiled slightly. "Here's hoping we get lucky."

Yost had made excellent time driving into the city. Traffic had been surprisingly light, and he had the good fortune to pass an intersection just prior to an accident. He had considered how he would contact Daniel, to inform him of the Fitzgibbons' action. It was possible, he thought, that Detective Callahan already possessed the pages. He hoped that was not the case.

Callahan would be impossible to deal with, and possibly had already alerted his superiors. Yost didn't believe for a second that they could eliminate the detective in the manner they had dealt with the men the other night.

Once over the bridge, in the city, the greater concentration of traffic and pedestrians slowed his pace.

Turning onto the street that housed the precinct, he began to look for a place to park. Seeing a spot he sped up, pulling his vehicle into the vacant area of the street. Surveying the area, he was glad he wasn't closer to the entrance to the station. He was also pleased to note that there were a couple of expensive cars parked on the street, no doubt important people doing business with the police department.

Sitting back, he watched the people coming and going from the station.

Inside the station, Callahan and Shaw were reviewing the statuses of other cases they had been working on. Finally, Callahan pulled the case folder for the murder of Eileen O'Sullivan.

Shaw spoke, "Any developments on the case, Mike?"

Before Callahan could reply, there was laughter and loud voices coming from the other side of the squad room. Callahan turned to see the cause of the disruption. He broke out in a smile. Walking into the room greeting people, shaking hands, was his partner, Doc.

Callahan rose, ignoring Shaw he walked over to his partner; the two men saw each other.

"Hey, you're not allowed back here, this is only for policemen."

Doc laughing gave it back, "Then how the heck did you get in?"

They shook hands.

Callahan asked "What brings you in, you coming back on some limited duty or something?"

"Not yet, I got one more doctors appointment before I can be cleared to come back."

Callahan looked his friend over. "You do look better."

Doc smiled. "Yeah, I almost died, you know."

They both laughed.

Other officers walking by slapped Doc on the back, offering greetings to the popular detective. Doc cheerfully acknowledged their good wishes.

"Well, look what the cat dragged in." Kroon stood a few feet away, a smile on his face. He walked over and held out his hand. "I didn't get any word about you coming back."

"No, sir, just had to get out of my apartment…I was going off my nut."

Kroon nodded. "I understand. It's good to see you, Doc. Say, did you hear about that cop shot in Queens?

Doc nodded. "Yeah, I saw that in the paper. Any leads?"

"Nothing yet, but we got a lot of men on it. Something will break." Kroon answered confidently. "All right, gotta get back to work. Good seeing you, Doc." Turning, he walked away.

Doc turned to Callahan, asking "What are you doing?"

Mike pointed towards his desk; Shaw still seated looking back at him. "Case review."

Doc lowered his voice, "That's gotta be the kid."

"Yup, come over, I'll introduce you."

"Okay."

They walked over to Mike's desk.

Shaw stood, trying not to appear too eager "Dan, this is Doc."

Doc held out his hand, smiling slightly "How's it going, kid? Mike been showing you the ropes?"

"Yeah, he's been great."

Nodding, Doc glanced at Mike, "Mind if I sit in on your review?"

Looking slightly surprised, Callahan shook his head. "Sit down. Dan, grab another chair."

"So, what case were you guys discussing before I came in?"

"Murder case, young woman, Eileen O'Sullivan."

Doc looked thoughtful for a moment, "Wasn't she the one who washed up on the beach in Rockaway?"

Callahan followed his lead. "Yeah, that's the one."

Sitting back, Doc raised his eyebrows, "Any developments?"

Callahan spoke, "Yeah, we have a positive ID on a man who was on the boat that the deceased was last seen on. Interestingly, I also got a positive ID on another man who tried to attend the deceased's funeral."

Watching Shaw, both men hoped for some telling reaction. Frustrating both of them, Shaw maintained a blank look on his face. Inwardly, he was emotionally wracked. They had identified Yost and Fitzgibbon, how close where they to his father?

Callahan decided to push it further. "The interesting thing here is that both of these men work for Dan's father."

Doc looked straight at Shaw. "That a fact, Dan?"

Shaw recovered quickly, appearing annoyed. "This is the first I'm hearing of this." Callahan turned to Shaw, a thoughtful look on his face. "You ever see the deceased at your dad's estate?"

Callahan handed Shaw a photo they had taken from Eileen's apartment.

Shaw, staring at the photo, thought for a second. "Nope, I don't recall seeing her."

He handed the photo back to Callahan.

Doc broke the silence. "Wasn't she one of Ginny Maitland's girls? Did she come up with anything?"

Shaw watched them both maintaining a strict poker face. He was silently glad that he had developed an ability as a child to lie to his father and to the people on the estate. Callahan spoke slowly, "Ginny didn't have anything on her personal life. The deceased is reported to have kept a diary, but we've been unable to find it."

"Too bad," Shaw commented.

Callahan replied sarcastically "Yeah, too bad."

34

Carefully parking the Packard down the street, away from the precinct, Yost was unwilling to chance having it seen by Danny's partner. Standing in the shadow of an awning, he watched the activity outside the police station. There was a steady flow of officers, into and out of the building. Street vendors hawked their wares to the public as they walked by. Considering his options prior to leaving the estate, he pulled an envelope out of his pocket. Danny's name was printed on it.

Yost watched some kids playing in the street. Making his choice, he called over, gesturing to one of the older boys. "Young man, I need your assistance."

The kid stopped, staring at him. "Oh yeah…what's the deal, pops, whatcha need me for?"

Yost slowly approached the kid. He showed him the envelope.

The kid laughed. "The post office is two blocks south."

Yost controlled his temper. "No, I need you to deliver this to the precinct," he said, pointing at the building.

The kid looked wary. "What's amatter…you can't go in there?"

Yost smiled. "I would prefer not to. If you deliver this, I'll give you a dollar." He could immediately see the greed in the young boy's eyes. Yost continued, "If you deliver it and no policemen follow you out, I'll give you another dollar."

The boy's eyes widened. "Two dollars for that?"

Yost Nodded, "Just for that."

"You gotta deal." Holding his hand out, Yost gave him the envelope and the dollar. Turning quickly, the boy ran towards the precinct. Bounding up the steps, he entered the building.

The sergeant at the desk noticed him as he approached. Putting down his pen, he looked at the boy. "What can I do for you, son?"

The young man held out the envelope. The sergeant took it, as he looked at the name on it, the boy turned running out of the building. Turning it over in his hand, he saw that it was sealed. The name was the young detective assigned to work with Mike Callahan. He recalled that Dan Shaw wasn't too popular, but that wasn't his problem.

Calling out to an officer passing, he held up the envelope "Hey, Schneider, do me a favor."

Stopping, the officer stared at the desk sergeant. "Sure, sarge, what do you need?"

He held the envelope out to him. "Deliver this to Danny Shaw; he should be in the squad room with Callahan."

The officer took the envelope. "You got it, sarge."

With the envelope in hand, the officer walked away. Going upstairs, he entered the squad room, not knowing Shaw, he looked for Callahan. Seeing him seated with two men and recognizing one as Callahan's partner, Holiday, he assumed the other was Shaw.

Walking over to the desk, Shaw and Doc noticed his approach. The officer gestured at Shaw. "Are you Detective Shaw?"

Shaw nodded. "Yeah, why?"

The officer held out the envelope. "The desk sergeant asked me to give this to you."

Shaw took the envelope. "Thanks." Mike and Doc watched as he put the envelope in his pocket.

Doc asked "You gonna open it? It might be important."

Shaw answered calmly, "Yeah, as soon as we're done here." Having recognized the stationery from the estate, he instinctively knew it was a message from his father, and he didn't want to open it in their presence.

Callahan spoke "Okay, let's continue."

They spent the next hour going over the statuses of the case load. Some of the cases dated prior to Doc's illness. As they finished, Mike looked at his partner, easily seeing he was tired. "I think you may have pushed it a bit, partner."

Doc gently rubbed his abdomen. "Yeah, I think you may be right, Mike. I'm gonna go lay down for a bit before I head home." He slowly rose. Mike thought about offering a hand, but decided against it.

Shaw stood up. "I'm gonna get a cup of coffee. I'll be back in a few minutes."

Callahan nodded, not bothering to look at him, more concerned about his partner.

Moving quickly away, Shaw found a secluded spot and quickly opened the envelope. Reading it, he was stunned by Yost's information. The missing pages from the dead girl's diary were in an envelope on Callahan's desk. He thought for a second, he hadn't seen any envelopes in his inbox. Walking quickly to the men's room, he went into a stall, tore up the note and flushed it.

Walking back to the desk, he was disappointed to see Callahan still seated, writing something. Stopping before the desk, he tried to appear casual as he looked at the contents of the inbox. There didn't appear to be any envelopes. He wondered if it was possible that Callahan had already opened the envelope, and was toying with him.

Callahan looked up. "Where's your coffee?"

"What…oh, I drank it already."

Callahan continued writing, "Anything important in the note?"

Fighting to remain calm he lied, "No, just a note from a lady I was with last week. She was wondering when I might call her again."

Callahan looked up, skeptical. "That a fact…good for you." He didn't believe him.

"While you were drinking your coffee, I got a call on the Spencer case. We gotta take a ride to Judge McNamara and get a warrant. We're going to bring in the suspect and book him on suspicion of murder."

Callahan finished with his writing rose, "Let's go."

Wanting more than anything to rifle through the contents of the inbox, Shaw nodded "Sure thing, Mike." The two men walked out of the squad room.

The envelope with the pages of the diary remained where they were, stuck between the desk and the wall.

Walking out of the station, Shaw stopped and put his hat on. Looking around for Yost, he saw him in the window of the stationery store across the street. He had to speak with him.

Turning to Callahan, he pointed at the store "I'm gonna grab a pack of gum, can I get you anything?"

"What? No, thanks…hurry up, I'll get the car."

Running between traffic, crossing the street quickly, Shaw entered the store. He grabbed a pack of Wrigley's and paid for it. Turning, he saw Yost leaning against the wall, reading a magazine. Walking over, Shaw pretended to look at the magazines.

"I didn't see an envelope in the inbox."

Yost raised his eyebrows. "Do you think he has the pages?"

"No, he would have said something. I have to go, tell my father I'll call him later." Watching him leave, Yost went to the telephone booth to call the senator.

Shaw ran across the street to the waiting car and jumped in. "Let's go."

Looking ahead, Callahan was annoyed "Took you long enough."

"Sorry," Shaw said, even though he wasn't. He was really beginning to dislike the superior attitude of his partner. *Wouldn't he be surprised if he knew what I'd done in the last few days,* thought Shaw. He was resolved to protect his father, and to secure his respect. He had no political ambitions, feeling his dad could pull the necessary strings to make him a captain, at the very least.

In the stationery store, Yost's call reached the estate.

The senator answered quickly, awaiting the call. "Yes, Gerhardt. Did you speak with Daniel?"

"Yes, sir, he said there was no envelope that he could see. He didn't have the opportunity to look through the mailbox."

Shaw swore. "Does he think that his partner has the pages?"

Yost spoke slowly, keeping his voice calm, "No, he thinks he doesn't have them yet. He is certain he would have mentioned it."

"What is Danny going to do…did he say?"

"He said he would call you later. He was in a rush; the older detective was waiting for him. I think he will look for an opportunity to search the box for the envelope."

Shaw didn't speak for a minute, then proceeded, "Listen to me, Gerhardt, if Daniel fails to obtain the pages, we may need to move forcibly to get them. Do you understand me?"

He understood, but, unlike Danny, he had no desire to murder a policeman. "I understand, sir, don't worry."

"Good…I knew I could count on you."

Yost hung up the phone, wondering how the elimination of that young girl on the boat had progressed to this point, two men dead with the distinct possibility of another man dying soon.

Who would have thought?

35

Tom Regan sat in Diamond's office, watching as Diamond counted out the payoff for the senator. As Diamond counted the money silently, Regan thought what he could do with such funds.

Diamond Laughed, "Getting any ideas Tommy," startled, Regan looked up to see Diamond watching him.

Regan smiled easily. "Does he really deserve that much of a cut, boss?"

Scratching his chin, Diamond thought for a second. "Yeah...he does." Sealing the envelope, Diamond handed it to his lieutenant.

He asked Regan "You meeting the Kraut at the usual place?"

Regan nodded "Yeah, same place, same time. The Kraut is nothing if not one heck of a predictable guy."

Diamond smiled. "It's a German thing, Tommy. They're very ordered."

Regan stood. "I'll see you when I get back, boss."

"Sure, take care, Tommy."

Regan left, and Diamond concentrated on the papers on his desk. He was pleased with the earnings numbers. The bootlegging continued to be profitable, while the income from the Hotsy Totsy had remained stable, even after the event of the other night. He hoped that would be the end of that, but it was well known that Lucky Luciano was an ambitious man.

Sitting back in the chair, Diamond stretched. Looking at his watch he thought he'd take Regan, and grab some lunch when he returned. He was feeling good. If the numbers stayed the same, he could begin to consider retirement pretty soon. He had vowed that he wasn't going to end up like so many other mobsters, shot to death in some alley.

He had been accumulating his retirement money for some time now. Since the Depression began, he hadn't kept all of his money in one bank, choosing instead to spread it around to a number of banks, using fictitious names.

He also kept a stash of ready cash on hand for emergencies. The stash was actually quite a lot of money, given the events of 1929; he refused to place all of his trust in banks. He had told no one about the apartment with the hidden safe. The vault in the concrete wall had the capacity to store a good deal of money. His private joke was that once the vault could hold no additional cash, he could disappear from the stage, so to speak. He found himself looking forward to that point in time with increasing longing.

Tom Regan had driven away from Diamond's office. At first, he had failed to notice the car that had begun to follow him, but after a few moments he realized he was being tailed.

The question was why. Were they interested in his meeting, or was it a hit? He quickly concluded it had to be a hit.

Luciano had been furious over the failed hit, recognizing that Regan had played a pivotal role in saving Diamond. He decided that removing Regan would greatly weaken Diamond.

Regan maintained his speed, considering his options. He had his forty-five with him, but if it was a hit, the shooters could have greater fire power that his handgun. He began to look for an option to deal with the men shadowing him.

Sarah Keegan walked briskly towards the courthouse. She was in a jovial mood, today being her twentieth anniversary of working in the state court system. She had also had the pleasure these past couple of years of working for Judge Joseph Crater.

Despite the reputation that he enjoyed with the press, she felt that he was always a gentleman. He was never rude or cross to her, and he never raised his voice. He was, she felt, dedicated to the law, always being one of the first to arrive and the last to leave. Any review of his calendar would show a dedicated man.

Greeting co-workers as she walked down the hall towards her office, she grasped the handle, surprised to find it locked. Jiggling the knob, she found it was indeed locked.

"That's odd," she muttered.

Opening her purse, she searched for her key. Finding it, she opened the door, and turned on the lights. Hanging up her coat, she walked into the judge's office. It was evident that the judge hadn't arrived yet.

Pursing her lips in thought, she stared into the office, trying to recall if the judge had mentioned any reason as to why he might be late today. Shaking her head, she walked over to his desk, opening his calendar.

Scanning the entries for today, she grew concerned "Oh my." Looking up at the clock on the wall, she walked briskly out of the office. Leaving her office, she bumped into a friend, continuing to walk, "Can't stop, I'll talk to you later, Louise." Her friend smiled, as she walked briskly past her, assuming she was on some task for her boss.

Sarah walked into the clerk of the court's office. The clerk's assistant looked up, smiling. "Good morning, Sarah, what can I do for you?"

"Jackie, the judge hadn't come in yet."

"Really...isn't he on calendar this morning?"

"Yes, that's the surprising part, he's never late."

The assistant opened her desk drawer, pulling out a black book. She quickly leafed through the pages, then stopping, placed the book on her desk. Dialing her phone, she sat back listening to the receiver. After a number of rings, she put the phone back in its cradle. "No answer, maybe he's en route?"

Sarah nodded. "I'll go back and wait for him. I'll call you as soon as he arrives."

"Thank you, dear, I'll tell his court that he hasn't arrived yet."

Sarah rushed out of the office. Arriving back at her office, she found that it was still empty. Sitting at her desk, she nervously drummed her fingers, waiting for her boss. She had a bad feeling about this.

Along the sand dunes in the Rockaways, the wind had blown the sand into a smooth natural pattern.

Tom Regan sped up. Looking in his mirror, he noted the sedan was keeping pace with him. Down the street, he noticed a brownstone separated from the rest of the block. Pulling his car over a little past it, he jumped out, running into the building. He quickly went to the mailboxes and began to press all of the buzzers. After a second, he heard the buzzer opening the hall door, allowing him to enter. If he could move quickly enough, he could turn the tables on the guys following him. He wasn't taking any chances; he was going to have to kill them. Running towards the back, he quickly went to the basement, hoping that there was a rear exit.

Smiling, he thought that his luck was still with him as he saw a door with light around the edges. Testing the door knob, he turned the lock and opened the door into the backyard of the building. Thankfully, no one was in the yard, laundry hung on clothes lines stretched across the space. Walking to the far side of the building, he hopped the fence.

Dropping down, he made his way cautiously up the alley. Drawing his gun, he screwed a silencer onto the barrel. At the end of the alley he stopped, peering around the corner. He could see the car that followed him, with two men seated in the front seat. Pulling his hat low to cover his face, he walked to the sedan, noticing the window was open. Grasping the handle for the back door, he opened it and jumped into the back seat with his weapon trained on the two men. Surprised, the men jumped, starting to turn.

His voice calm, he held his weapon high "Don't turn, hands on the dashboard. Talk quick, why you following me?"

The men were silent.

Regan stuck the barrel into the ear of the passenger. "I won't ask again."

"We were told to keep an eye on you."

"Liar." Regan shot the man in the head. The gun made a soft sound with the silencer in place. The driver jumped, speaking quickly in Italian.

Regan calmly shot him in the face as he turned towards him.

Quickly noting that the sidewalk was empty, Regan got out of the car, walked quickly to his vehicle and drove away.

It would be an hour before a passerby noticed the two men slumped over in the car. The police were called; while investigating the crime, they spoke to all of the neighbors. Nobody saw anything.

The morning had passed with no word from the judge. Sarah had spoken to a few of his friends, asking if they had seen him yesterday. They each replied, saying they hadn't, a couple of them smiling insinuating that perhaps "Good Time Joe" had spent the night somewhere other than his apartment.

Sarah arranged to have the police stop at his apartment to see if he had suffered some sort of medical problem and couldn't answer the phone. She shuddered at the thought. Sarah had grown accustomed to working for the man. He was always a gentleman, and there were growing rumors that he was destined for the Supreme Court. At her age, she didn't relish the thought of breaking in a new boss.

Sarah had placed calls to the local hospitals, inquiring if a middle aged man had been admitted due to an accident or some other problem. All of her inquiries had produced no one even remotely close to the judge. Sitting alone in her office, she quietly prayed for him to walk into the office, apologizing for his lateness.

The phone rang, startling her, quickly grabbing the receiver "Yes?"

Listening silently, nodding, her face solemn "Yes, I understand…of course…if that is the procedure, I understand…thank you, officer."

The police had entered the Judge's apartment finding that he had not slept there last night. The room was made up, the landlady informing them she hadn't made the bed this morning. She assumed that the judge had spent the night with friends. The police had instructed her to contact them in the event she heard from the judge and that they had to wait forty-eight hours, before a missing persons report could be filed.

She desperately wanted to file the report now.

Snapping her fingers, she realized there was something she could do while she waited. Picking up the phone, she dialed a reporter whom the judge often used for friendly pieces in the press.

"Franklin Pierce, please," she said and she waited to be connected. "Good morning, Mr. Pierce, this is Sarah Keegan, with Judge Crater's office."

Immediately cordial, he replied "Good morning, Miss Keegan, what can I do for you today?"

"Well, you've always been a friend of the judge, so I thought perhaps I should call you first."

Unsure where this conversation was going, "Is there a problem…is the judge alright?"

Relaxing, she opened up, speaking emotionally "That's just it. Mr. Pierce, we don't know."

The reporter spoke slowly, "I'm not following you...what are you trying to say?"

"Well, the judge didn't show up for court this morning. The police went to his apartment, and he hadn't spent the night there either."

Pierce let out a breath. "Well, as you know, Miss Keegan, the judge has a number of...friends, perhaps he spent the night with one of them."

"Mr. Pierce, I'm aware of the judge's reputation. What you don't seem to understand is that he was on calendar this morning, and he failed to show up or to call in sick. That, Mr. Pierce, is something he has never done."

Pierce was silent for a moment. "No...I'd have to agree with you. He is one of the most dedicated jurists I've ever dealt with; I don't believe he's ever missed a day on the bench."

Hopeful at hearing his words, Sarah continued, "There, you see? I can't help but feel there is a problem."

"I assume you checked with the local hospitals?"

"Yes, of course, no one was admitted yesterday even remotely resembling the judge."

"Was the judge handling any high profile cases...you know, any gangsters?"

"No, he wasn't presiding over any such cases."

Thoughtful he considered his words, "I'll tell you what, Miss Keegan, I'll make some calls. I'm sure he'll turn up; it will probably be some innocent misunderstanding."

"That would be wonderful, Mr. Pierce. I'd be ever so grateful."

"Not at all. I'll call you back; let you know if I get anything."

Thanking him again, she hung up.

36

As was her custom, Claire arrived at her office early, and, as always, she saw the light on in Ginny's office. Hanging up her coat, she walked over, knocking gently on the door.

Writing at her desk, without looking up, Ginny responded "Come in, Claire."

Walking in, Claire smiled slightly. "Good morning, Ginny."

Sitting back, Ginny smiled. "How was your evening?"

Thoughtful she considered her response, "Very nice, he was a real gentleman."

Nodding, Ginny agreed "He's a fine young man, with a solid future. His father's business interests are diverse."

Sitting, Claire seemed lost in thought for a second.

Smiling wistfully, "He's not too bad on the eyes either."

Ginny returned her smile. "Yes, there's always that."

Ginny had casually suggested to Claire that she have dinner with the son of a business acquaintance of Charles. It had been evident to Ginny for some time that she cared for their mutual friend, Michael Callahan. Knowing this and caring deeply for both of her friends, she doubted that Michael would remarry, after the tragic death of his young wife. Additionally, feeling that a woman as fine as Claire deserved a man who would care for her, Ginny had arranged a reception at her home, with Claire and the young man in attendance.

It had been easy to introduce the two of them; keeping an eye on them she was pleased to see that the young man was quite interested. *And why not*, she thought, *Claire was an attractive, intelligent woman.*

Ginny sat back in her chair, a playful smile on her face. "So, do you plan on seeing him again?"

"Yes, he's taking me to the Paramount on Friday; Duke Ellington's band is playing."

"Yes, Charles and I are attending the Saturday night show. Did he mention where you are seated on Friday? If you need better seats, I could make a call."

Smiling gratefully at her friend, she shook her head slightly "I appreciate the thought, but I'm certain the seats will be good."

"Of course, I understand."

Changing course, Claire was curious "Have you heard from Mike lately?"

Thoughtful, with mild concern in her voice "No...and if I don't hear anything today, I'll call him at his office."

Claire leaned forward in her chair, her voice even "Do you really believe that the senator had something to do with Eileen's murder?"

Picking up a letter opener, Ginny played with it while she spoke, "I'm convinced; but you know Michael, he said we have a lot of circumstantial evidence against one of the most powerful men in the state. If they could find her diary, it might just provide the information to bring that man down."

Placing the letter opener back on the desk, she said "I'll let you know when I hear from Michael."

Claire rose, ending their conversation "Okay, I'm going to finish tallying up the numbers for the month." She stopped at the door, a smile on her face "Paul is very nice. Thanks again, Ginny."

Looking at her, Ginny returned her smile. "I'm glad you're happy."

Callahan and Shaw had taken Earl Spencer into custody at his apartment, then deposited him at central booking at the court house.

Driving back to the precinct, Callahan spoke, "Do you think you have it in you to truly uphold the law?"

"Yeah...why do you ask?"

"You know I consider your father a suspect in the O'Sullivan murder."

Nodding, he was slightly surprised at the admission "Yeah."

"We have a witness that places your father's man on the boat the night of the murder. Also, the caretaker at your father's estate went to her apartment after the murder, and we believe that she sent her diary to him, before her murder."

"Yeah…that is interesting, Mike, but how does it prove that my dad was involved in the murder of the girl?"

Watching the road, he glanced quickly at Shaw, "I know, it doesn't, but if we can get the diary, it might have information that could lead to an indictment for your father."

Danny wanted to laugh; however, containing himself, he appeared emotionally torn. "Mike, I promise you…you find that diary, and if it has information of criminal conduct against my dad, I'll slap the cuffs on him myself."

Callahan gave him a quick glance, surprised. "Good. I'm glad I can count on you."

Turning, Shaw stared out the window, thinking, *Good luck finding that diary, hotshot.*

"You know Doc will be back next week. I'm gonna speak with Kroon about getting you a permanent partner. I was thinking Harris might be willing to work with you. His partner is due to retire shortly, and he still has a couple of years to go. He's a good cop; you could learn a thing or two from him."

Shaw looked at him, surprised. "Yeah, he's a good guy. Thanks Mike."

Once Callahan pulled the car into a parking space at the precinct, they got out and walked into the building.

Shaw was thinking furiously how he could look for the envelope with the pages torn from the diary. If he could get those pages, the investigation would end and his father would be safe. He envisioned how grateful his father would be when he presented him with the pages.

Tom Regan had waited for an hour at the place where he was supposed to meet Yost. Glancing at his wristwatch again, he shook his head. The German had never been late for one of these meetings. With everything that had been happening lately, he wondered if the German had met some misfortune.

Knowing that Legs was expecting a large shipment soon, he needed to be certain that payoffs were made. It would be very inconvenient if angry law enforcement officials confiscated the shipment. That would impact the business at the club, angering the clientele.

Deciding he had waited long enough, he started the car. Pulling away, he sped back towards Leg's offices. He'd have to tell the boss, leaving it to him to call the senator to see why his man had failed to pick up their cut.

Regan shook his head slowly. Things were getting out of hand, and if Luciano was still making a play for Leg's rackets, people were going to die. The press would love it as they always do, mob murders always sold newspapers.

Arriving at the estate, Yost went quickly to the study to inform the senator of the current state of affairs. Sitting behind his desk, Shaw listened quietly as the German spoke.

"So...Daniel said he would try to find the envelope when he returned?" Shaw asked.

Standing before the desk, Yost replied, "Yes, sir."

"He said he would call once he finds the envelope that Benny left?"

"Yes, sir." Yost stood rigidly before the desk.

Shaw gazed about the room. "Then, I guess we have to wait."

The phone rang, startling them both. Shaw quickly grabbed the receiver. "Yes...Daniel?"

"No, it ain't Daniel, senator, It's Legs Diamond."

Surprised, Shaw asked, "Why are you calling me here, Mr. Diamond?"

"Your man failed to meet with my man today."

Shaw thought for a second, recalling the meeting date "Dammit." Holding the phone away from his face, his hand covering the speaker "You didn't meet with Mr. Diamond's henchman."

Gerhardt rolled his eyes, angry over having forgotten of the meeting.

"Hey Shaw, are you still there?"

Calming himself, Shaw spoke, "Yes, I'm here, Mr. Diamond. I want to apologize for missing the meeting. We had some concerns we needed to take care of here."

"Oh yeah, well…we're still good?"

"Yes, Mr. Diamond, we are, as you say, still good. If you'd like, I'll arrange to have my man meet with your man at ten o'clock tomorrow morning, at the usual place. Is that satisfactory?"

Shaw could hear Diamond speaking with his henchman.

"Yeah, that would be fine. I appreciate it."

"Goodbye, Mr. Diamond."

At the other end of the line, Diamond hung up the phone.

"I swear, Tommy, if I didn't need that guy, I'd hit him myself, the arrogant bastard."

Regan sat across from Diamond, sipping his drink.

Diamond looked at him intently. "Tell me again what happened with the two Italians."

Regan went over the events of the morning in detail. When discussing the events in the car, he embellished their responses somewhat, to make their murders seem to be a reasonable action.

Diamond clenched his fists in anger. "That sonofabitch, I tell him I want peace and he tries to take out my top guy. Well, the gloves come off now. If he wants a fight, so be it, Tommy. I want Luciano followed. I want to know his daily routine better than he does. I want to know where he has any ladies he spends time with and, if he eats out, I wanna know where. You got me?"

Regan nodded. "Yeah boss, I gotcha."

"Good, I want you handling this personally, Tommy, no screw ups."

Smiling, as always Regan was confident "Trust me, boss, his luck just ran out."

Grabbing the bottle on the table, Diamond poured Regan another drink.

Across town Lucky Luciano raged at his lieutenants. They all sat silently, knowing better than to speak, until he had vented his anger.

"That Irish sonofabitch kills two of my men! I want him dead! I don't want to hear that he is walking around still breathing, still enjoying himself. I don't care how many men you put on him, I want this done, and done soon, am I clear?"

They all nodded.

"Good; and I want his boss, that sonofabitch Diamond taken out too."

He paused, thoughtful, considering the action "With him we gotta be more prepared. We gotta have a plan. That guy is more lucky than I am." He stared intently at his men.

A couple of them smiled at what they thought was a joke.

Luciano smiled, opened his arms gesturing at his men. "What's the matter, you guys got no sense of humor?" They all laughed.

Smiling, Luciano sat down. Pointing to a man on his right, His voice commanding "Gino, I want you to set up Diamond for a hit." He was lost in thought for a second, then he snapped his fingers, liking the idea "A broad, that's it! We'll use a broad."

Gino was confused, as he stared at Luciano "You want a broad to hit Diamond?"

Glaring back at him frustrated "No, stupid. We use a broad to set him up. He has always had a weakness for the ladies. We have her party with Mr. Diamond; get him to a location where we can take care of him. It will need to be a location where the cops are friendly to us."

Smiling, his voice menacing "You think you can handle that, Gino?"

Nodding, slightly fearful "Consider it done, boss."

"Good, I want to know when the hits are planned. I want to set up a good alibi, and I'll want to drink some toasts to the dear departed." Glancing about the room, he eyed each man before continuing. "Regarding that bastard Tom Regan, I don't care how or where it's done. You know, in fact, the louder the better. I wanna send a message to everyone that no one, and I mean no one, hits my guys and lives to talk about it." Readily agreeing, the men were angered at having to attend two funerals.

Luciano nodded, ending the discussion "Good, all right. Any other items for discussion?"

Looking around the room, the men were silent.

Luciano rose, with his men following suit, and they filed silently out of the room. Luciano allowed a maid to help him with his coat. Mumbling his thanks to her, he followed his bodyguards down the hall, exiting the building.

The maid, an attractive young Italian girl, trembled at what she had overheard. During the meeting she had been working in the kitchen. The old house had a central heating system with ductwork going to various rooms from a fireplace in the main dining room, where the meetings were held.

She had met Tom Regan, or, more accurately, Tom Regan had recently met her, and he had been very effective in romancing her. He had used all of his charm to develop the girl as a potential source. The girl was desperate to escape from her family, specifically from her father. He was a man who, failing in life, had begun to try to seek solace with his daughter. Her mother proved blind to the situation, and would hear nothing of it from her daughter. Searching for an escape, she had felt that Tom Regan provided the answer to her problem. She was certain that this information would seal the bond of affection between them

Regan, for his part, found that he actually felt something for the girl. He wasn't certain that he could say it was love. His mother had died when he was very young. He barely remembered her. His father had spent his time working to support his children, often being so tired he had little time to offer his children any sign of affection. When he was old enough, he had struck out on his own, using his charm and his street smarts to advance in the growing world of organized crime.

Finishing her work, the young woman told the butler she was leaving for the day. He acknowledged her with a wave, while he read the newspaper. Moving quickly down the street, she headed for the local drug store. It had the closest phone booth she knew of in the area. Walking into the pharmacy, she quickly made her way to the booth in the rear.

She stopped, there was a man using the phone. Standing in front of the booth, she anxiously tapping her foot. After a couple of minutes of watching the man put coins into the phone as he continued to speak, she tapped on the door. Startled, he looked at her for a second, holding up two fingers, indicating the remaining time he'd be on the phone. Nodding, she watched him turn and resume his conversation. Good to his promise, within a couple of minutes, the man hung up the phone.

Thanking him as he passed her, he nodded, mumbled something and was gone. Sitting in the booth, she found the phone number Regan had given her. Dialing the number, she nervously twirled her hair, a habit from her childhood, and counted the rings.

A male voice answered, "Yeah?"

Anxious, she forced herself to speak clearly "I need to speak with Tom...Tom Regan, I'm a friend."

"Hold on." She heard the phone being placed down.

Shortly, a familiar voice spoke to her, "Who is this?"

Relieved, at hearing Regan's voice "Tommy, it's me, Carla. I've got to talk to you, it's important."

Hearing the urgency in her voice, he spoke calmly, "Okay honey, why don't you tell me what's up."

She proceeded to tell him what she had overheard at Luciano's building. Once she had finished her tale, she waited for him to respond.

"Tommy, are you there?"

"Yeah, I'm here, babe, just thinking for a minute." More angry than surprised at her comments. "OK, now listen to me, Carla, for the next few days we can't be seen together. I need to take care of certain individuals before they take care of me. Do you understand?"

"I think so, Tommy."

"Once this…situation has resolved itself, I wanna be with you, you know, like a steady girl."

Her heart raced. "Oh Tommy, I'd like that a lot."

The words surprisingly came to Regan, finding that he cared for her "Yeah, me too, and who knows what can happen after that."

The words caught her totally by surprise, emotion in her voice "Sure, Tommy, sure. What do you want me to do?"

Regan spoke calmly, "You go home, you go to work, you act like nothing's wrong. Can you do that for me?"

"Sure, Tommy, I can do that."

"Once we've resolved this situation, I'm gonna come for you. In the meantime, you tell your father if he lays a hand on you…I'll kill him."

"Okay, Tommy, I love you."

"I love you too, take care," holding the phone tightly she heard him hang the phone hang up.

37

Diamond sat quietly, listening to Regan. His face showing little emotion. "You sure this information is solid?"

"Yeah, boss. Trust me, it's golden."

Diamond stared at his friend. "You say it's a broad who works for Luciano?"

Regan, shrugging "Yeah, we kinda got a thing going."

Diamond knowingly smiled, speaking to his friend "Tommy, you got more *things* going than anybody I know."

Getting up, Diamond walked to the window. Looking out at the city, he seemed lost in thought for a minute. "I'm gonna tell you something, I've been considering for a time now." Curious, Regan leaned forward in his chair. "I've been speaking with people in Albany about expanding our operations in that town."

"Albany, boss?"

Diamond turned facing his friend. "Yeah, the town is ripe for the picking; they don't have any of the major mobs up there."

Regan nodded. "Yeah, I've heard that too, boss, but you'd have to deal with the local political machine, word is they're a bunch of greedy bastards."

Diamond laughed. "Show me a politician who isn't a greedy bastard." Stopping, he thought for a second. "Listen to me. Tommy. I've got a stash of cash in town that we'll need to make our initial payoffs. I'm gonna get out of town for a few days to begin to set up the necessary contacts. You can't tell anyone where I've gone. Hell, with what's been going on people are gonna think I'm just hiding out."

Understanding, Regan asked, "Gotcha, boss. Where you gonna be, in case I need to get a hold of you?"

Taking a card out of his shirt pocket, Diamond handed it to Regan. The card had an address and a phone number in Albany. Normally, Diamond would not have shared such information with anyone, but he had reached a point where he felt he had to trust someone, and Regan was his man. Tom had proven himself many times.

Diamond continued "I'm gonna leave later today, drive around the city a bit in case I'm being tailed, then head upstate.

Regan was concerned. "You going by yourself?"

Diamond held up a hand to silence his friend. "I ain't crazy, I'm gonna have Eddie with me."

Regan considered that a good choice, Eddie was fiercely loyal and he was a crack shot. "When do you expect to be back?"

"A couple of days at most; I'll buy you dinner at the club next weekend."

Regan got up, realizing their conversation was over "Sure, Legs...sounds good."

They shook hands and Regan left.

Alone, Diamond thought that if Luciano had simply offered to buy him out, he might have sold everything to him. Hanging his head he shook it slowly, thinking, *what the hell, he was a businessman.*

Diamond followed Eddie down to the car, Eddie had put their suitcases in the car earlier. Both men stared about, looking for anything suspicious. Seeing nothing suspicious, they drove out of the garage. Diamond hoped for a quiet uneventful trip.

Regan waited in his car for the German. As punctual as ever, he saw the black sedan turn the corner, slowly approaching his car. The two men made eye contact, the German parking a short distance from him. Casually getting out, Regan walked towards the Packard.

As he expected, the man was alone. Regan got into the car. Reaching into the inside pocket of his suit, he withdrew the envelope with the cash. He placed it in the hand of the German, and waited while the man counted the money. Finishing the count, the German put the money back into the envelope, nodding at Regan. Their business completed, Regan opened the door and got out. Looking back in at the German, he smirked, muttering "You're a real chatterbox, you know that?"

Looking at him confused for a second, Yost then surprised Regan by laughing. Closing the door, Regan stood while the black Packard slowly pulled away from the curb and drove off.

Regan drove back to the office, considering his plan to hit Luciano, having already gotten more information than he expected. Luciano, while feared, was a man with many enemies. The story of the bad blood between him and Diamond was common knowledge on the street. It appeared that Luciano did very little with any repetition or regularity. *Well,* Regan thought, *I didn't think it was going to be easy.* He thought again about Diamond's trip and the possibilities that might offer. He had to find out more about the political machine in Albany, but first things first.

Callahan and Shaw sat facing each other. Callahan asking "Does the caretaker cottage at your father's estate have a telephone?"

Surprised, Shaw wondered where he was going "Ah...I think so, why?"

"I want to ask the caretaker to come in for a chat. If they have the diary, they may fear giving it up."

Shaw's mind was racing. "I don't know the number offhand... I'm supposed to have dinner with my dad tonight. I can get the number and give it to you tomorrow."

Callahan nodded. "Okay, that'll be fine. What time are you leaving?"

Shaw looked at his wristwatch thinking he'd have to alert his father, "About five, okay?"

Callahan spoke again, a warning tone in his voice, "Yeah, that's Okay with me. Don't tell your dad anything."

"Sure, Mike."

Callahan smiled. "Why don't you head out a little early? I'll finish up here and tell Kroon I sent you on an errand."

"Thanks Mike." He thought, *what a trusting jerk.* Shaw quickly left the office.

Watching him leave, Callahan still wasn't sure about the kid. His telephone rang.

"Detective Callahan, can I help you?"

"Hello Michael, it's Ginny."

Smiling, glad to hear her voice, "Ginny, hello."

He quickly updated her on the status of the case.

Disbelief in her voice "You honestly think Danny would arrest his father?"

Exhaling, Callahan was unsure, "I don't know. He always seems so earnest on one hand and so full of shit on the other." Callahan stopped. "I just got an idea."

"What would that be, Michael?"

"If I get the diary and the caretaker will testify against the senator, would you offer him and his wife protection against Shaw?"

"Certainly, Michael. I could help them obtain employment and, if need be, help them relocate to another state. I'm certain Charles would know someone who could use a capable couple."

"That's it, then. Have I ever told you what a wonderful woman you are?"

Ginny was surprised by his emotional statement. "Michael, you know I'd do anything for you."

"I know Ginny…I know. I gotta run. I'll call you once I've spoken with the caretaker. Take care."

"You take care of yourself, Michael…and watch that little bastard."

Laughing slightly, at her stern tone "Yes, ma'am." Hanging up the phone, he straightened the papers out on his desk. The envelope with the missing pages remained stuck between his desk and the wall.

Danny Shaw drove out to his father's estate, wishing he had the missing pages with him.

At the estate, Benny and Rita put their overnight bags into the pickup truck. The call regarding the death of Rita's cousin had been a shock. The man had been killed at his job in a slaughterhouse. The manner of his death had been quite gruesome. The senator drinking gave his permission for them to leave for two days, with a wave of his hand. He hoped that Danny would soon produce the missing pages, ending this affair. He was tired.

Benny quickly drove away from the estate, failing to notice Danny as they passed each other on the road.

Danny pulled into the estate, speeding up the driveway unconcerned with his or anyone else's safety. Pulling up to the main house, he bounded out of his car, quickly walking into the house.

Looking about, he made his way towards the study, knowing that his father spent the majority of his time there. Entering the study, he saw his father seated behind his desk, to his left was a decanter of brandy along with a half full glass.

Stopping abruptly he asked, "Dad, how many have you had?"

Looking up, the senator studied his son for a moment. "A few, what brings you out to the estate…son?"

Danny could see that his father had been drinking probably for some time, and that he had definitely had more than a few. Standing straight, Danny almost laughed. "What the hell do you think brought me out here?" The senator sat silently staring at him.

Danny continued "I noticed the truck is gone, the cottage is dark. Where are they? Have they left the estate?"

Furrowing his brow in concentration, the senator looked slightly downward, deep in thought. Danny waited impatiently. His frustration growing. "I asked you a question, dammit!"

The senator looked up sharply. "Just who do you think you're speaking to, young man?"

Danny was instantly taken back to his youth, cowering before his father's anger. "I'm sorry...I didn't mean nothing."

The senator silenced him with a wave of his hand. "Benny said something about a death in the family. They were going into the city and would be gone a couple of days. Why do you ask?"

Taking a breath, Danny spoke slowly, "Callahan wants to speak with them. He wants to talk about the diary, to see if they have it. He wants me to give him the phone number for the cottage, and not tell you."

The senator gave a low, guttural laugh. "Really? How naive."

Danny grabbed a glass off the bar and poured himself a drink from the bottle on his father's desk. Sitting, he took a long drink. Exhaling he added, "Yeah, he's pretty full of himself."

Leaning forward, the senator stared intently at his son. "Now listen, Daniel, you'll tell the detective that the phone is out in the cottage, that it is scheduled to be repaired in two days."

"What reason do I give him?"

"Make something up...you're a good liar."

Danny took that as a compliment. "Okay, leave it to me, but why two days?"

"That is how long you have to find the two missing pages that the Fitzgibbons left at the police station."

Nodding, accepting the time limit "Okay, two days should be enough."

"See that it is."

38

Diamond had made good time, arriving in Albany ahead of schedule. He and his man booked rooms in a modest hotel on Dove Street. Telling his man to get some rest, Diamond made some phone calls. He checked the small satchel he had brought with him, wondering again if the money was enough.

He had made a list of the local politicians to whom he was going to offer money. If anyone got too greedy, he would address them separately, later. He placed his handgun easily within reach, as he lay down on the bed. He hoped he could grab some sleep but his mind was racing with thoughts and plans.

A knock on the door startled him awake.

Grabbing the gun, he asked "Yeah, who is it?"

"It's me, boss, Eddie. I'm by myself."

Relaxing, but still holding the gun, he went to the door, opening it slightly to see his man standing in the hallway.

Opening the door wide he relaxed, "Come on in, Eddie, thanks for waking me up."

"Oh yeah, you were sleeping, boss?"

"Yeah, give me a minute to wash up."

"Sure, boss." Eddie sat on a chair facing the door, opening his suit jacket to allow quick access to his handgun.

Minutes later, the two men left the hotel, Diamond with his satchel in hand. As they drove past a man stepping out of his car, he glanced their way. There was no mistaking; the man was certain it was Legs Diamond. The man, a member of Lucky Luciano's organization, was in Albany to meet with his Canadian bootlegging contacts. He was aware of the situation between his boss and Diamond.

Watching them pull away, noting the license plate he made his way quickly into the hotel to a pay phone in the lobby. Dialing Luciano's private number, he spoke as soon as he heard the familiar voice. "I got some hot information for you, Lucky."

"Oh yeah? I hope we don't have any problems with our friends to the north."

"No, boss, nothing like that. I was getting out of my car at the hotel here and I saw Legs Diamond and one of his boys leave the hotel and drive off."

Luciano spoke slowly, "Al, are you sure it was Diamond? I mean…what the hell is he doing in Albany?"

"I don't know, boss, but he was carrying a satchel."

"Okay, listen, whatever else you're doing, stop it. I want you to tail him, find out what he's up to. If possible, I want you to set him up with a broad. I want him drinking. I'm gonna send a couple of boys to pay him a visit."

"Okay Lucky, I gotta run to see if I can catch up to him."

"Well stop talking and start running."

Sprinting out of the hotel, the man looking up and down the avenue, cursing; there was no sign of Diamond's car. Getting in his car, he drove down the street. Not believing his luck, he saw the car parked up ahead. Quickly, he called the escort service he used whenever he was in the city. It was run by an Italian and his girls were discreet and reliable. If he could arrange for his boss to take out Diamond, it would really boost him within the organization.

Luciano yelled for his man in the next room, who came on the run.

"What's up, boss?"

"I want you and Charley to get a car and get up to Albany, as quick as you can."

The man seemed confused for a moment. "Albany… what do you want us to do in Albany, boss?"

"I just got a call from Alphonse. He saw Diamond up there, and he's only got one of his guys with him. I want you to hit him. Al is going to try to set him up with a broad; we want his guard down and him drinking. If it works out, you hit him once he's sleeping with the broad. You got that?"

"Yeah, I got it."

"Good, get going."

In the hallway, the maid, Carla, had overheard the conversation. Maintaining her demeanor, she continued her cleaning. She would be ending her shift in three hours, and then she would call Tommy from the stationery store. He was always in control; he would know what to do. She knew he would be interested in this information.

She hummed a favorite tune as she cleaned.

At the courthouse Sarah Keegan was truly beside herself with anxiety. Picking up the phone, she dialed the newspaper "Mr. Pierce, please."

Franklin Pierce came on the line, after she greeted him "Hello, Miss Keegan. Am I safe in assuming that the judge has turned up?"

Slightly annoyed she remained calm, "No, Mr. Pierce, he hasn't turned up."

"That's surprising, and I think worthy of some investigation. I will look into this, and I'll keep you posted. Oh, do you have his schedule for the past few days? Yes…the last couple of days would be the most critical. No, I don't need you to drop it off. I'll send a runner around to pick up the information. Thank you, Miss Keegan. I'll be in touch." Franklin Pierce hung up the phone, wondering what could have happened to Judge Joseph Force Crater.

At the precinct, Callahan was putting in overtime, greatly looking forward to Doc's return. It would be good to have a real partner again and not some rich kid with a silver spoon in his mouth, whose father was a key suspect in the murder of a young woman.

Callahan looked up as a man approached; it was another detective in the unit, Joe Penny. The man stopped at his desk. "Something I can do for you, Joe?"

"No big deal, I was just curious what was in the envelope that was left for you."

Callahan was at a loss. "Envelope...what are you talking about?"

"That Irish couple, the envelope they left the other day. You weren't here so I put it in your inbox."

Callahan stood slowly, controlling himself "Joe, I haven't seen any envelope. Was the guy kind of average height, brown hair, on the thin side?"

Nodding Penny answered, "Yeah that sounds like the guy."

"What color was the envelope?"

"Just a white one, I got it off the desk sergeant."

Sitting, Callahan began going through his inbox.

Penny still stood before him. "Was it important?"

Without looking up, Callahan answered as he continued searching "You have no idea. Thanks for letting me know, Joe."

"Yeah, sure, I hope you find it."

Callahan searched through all the papers on his desk, no envelopes. His frustration and his anger growing, he thought, *it had to be Danny*. Who else would have taken the envelope? He would confront him when he came in, and if need be he would take him downstairs and go at it.

Finally done with her shift, Carla made her way quickly to the stationery store, down the street from the house. She dialed the number Tom had given her. After a couple of rings, a man answered.

"Tom Regan, please."

"Hold on, I'll see if he's here."

After a few moments, the man came back on the line "Tom's not here; can I take a message?"

Considering, she replied, "Tell him Carla called. Tell him it's very important. He should come to my house, park out front and beep the horn twice. You remember, I have information he will be very interested to know." The man continued to answer her questions

"Yeah, I gotcha, you say he knows where you live?"

"No, I don't know when he'll be back."

"Yeah, I'll make sure he gets the message, don't worry."

Staring nervously at the phone, she hoped that Tom would get in touch with her soon.

In Albany, Diamond's meetings had gone well. He kept careful records of the money paid to the local officials. Feeling that two of the men were going to be a problem, he considered his options regarding them. It had been obvious from the start that the local political machine controlled all of the rackets in the town. He was offering a larger percentage of the take to get his foot in the door.

Leaving the last meeting, the two men drove back towards their hotel. Pulling into the parking lot, they parked the car and walked casually into the hotel. In the lobby, off to the side, Luciano's man sat and an attractive young woman sat with him.

"The man on the right, the tall one with the dark hair, he's the target. Your job is to get him interested, get him drinking, and then get him back to his room. You understand that he is going to be hit...good. If this goes down as we want, you will receive $5,000, and if you keep quiet for six months you'll get another $5,000."

Diamond and Eddie walked through the lobby, entering the elevator. Recognizing her opportunity, the young woman spoke confidently, "Don't worry; I'll make certain he's good and drunk by the time your men come for him. I understand that these things are sometimes necessary." The man smiled slightly, making a mental note to thank the escort service manager "Good...very good."

Later that evening, as Carla sat in the living room of her house, she heard a car horn beep twice. Jumping up, she ran to the door, opening it quickly. Looking out she saw Tom's car. Bounding down the steps, she ran up to the car, opening the door she jumped in. Regan sat with a smile on his face. She hugged him and they kissed. After a moment, he gently disengaged from her and stared at her intently.

His voice calm, "I got your message. What's the news that you said would be so interesting?"

Taking some deep breaths, she calmed herself. Seeing that she was agitated, Regan grew increasingly curious as to the nature of her information. "Tommy, Mr. Luciano is going to kill your boss, Mr. Diamond.

Regan smiled gently, holding her hand. "We know that, but it's okay, Legs is outta town."

Nodding, she spoke quickly "I know...he's in Albany."

Regan grabbed her by the shoulders. "How do you know that?"

"One of Mr. Luciano's men called from Albany saying that he saw Mr. Diamond with another man. Mr. Luciano ordered his man to follow him, and to set him up with a woman. He said the woman should work on getting him drunk."

"Carla...what else did he say?"

"He sent two of his men by car. When the woman has him in bed, drunk, I guess that is when they will kill him."

"When did these men leave?"

She considered for a second. "About an hour ago."

Staring downward, Regan muttered a curse. He had to get to Albany, and quickly.

"Listen, doll, you've done great. I gotta get to Albany to protect Legs. You go back inside; you go to work tomorrow like nothing's happened. I'll see you when I get back. Okay?"

She gathered strength from his confidence. "Sure, Tommy, whatever you say."

"Good girl, now scat."

She watched as the car drove quickly away. Turning, she walked back into her house. Her father watched her from an upstairs window. Having heard her threat from her boyfriend, his anger fueled a desire to put his daughter in her place.

39

Regan drove furiously. Having recognized some time ago that Diamond was both a friend and his boss, he had to do whatever he could to save his life. He had no desire to start over again as one of the junior men in some other organization. It would be different with Diamond still alive. He could negotiate his own deal with another mob, but not if Diamond was dead. Also, he felt that Luciano was a man who held grudges, and would not soon forget the two men he killed. *Yeah,* he thought, *at the moment, his future hung on the events of the next 24 hours.* Watching the road signs he cursed, wishing he could travel faster.

In Albany, Diamond and Eddie had just finished dinner and were discussing the day when Diamond caught the eye of an attractive woman at the bar. The woman smiled seductively at him, slowly turning away. She was playing cat and mouse with him. Her employer had told her that the man had a big ego when it came to the ladies. She would let him think of her as a challenge.

Diamond spoke, "Eddie, why don't you head back to the room? I'll see you later. It looks like I got something waiting for me at the bar."

Turning, Eddie saw the lady at the bar, and gave a low whistle. Turning back, "You sure you want me to leave, boss?"

Feeling good, he nodded, dismissing any danger "Yeah, I don't think we gotta worry about anything in this burg."

Bidding his boss goodnight, Eddie left.

Looking back, Diamond made eye contact again with the lady, gesturing towards the empty seat. She seemed to consider for a moment then gathered her things, and alluringly she walked over to his table.

Stopping before his table, she cocked her hips in a bewitching pose. "Buy a lady a drink?"

Smiling, Diamond turned on the charm, "Please join me." He snapped his fingers at the waiter. The waiter came over, and Diamond ordered drinks. Waiting for their drinks, Diamond asked. "So what's your name?"

"Connie, what's yours?"

"Jack."

Staring at him, her eyes mesmerizing, "I haven't seen you around town, you passing through?"

"No, I've got some business to take care of, some people to meet."

She took a sip of her drink, never breaking eye contact. "Oh yeah? What type of business are you in, Jack?"

Diamond smiled, his answer a joke among bootleggers "I'm a salesman."

She smiled; appearing interested "What do you sell?"

Diamond cocked his head slightly; seeming thoughtful "I take care of peoples' needs."

She laughed gently, her mood playful "Sounds good, any money in it?"

Diamond's smile was constant, his desire growing "Some, it keeps me going."

She smiled gently rubbing his hand, "You wanna have a good time, Jack?"

Aroused, the drinks and her actions were having their intended effect, "Yeah…that sounds like a good idea."

"I know a place that's better than this. You wanna try it?"

Diamond looked about, the room was quiet. There seemed to be no one in the room who would pose him a threat, and he was also carrying his gun, as always. He had developed an attitude, after the numerous attempts on his life, that he was destined to have a long life.

"Sure, why not, let's give it a go." Taking her arm, he escorted her from the dining room. As they walked outside, Luciano's man, Al, watched from the shadows. The club she was taking him to would serve him doubles while Connie was served little alcohol. Before midnight, she was instructed to get him back to the room and into bed. Al had been informed that two men were on their way, to end the life of Legs Diamond.

Diamond's men approached the outskirts of the city. Their travel to Albany had been slowed by an accident on the road. Following the instructions given to them over the phone, they exited the main highway and turned down a side street, heading towards the hotel. Neither man spoke. They were professionals, each having been involved in a number of murders for their organization. Knowing the plan, each felt if the woman did her job, this would be an easy hit. They would do the job, quickly leave the city, and drive back to Manhattan. Their alibis were being set up.

Tom Regan had made great time on the road. The two men before him had maintained a reasonable speed limit, not wishing to attract the attention of any local police departments. Regan had no such concerns. Good fortune had been with him; he had escaped the scrutiny of law enforcement for the length of his trip.

The local club was jumping. Diamond was in his element, having enjoyed his time at the Hotsy Totsy Club, he surveyed the scene with the eye of an owner. Once he was firmly in place here, he would make the owner an offer for a piece of the action.

The wait staff had seated them at a table off the dance floor, Connie impressed as the man seemed to be holding his liquor.

"So, Jack, you gonna be setting down any roots up here with your businesses and all?"

Nodding, Diamond was relaxed "Yeah...I'm beginning to like this town. Maybe you and I could see more of each other. I'm due back here in a couple of weeks."

She put her hand on his arm gently caressing it. "I'd like that, Jack, I really would." *Too bad you won't be alive after tomorrow,* she thought to herself. She thought she should have felt bad, but life hadn't exactly been kind to her. The few men in her life had been all about themselves. It was time she had done something for herself. The money she was getting could set her up in another city, allow her to start a new life.

She glanced at her wristwatch; it was time. "Say, honey, you know what I'd like?" She began to caress the back of his neck and they kissed.

He stared into her eyes. The alcohol had lowered his guard effectively. "Yeah, let's go back to my place."

Diamond paid the check and they walked to his car. Connie was afraid that he might not be able to drive but he seemed to be okay. It was no matter, she had a flask in her purse and she would pour him a nightcap.

The car veered but stayed on the road. Back at his hotel, she helped him to the elevator. Getting to his floor she guided him into the hallway, towards his door. Aware of his man in the next room, she made an effort for them to be quiet. Entering the room, she dropped her coat on the floor, and began to kiss him passionately. He smiled at her, obviously drunk. "You're all right, baby. I really like you."

She maneuvered him onto the bed. Once he was on the bed, she began to undress in front of him. Smiling, she could see that he was aroused. She used all of her charms to keep him focused on her. Once she was naked, she went to work on him.

In the lobby, the two hit men from Luciano walked in. Seeing Al seated in the far corner of the room, they walked over and sat, waiting for him to speak.

Al spoke softly, "She has him in room 412. He's been drinking; she has done her job there. They just went up not too long ago. You should wait a bit before you go up. Give her time to do him before you do." He smiled at his attempt at humor.

The men nodded, the one next to him spoke, "Okay, you can leave. We'll tell Lucky what you did here. We're sure he'll be grateful."

Al looked around the room, nodded, got up and walked out.

While the men sat and waited, in the room Connie worked to give the man a proper sendoff. She was pleased that he seemed to be responding better than she would have anticipated.

Tom Regan had reached the outskirts of the city. Realizing he didn't know where the hotel was, he drove towards the center of town. Up ahead he spied a police car on the side of the road, and he pulled over behind it. Getting out, he affected a calm manner, walking up to the driver's window.

Tapping gently on the window, he tried to look confused. "Boy, officer, am I glad I saw you." The police officer calmly returned his stare. "I'm supposed to meet a friend at a hotel on Dove Street, and I lost the directions."

The police officer nodded, knowing the hotel "That would be the Albatross. Go to the second light, make a right, go three blocks, make a left and it's just up on your right."

Regan repeated the instructions. "Thanks very much, officer, you have a good night now."

The officer acknowledged his thanks and rolled up his window. Regan walked calmly back to his car, driving slowly away. Once he had made the turn he sped up. Making the turn onto Dove Street he pulled into the parking lot.

In the lobby, the two men looked at the clock on the wall, then at each other. In silent agreement, they stood, making their way towards the elevator. In the room, Connie lay next to a sleeping Legs Diamond. She smiled, thinking if he could perform like that drunk, she wondered what he would be like sober. The two men stepped off the elevator into the hallway.

Pulling into the parking lot, Regan jumped from the car, running into the building.
Entering the lobby, he ran to the front desk. "What room is Mr. Diamond in?"

The startled clerk responded, "412." Not wanting to wait for the elevator, he headed for the stairs. Taking them two at a time, pulling his gun, he continued up the stairs. The two men stood before the room. The deal was that the girl was to make certain the door was open. Looking up and down the hall, they drew their weapons.

Slowly opening the door, they noted the chair under the knob to the adjoining room, blocking that off. As insurance, a bottle sent to Eddie's room had been drugged. The girl saw them as she dressed, wanting to be out of the room.

Walking to the foot of the bed, they held their weapons on the sleeping man. Their boss had insisted that Diamond know who was responsible for his murder.

One of the men hit Diamond in the ankle with his gun. "Wake up, Legs, we gotta a surprise." Diamond opened his eyes, recognizing his problem at once. "Lucky says goodbye." They opened fire, hitting him three times in the torso. The woman cowered in the corner.

As they stopped to survey their work, shots erupted from behind taking both men down, surprised looks on their faces. A furious Tom Regan walked into the room holding his weapon on the woman.

Connie spoke quickly, "Hey, I'm just an innocent working girl; I just wanna get outta here."

Staring at her, Regan remembered Carla's story, and calmly shot her in the chest. She flew back against the wall a stunned look on her face. He walked over to her, furious at arriving too late to save his friend "He was my friend, you bitch." He shot her again in the head.

He turned back to his friend, kneeling by him. "Ah Legs, I'm sorry; I couldn't get here soon enough."

Diamond opened his eyes. "Tommy...did you get them?"

"Yeah, I got them, Legs. Don't talk; I gotta get you to a doctor."

Diamond weakly shook his head. "I'm done, Tommy. You've been my one true friend." He pointed weakly at the night table. "Get my wallet ... address... safe... money...I'm giving it to you." His head fell to the side, he was dead.

Regan grabbed his wallet off the table. Before leaving, he put another bullet into each of the men on the floor. Wiping tears away, he walked quickly from the room. Going down the back stairs, he went around the building to the parking lot. In the distance, he could hear police sirens approaching. He walked casually to his car and got in, slowly driving towards the sirens. The police cars passed him quickly, and in his rear view mirror, he saw them pull into the parking lot for the hotel.

40

Callahan waited impatiently for Danny to arrive. Seeing him walk through the doors to the squad room, he stared intently at him as he walked over to the desk.

Danny staring, looking curiously at Callahan "You look like hell. Been here all night?"

Callahan spoke with a menace in his voice. "Yes, I've been here all night. I heard an interesting piece of information which really surprised me. I want to talk to you about it. Let's go downstairs where we can talk in private."

Shaw stared at Callahan, unsure as to how to proceed. Tentatively, he said "OK, Mike, let's go"

Shaw followed him out of the room, while the other men continued about their business. Callahan didn't bother to look behind him, hearing the young man following closely at his heels. In the basement, Callahan walked towards the rear interrogation room, which was noted for its privacy. Knowing the reputation of the room, Shaw began to grow nervous, wondering if Callahan had found the missing pages of the diary.

Opening the door, Callahan saw a man writing at the desk. The man looked up, surprised.

"Barney, I need this room for a few minutes, okay?"

The man nodded, gathering his papers, annoyance in his voice "Can't get any privacy to get this damn paperwork done. You gonna be long, Mike?"

"Nope, shouldn't be long at all."

They stood by the door as the detective left. Callahan gestured for Shaw to enter, noticing how Shaw's eyes darted about, Callahan's anger growing. His plans to quietly question the young man vanished, as he grabbed him and threw him over the table. Shaw let out a yelp as he landed, with Callahan was moving quickly towards him.

Shaw quickly recovered, fearfully asking "What the hell is wrong with you?"

Grabbing him, Callahan pulled him up, punching him hard in the stomach. "Where are they, you little bastard, where are they?"

Shaw was in complete panic. "Where are what?"

Drawing his fist back, Callahan punched him in the face hard. Shaw went flying across the room, landing roughly on the floor. Mike's anger seething, he snarled "The pages, you little bastard, you know what I'm talking about."

Callahan moved towards him again, with Shaw trying to scurry away like a crab.

Quickly closing in on him, Callahan pulled him off the floor again. Shaw began to whimper as Callahan punched him hard again in the stomach. Shaw collapsed on the ground, gasping for air. Callahan moving menacingly towards him, and Shaw held out his hand.

Shaw desperately yelled "Wait, for Christ's sake; wait a minute!"

Callahan stopped short, barely containing himself "You gonna tell me what happened to them pages, or do we continue?"

Breathing heavily, fear in his eyes "Mike, I swear I don't know what you're talking about."

Callahan watched him intently, his anger ebbing "Get up, sit there," pointing at a chair. Callahan stood near him, assuming a commanding position over the frightened, young, man.

"A detective told me that the caretakers from your dad's estate dropped off a note of some sorts, which he put in an envelope, and left on my desk. I'm betting they were pages or had something to do with Eileen's diary, and I think you took them." His voice was full of menace.

Shaw couldn't remember being this scared. "Listen to me, Mike, I swear on my mother's grave, I did not see any envelope and I did not take it."

Almost snarling, his anger rising again "I think you are so full of shit and, if I have to, I'll beat it out of you."

Pathetically, resignation in his voice "You do what you feel, Mike, but I gotta tell you that when you're finished, you still ain't gonna have anything, cause I ain't got whatever it is you're looking for."

Frustrated, unsure as to whether or not the young man was telling the truth, Trying another approach "All right, come on, smart guy, let's go to my desk." Turning, Callahan walked to the door.

Opening the door, he saw Barney standing there. "Everything okay, Mike?"

Walking past him, Callahan kept his eyes on Shaw "Yeah, couldn't be better, Barney."

Walking quickly upstairs, they were back in the squad room. A couple of men looked up, and upon noting the condition of Shaw's face, they smiled.

As they stood at his desk Mike gestured at it, speaking as though to a child "Where could the envelope go, Danny? Where could it vanish to?"

Shaw looked furtively about the desk. "I dunno, Mike."

Still angry, Callahan walked over to the desk and grabbed it. He lifted the desk in a jerking motion, moving it slightly then stopping. They both heard the slight noise of something dropping between the wall and the desk. Grabbing the side of the desk, Callahan moved it a couple of inches away from the wall. Looking down, he saw a white envelope with writing on it. Kneeling down, he picked up the envelope, and pushed the desk back against the wall. Callahan wanting to see the contents of the envelope "C'mon, back downstairs."

Walking downstairs again, the two men entered the first interrogation room. Pulling a penknife, Callahan carefully opened the envelope. Shaw sat quietly across from him as he read the pages of Eileen O'Sullivan's diary. After a few minutes, Callahan slowly looked up at Shaw.

Shaw had an angry look on his face. "I told you I didn't have the damn pages."

Callahan was slightly taken aback, replied "Yeah…I'm sorry about that. You gotta admit you were the logical suspect."

Shaw looked like he might cry. "Yeah, pretty convenient for you." Pointing at the pages on the table, he wanted to know "What do they say?"

"They say enough to bring your father in for questioning on a number of issues including Eileen's murder."

Shaw drew in a breath, actually surprised "Really…my dad?"

"Yeah, Dan. Your dad."

Tom Regan drove at a leisurely pace back to Manhattan. His thoughts kept returning to the scene in the hotel room, and the look on his friend's face as he died. *If I had only gotten there a few minutes sooner*, he kept thinking.

At a diner where he had stopped for a cup of coffee and a sandwich, he looked through Legs' wallet. He had found a small piece of paper with a street address, and what appeared to be a combination. Smiling, Regan recalled the numbers to be Legs' lucky numbers, thinking that while most men had a number or two they considered lucky, Legs had a handful of them. He thought with sadness that 412 certainly wasn't among the numbers Legs considered lucky.

He had never heard Legs mention the address on the paper. That was fine with him; his friend was entitled to his secrets. Without thinking, he reached again under his coat to feel for his gun again, touching it giving him a feeling of security. He knew now with Legs out of the way that Luciano would come looking for him. He would get whatever money Legs had stashed in the safe, get Carla, and leave town.

He had some contacts in Philadelphia; he would start a new life with her. He was going to stop by the office, and tell whoever was there what had happened. Legs' men would need to fend for themselves.

They had been living on the edge since Rothstein's murder; it was Legs' relationship with the senator that allowed them to continue in business. Briefly, he had considered approaching the senator for his support, but had decided against it. He had no desire to lead a mob, especially with a man like Luciano after him. Looking at his wristwatch, he saw that he was making good time. His first stop in the city would be at Legs' place to get the money. Once he had that, he would go to Carla's.

In Manhattan, Lucky Luciano listened to his man in Albany as he related the events of the past evening to him. Wondering, *who had taken out his men?*

He knew that Diamond's bodyguard had been drugged, and that no one else was there. It wasn't a cop, according to his man, or the reports coming over the radio. They said that a *mystery man* had shot and killed the murderers of the infamous Legs Diamond. It was also noted that a woman had been killed in the room with Diamond and his men. Al had said that the local, who had provided the woman, was upset over losing his *merchandise.* Luciano understood the man's feeling and agreed to pay the man for his loss.

There was a knock on his door. It roused him from his thoughts "Come," and the maid Carla entered. She gave him a slight curtsy, and he waved for her to go ahead and clean.

"All right Al, all things considered, you did good. I want you to spend a couple of days there, see if you can find out anything else. See if they get any leads on the shooter of our guys. How the hell do I know? Tell em you're a reporter, do I have to think of everything?"

He hung up the phone. If he had to, he would have bet money that somehow Tom Regan was involved. He watched the maid as she cleaned, his thoughts wandering.

Another knock on the door. He grew slightly annoyed. "Yeah, come in."

"Excuse me, boss, someone wants to see you."

Frowning, his annoyance grew "Is this necessary?"

"I dunno, boss. He says he has some information for you."

Sighing, waving his hand at the door "Okay, bring him in."

Opening the door, the guard ushered an old man into the room. Cleaning, the maid turned to see the man and uttered, "Poppa, why are you here?"

Glancing at her, the man walked past her. Hat in hand he stood before Luciano's desk.

Staring at him curiously, he asked, "You're Carla's father?"

The man nodded.

Luciano gestured to a chair, wondering why the man was here "Please sit down."

Gesturing, his hands open wide; he asked "What do you have to tell me?"

Carla began to fear what she might hear. She knew that her father hated Tommy, for what she had told him, and of his threat against him. She began to pray that her father wasn't about to say something that could never be taken back.

Luciano waited quietly.

The man coughed slightly. He hadn't expected his daughter to be present "Sir, my daughter has betrayed you."

Luciano stared at the man and smiled. "What the hell are you talking about? She's only the maid."

Carla stared at him, unbelieving that he could do this.

The father continued "She has been seeing a man who works for Legs Diamond; she tells him what she hears in here."

Luciano's demeanor turned to ice. Looking at the young girl, noting the look of shock on her face, he thought the man spoke the truth. "Carla, is this true?"

As if in a daze, she shook her head. "No, sir, he works on the docks. He's not Italian, but he is a good man."

Anger rose in the father, he spat out "Why does he drive the nice car? Answer that!"

"His boss lets him take it sometimes when we go out. Poppa, you are only doing this because he said if you touched me again, he would kill you."

The man shot up, his face livid "Liar...whore, you know I speak the truth."

Luciano raised his voice, "You sit down. You try to touch your own daughter?"

"She lies, Mr. Luciano, because I confront her and I want her to marry a good Italian man."

His opinion of the man had fallen to an absolute low, given the daughter's accusation. Filled with rage the daughter drew close to the father, her anger coming out "You're sick, you disgust me. After today, I'm leaving with Tommy, and I will never see you again."

Luciano jerked at the mention of the name. "Carla, what did you say your boyfriend's name is?"

She looked around surprised, realizing her mistake "Joe...its Joe."

Luciano got up from behind his desk and walked around to her. Standing in front of her, he spoke in a low even voice, "You just called him Tommy a few seconds ago. So...which is it? Joe or Tommy?" Turning to his man at the door he pointed at the father. "Take him to another room and hold him."

Carla turned to leave, but Luciano grabbed her arm, hard. Alone with her, he held her arm in a viselike grip. "You haven't answered my question. What is your boyfriend's name? I want to know, and I want to know now."

She began to whimper. "Please, sir, you're hurting me."

He increased the pressure on her arm, a cruel smile on his face, enjoying himself "You think this hurts...you ain't seen nothing yet." In a lightning fast motion, he slapped her hard across the face. The blow stunning her, she went weak in the knees. Grabbing her other arm, he held her up. "I'm gonna ask you one more time...what's your boyfriend's name?"

She began to speak, and he drew back his hand to strike her.

"It's Tommy."

"Would that be Tommy Regan?"

Looking at him surprised, she slowly nodded.

Punching her hard in the stomach, he let her drop to the floor.

Gasping she lay at his feet.

"So your father wasn't lying. What did you tell Mr. Regan?"

Trying to catch her breath, her voice desperate "Just that...just that you were mad at his boss and wanted to kill him."

Luciano shook his head disbelieving, "Hell, Diamond knew that already. What else you tell him?"

"Nothing...I swear it."

He slowly shook his head. "Why don't I believe you? A young woman in love with a smooth operator like Tom Regan, I'm betting you told him a lot more."

He grabbed her by the hair and pulled her up, shoving her into one of the chairs by his desk. Turning to the door, he spoke to his man quietly watching the scene "Tell Pete to bring the old man back."

Entering the room, the guard moved the father to the chair next to his daughter. Luciano stared at them, a disgusted look on his face. He spoke to them both "What am I gonna do with you?"

The father stared at him, questioning, "What do you mean, sir? I will take my daughter; you will never see us again."

Luciano seemed to consider that for a moment. Shaking his head slowly, he disagreed "I don't think so. I do owe you a debt in that you revealed a traitor to me. I won't forget this...and you don't forget who I am."

Staring at Carla, his face took on a hard demeanor. "I give you a good job, and this is how you repay me? You tell my business to a rival for a roll in the sheets. I'm sorry...but you are going away forever."

Carla stared at him in shock. She turned slowly to her father, her voice venomous "I hope you're happy, you bastard."

Looking at the father, he was done with him "You're free to leave. If you ever mention this to anyone, you will die badly. Do you understand me?"

The old man nodded slowly. He looked at his daughter, who refused to return his gaze.

Luciano yelled at the father, "Get out of here."

The father quickly got up and left.

"Now, Carla, I'm sorry...I always liked you, but you know what I have to do."

Leaping out of her chair like a cat, she was on Luciano in an instant, clawing at his face. Luciano fought to fend her off as his man came around and struck the side of her head with his gun. She fell to the floor limp.

"Sorry, boss, I..." Luciano waved him off. Laughing, Luciano was impressed, "What a tiger...too bad. Get one of the boys. I don't want her to suffer; a clean kill, and bury her. I don't want the animals picking at her, you hear?"

"Yeah, boss, I hear you." Picking her up, he carried her out of the room.

Sitting back down at his desk, Luciano wondered what he would have for lunch.

41

Tom Regan pulled up to the address on the piece of paper from Legs' wallet. It was a quiet neighborhood, with everyone seeming to be going about their own business. Again, he touched the gun in his shoulder holster, his personal security assurance. Casually getting out of the car, he walked into the building, hoping he wouldn't meet any of the tenants as he made his way to the door of the apartment. Taking out the keys he had taken from Legs along with the wallet, he took a second to look at them. Upon inserting the likely candidate into the lock, the door opened.

Regan looked up and down the hallway. Again seeing no one, he entered the room. Shutting the door, he stared around the apartment. The room was sparsely furnished; he smiled, thinking it wasn't like Legs, who enjoyed more style. He began to move slowly around the room, looking about, as he searched for the safe.

Walking into the bedroom, he spied an extremely bad painting on the wall, above the bed. Moving towards it he stepped onto the mattress, kneeling on the bed, he lifted it off the wall. Placing the painting on the bed behind him, he turned to see a wall safe. Smiling, he got out the paper and studied the numbers.

Working the combination to the safe, he quickly had it open, gasping slightly at the stacks of dollars inside. Staring at the money, he chuckled to himself; looking again to be sure he was alone.

Stacking the money on the mattress, when the safe was empty, he moved off the bed. He began to count the money. When he was finished he whistled, he was filled with gratitude "Legs, if you can hear me, you are truly the best friend I ever had. I don't think I can ever thank you enough."

He looked quickly about the room for a suitcase, knowing he didn't want to leave the apartment carrying the money in a bedspread. Walking quickly over to a closet, he found a satchel. Laughing, he shook his head "You were always prepared, Legs." He began to neatly stack the money in the suitcase. He thought happily that this would more than give him and Carla a new start somewhere else. He could picture her face when he told her about the money and his plans for the two of them. Feeling as happy as he could remember, everything would all be different now. His friend had given him the opportunity to start fresh, with a woman he loved. The suitcase full, he closed it. Closing the safe, he re-hung the painting, and gave the room a final check, touching his gun as he did.

Smiling, he walked towards the door, opening it slowly. Sticking his head slightly out, he looked up and down the hallway. Seeing no one, he stepped out into the hall, quickly making his way to the door. Opening the front door, he looked up and down the street. Seeing nothing to concern him, he walked quickly down and to his car.

Driving away from the apartment, he gave a silent prayer of thanks to his friend again. Stepping on the gas, he drove towards the warehouse to tell the men what had happened in Albany.

Callahan sat in the interrogation room with Danny. He spoke kindly "We're going to bring your father in for questioning. You feel you're up to that?"

Shaw thought for a second and nodded, he easily lied "Yeah...I can do that. If he's guilty of a crime, I can't protect him. It would be wrong."

Staring at him for a moment, Callahan nodded. "Okay then, partner, let's go see your father." Taking the pages from the diary, Callahan put them in his pocket. Standing up, he told Shaw "I'll tell Kroon where we're going, you wait by my desk."

The two men walked upstairs, with Shaw heading towards the front of the building where the payphones were located. Looking about quickly, he jumped into a booth, dialing his father's number. Waiting impatiently while the phone rang, he looked nervously about.

"Shaw," his father's voice.

"Dad, listen, Callahan found the pages. There was nothing I could do; we're coming out to see you. He wants to bring you in for questioning."

Unusually calm, he replied "Thank you for the warning, Daniel. We'll see you soon." He hung up the phone.

Hanging up the phone on his end, Shaw almost jumped out of the booth. Looking about, he breathed a sigh of relief as he didn't see Callahan. Moving over to a bench, he sat, trying to affect a casual attitude. Within a few moments, Callahan came walking into the room.

Shaw asked casually "Did you tell Kroon?"

"He wasn't in, I left a note. Did you sign out the car?"

Shaw looked at him, surprised "Mike, the senior man has to do that, you know that."

Callahan gave a shake of his head, accepting the comment "All right, I'll take care of it."

Shaw moved towards the inside of the building.

Callahan asked "Hey, where you going?"

Without looking back, Shaw raised a hand waving "Gotta hit the can quick, sorry."

Shaking his head, Callahan went back to signing out a car.

Shaw moved quickly through the squad room. Looking into Kroon's office, he noted it was empty. He casually walked in and looking about he noticed an envelope on the desk with Mike's name on the bottom. Glancing about, he casually palmed the envelope, putting it in his pocket. He made his way back to the front of the building, seeing Mike waiting for him.

Smiling, Callahan asked "Everything come out OK?"

Confused for a second he smiled back, glad that Mike had calmed down "Yeah...I'm ready to go."

Callahan nodded. "Good, let's go."

Pulling up in front of the warehouse, Regan got out of his car and walked quickly into the building. The men were working. A couple of them looked up, seeing him, they called out greetings.

Regan went to the office. Seeing the foreman, he called out "Marty, get the guys, I got something to tell everyone."

After a few minutes, the men were standing in front of the office. Regan stood and spoke, "I got some bad news boys. Legs is dead."

The men looked at each other in confusion, unsure of how to react.

One of the men asked "What are you saying, Tom? We ain't heard nothing"

"Bobby, trust me, I held him in my arms as he died. Two of Luciano's men did the hit. I got em both, and the bitch that set him up."

Another of the men asked "What are we gonna do?"

"Luciano is going to move in hard on us. You guys gotta make other plans."

"Tom, why don't you take over?" A couple of the men nodded, voicing agreement.

"Thanks, guys, but I ain't a leader, not like Legs. I'm gonna blow town. Luciano has a contract out on me. I wanna live a little bit longer. There should be some payroll in the safe. I'm gonna split it up between everyone, fair and square."

The men nodded and began to roll down their sleeves. Looking about, Regan thought *they were all considering their options.* Opening the safe, Regan divided the money giving the men their walking money. They all wished each other well and some left the building. A couple of the men stayed to drink a toast to their late boss.

When the last man had been paid off, Regan went back to the safe, removing a notebook from the bottom shelf. Looking through the book, Regan smiled as he read the ledger of the payments made by Legs to the senator and to other local politicians. He whistled as he saw some of the names in the journal. Quickly checking the remaining documents in the safe, he noted there was nothing of interest and he closed and locked the safe.

Saying his goodbyes again to the few men remaining, he got in his car and drove away. Knowing that today was normally Carla's day off, he hoped she would be at her house. Making good time, he pulled over, stopping a few houses away, wanting to be certain that no one was watching the house.

Stepping out of his car, he walked up to the house and knocked on the front door. Feeling good, he thought if the father gave him any lip, he would ignore him for Carla's sake. Knocking a couple of times, he listened for any sign of activity inside. He thought he heard a radio playing, so he tested the door handle and it opened.

Sticking his head inside, he called her name. No answer. Hearing the radio playing in the back room, he walked towards it. Entering the room, he saw her father sitting alone in a chair, with a half empty bottle of liquor on the table next to him.

The old man looked up at him; bleary eyed, he appeared to have been crying. Regan grew concerned, moving closer to him "Mr. DiSomona is there a problem? I'm here to see Carla."

The old man stared at him, not speaking. His face grew hard. "Problem...yeah, there's a problem. You are the problem."

Shaking his head, Regan had no desire to get in an argument with the old man. "Look, sir, I just want to speak with your daughter; then we're outta here."

The man laughed a sad hollow laughter. "No, Irishman, she won't be going anywhere with you...or anyone."

Regan's concern grew his tone fearful "What have you done? Where is Carla?"

The father started to sob. "It's your entire fault...your fault."

Walking over, Regan grabbed the lapels of the man's jacket, lifting him out of the chair. Eye to eye, his voice full of menace, afraid of the answer, he asked "Where is Carla?"

The old man stared down to the floor, unable to maintain eye contact with Regan. "Her boss, he find out that she speak with you. He did what he had to do."

A cold stab of fear pierced Regan's heart. Shaking the man to get his attention, he asked roughly "How did Luciano find out about me?"

Defiance, her father spat back "I told him. I thought he would let her go, then she would be here where she belongs."

The fear in Regan's heart turned to anger. Incredulous, torn between rage and disbelief "You ratted out your own daughter?" The old man started to cry. Shaking him harder, Regan pressed the broken man "What did Luciano say, what did he say?"

The old man was crying freely, realizing his loss "He say she goes away, forever. It's all your fault."

Releasing the old man, he tossed him back into the chair, unable to believe what he had just heard. Her father had ratted her out to Luciano, and she was now most probably dead. A dark emptiness overwhelmed Regan, he wanted to scream. Looking down at the old man, his hatred grew to consume him. Looking about the room, he walked over to the couch, and grabbed a pillow. Walking back to the old man, who was crying, Regan pulled his gun and, using the pillow to muffle the noise, shot him in the face. Pulling the pillow away, he saw that the bullet had done its job. Carla's father was dead.

He stared at the dead man for a few moments. "Now, apologize to your daughter."

Regan walked out of the house, pulling the brim of his hat down to hide his face. Getting into his car, he began to drive away, wiping tears from his eyes.

42

Shaw looking for Mike's strategy in dealing with his father "So, Mike, you're going to confront him with the pages from Eileen's diary?"

Confident with the diary pages in his pocket, Callahan replied "Yeah, it seems pretty clear; he had the large guy that works for him kill Eileen on that party boat, never expecting that a storm would wash her body to shore. It may not be a rock solid case, but I'm willing to go with it, and at the very least, it will probably end his career in the Senate."

Shaw whistled slightly, feigning support "Hell that alone will kill him. He loves being a senator."

Callahan gave him a hard look. "Too bad about that."

"You don't gotta worry, Mike. I'll have your back on this. Yost can be an unpredictable guy."

Callahan looked at him confused, asking "Who?"

Shaw smiled, enjoying his confusion "The big guy."

Nodding, Callahan simply said "Oh."

Considering the situation, Callahan added "We're also going to take the Irish couple in for questioning. They can follow us back to the city."

Shaw looked out the window thinking the Fitzgibbons were probably still away at their family funeral. *The Irish were very big on funerals,* he thought.

Up ahead, they saw the entrance for the road to the estate. Slowing down, Callahan noted that traffic was heavier than he expected. Every time he drove, it seemed that there were more automobiles on the road.

Looking over at Shaw, Callahan saw that he didn't seem to be agitated, which was good. If there was a problem, he had to count on the kid. He couldn't wait until next week, when Doc was due to return full time, and then he could put the last couple of weeks behind him

Driving around a slight bend, he came up to the entrance for the estate. Slowing down, he made the turn and drove up the driveway to the main house.

Looking about, Callahan was impressed by the house and the grounds, wondering how, with all of his advantages, Danny didn't turn out better. They walked up to the front door and Danny went to open it. Callahan grabbed his arm and Shaw looked at him, confused. "What?" he asked.

"We're on official police business. We have to be invited into the house."

Shaw steeped away from the door. Callahan knocked, hearing the echo in the house. After a few moments, the door opened and the German stood there looking at them. Seeing Danny, the German smiled. Seeming cordial "It's good to see you, sir. Is your father expecting you?"

"No, Gerhardt, Can we come in?"

The German looked a little confused. "Of course, sir, you live here."

Gesturing towards Callahan, Shaw added "This is my partner, Detective Callahan."

Yost nodded, he spoke respectfully "Detective."

Callahan sized up the large man, thinking that even with a bad leg he would be a formidable opponent in a fight.

Yost spoke to Shaw "I will inform your father that you are here. I was preparing a lunch; he wanted to take the boat out and have lunch on the water."

Shaw took the lead, gesturing to Callahan "We'll wait in the study."

"Very good, sir."

Callahan followed Shaw into the study. Looking about the room, he was impressed, thinking it reminded him of the New York Library.

After a few minutes, Senator Thomas Shaw walked into the room smiling, at ease. He walked over to his son and gave him a warm embrace, smiling broadly "Good to see you, Dan, what brings you out here?"

Shaw pointed to Callahan. "This is my partner, Detective Michael Callahan, dad. He'd like to speak with you."

The senator, still smiling, looked at Mike, "Certainly, but why don't we take this out on the boat? It's so hot; I thought that lunch out on the water might be more comfortable."

Seeming to think for a second, Callahan shrugged. "Certainly, senator."

Shaw seemed pleased, gesturing "Good, then, let's head down to the dock."

As they walked, Shaw controlled the conversation, working his audience "Detective, it's a pleasure to meet you finally. Dan had spoken very highly of you." Giving him a conspiratorial wink, feigning friendship "If there is ever anything I can do to assist you in your career, you just have to ask. It's the least I can do, after the way you've worked with my son, showing him the ropes, so to speak."

Callahan took in the modest yacht thinking it probably cost as much as a small house. The men boarded the yacht easily. With Yost expertly casting off the lines, they were shortly under way. Walking to the aftdeck Shaw gestured to them, saying "Please be seated. Can I get you a drink?"

Callahan spoke, "Nothing for us, we're on duty."

The yacht cruised smoothly in the calm waters of Long Island Sound. Callahan noted the lack of other boats in their immediate area.

The senator smiled, asking almost playfully "Well, you won't mind if I have one, will you?"

Callahan replied blandly, "Not at all, senator, it's your boat."

After a short time, the engines slowed and the yacht stopped. The German reappeared and began to set the table for lunch. The lunch set, the German disappeared into the cabin.

Playing the host, the senator continued "Please, help yourselves. So, detective, what is it you wish to speak with me about?"

Callahan took a bite of a sandwich and swallowing; Callahan spoke slowly "A couple of weeks ago, the body of a young woman washed ashore on the south shore of Long Island. She had been murdered."

Shaw seemed to think for a moment then nodded. "Yes, I recall reading about that in the papers, a tragic event."

"We have reason to believe that you were acquainted with this woman."

Surprisingly, he admitted "Yes...I knew her. I was terribly sorry to hear what had happened."

"Would you mind discussing the nature of your relationship with the young lady?"

Uncomfortable, with a note of sadness in his voice, he glanced quickly at Callahan "We had dated a couple of times. She was a delightful young lady." Shaw looked directly at Callahan, casting a knowing glance "My wife died when Daniel was quite young. I've devoted my life to public service. What can I say? I enjoyed the company of an attractive young lady." Shaw seemed lost in thought for a moment. "After we had dated a few times, she approached me and said that she had met a young man. She said they were happy together. Well...there was nothing to say? With the difference in our ages, I wished her the best and we parted as friends."

Callahan nodded, continuing the discussion "Were you aware that the young lady had kept a diary?"

Shaw seemed genuinely surprised, and excited "Excellent. Has it provided any clues as to her killer?"

Watching the senator, Callahan replied "Sadly, no, we weren't able to recover the diary."

Shaw had a momentary thought of the ashes of the diary, in his fireplace. "That's too bad. What is the status of the investigation?"

Callahan kept an even tone, his eyes clearly on the senator "Well, it seems that your retainers provided us with a couple of pages from the diary."

Surprise, Shaw continued "Really, how did they come by it?"

"It would seem they were friendly with Eileen."

Shaw thought for a second, looking innocently at Callahan "Imagine that."

Callahan took control of the conversation "Senator, we have reviewed those pages and you are mentioned quite prominently. In fact, there are a number of references to you receiving payoffs from Legs Diamond, and to your threat to kill her if she ever told anyone of your dealings with the mobs."

Shaw's pleasant demeanor dropped, all pretense of friendliness gone "You would, of course, have a difficult time proving the veracity of those pages in a court of law."

Callahan nodded, meeting his gaze "Agreed, but it would be interesting to audit your finances to see if any unaccounted money turns up."

Standing up, Shaw walked over to the drink table. When he turned, he held a small handgun, pointing it at Callahan. "Take his weapon, Danny."

"Dad?"

"Do it now, son." Walking over, Danny removed Callahan's weapon from his holster. Callahan stared at Danny, fury in his eyes. Callahan fought to contain himself. "Does he have the pages with him?"

Danny replied "Yes."

The senator spoke confidently "Good, get them too, please."

Shaw reached in and took the diary pages, handing them to his father.

Callahan glared at Danny, his voice full of contempt "Kroon knows we're here. I left him a note."

Danny smiled, pulling the envelope from his pocket. "You mean this note?"

"You miserable little bastard."

"He's my dad."

The senator spoke "Detective, I won't insult you by asking how much money it would take to make this all go away. Daniel tells me you are quite incorruptible and, of course, there is the personal nature of this investigation." Shaw smiled, keeping his weapon trained on Callahan. "Now that I have these pages, your investigation is, I think, over."

Controlling his anger, Callahan spoke slowly, "I won't let this go. You didn't have to kill her, you bastard."

Shaw appeared confused, his eyes wild "Kill her...I didn't kill her. Why would I kill her? I loved her." He grew angry, his emotion taking hold "You think I had her murdered? What type of man do you think I am?"

As he spoke, he gestured to Callahan using his gun, his face red with anger, and then he gasped, as if struck. He stared at the two men, a look of surprise on his face. Taking a few stutter steps backwards to the rail, he sat against it. Looking down at his chest, a red stain began to blossom below his heart. Looking back at the two men he gave a half smile, and as his eyes rolled back he fell overboard.

Danny shouted "Dad!" Shaw and Callahan ran to the rail, watching as the senator's body slowly sank into the waters.

On the beach, Lucky Luciano's man watched the scene through the scope on his high-powered rifle. His instructions had been clear, if the cop was in danger, he was to do whatever was necessary to protect him. Quickly walking to his car, he put the rifle in the trunk and drove off.

On the yacht, the German, having watched from the cabin, came out on deck. Staring at Callahan he asked "What have you done?" He took a step towards Callahan, and a shot rang out, the German dropping to the deck.

Startled, Callahan turned to see Danny, weapon in hand, staring at the fallen man. Grabbing the weapon, he asked, amazed "What the hell did you do that for?"

"I thought he was going to attack you."

Callahan walked over to the German who was having trouble breathing.

Yost stared up at Danny, seeing the smug look on his face. Looking at Callahan, a look came into his eyes "Detective...that motorcycle police man that was murdered, Danny did it."

Callahan was stunned, asking "Are you saying he killed a cop?"

"*Ja*, I vas there...he did it with that gun."

Callahan turned sharply, glared at Shaw "Stand over there, you little shit. You move and I'll kill you." Turning back to the German, he moved closer to the dying man "You are saying that Daniel Shaw murdered that cop on Long Island with this weapon?"

Yost continued "I want you to know... the senator didn't order the girl's death. I took it on myself to free him from her. He was a great man; she was bad for him"

Staring at the dying man, Callahan was stunned "History will judge him. You saw Danny shoot that police officer?"

Weakly, Yost spoke "Yes, I'm saying that...also...he...killed...," and he died.

Callahan stood up, stunned at the events of the last few minutes. Turning towards Danny, he took out his handcuffs and cuffed him behind his back.

"Mike, come on, be smart here. I'm the sole beneficiary; I can make you very rich. All we need to do is to get our stories straight."

Callahan turned Shaw around and punched him in the face. Looking down at him, contempt dripping from his voice "You shot a cop; you're going to get the chair." He picked up the diary pages from where the senator had dropped them. He then picked up his weapon and put it back in his holster.

Not being much of a sailor, it took a while for Callahan to free the anchor and to drive the boat back in, choosing to beach it rather than go through the trouble of docking it. Damaging the boat didn't concern him, since the senator was dead. Danny had kept asking for help up to sit in a chair, but Callahan had ignored him.

Walking him up to the estate he called the local police, who, once they had arrived, took command of the crime scene. Callahan explained the situation to the officer in charge, saying that he was taking Shaw into custody.

Driving back into the city Shaw had sat silently, his eyes darting , he avoided looking at Callahan.

Arriving at the station, Callahan walked Shaw into the building. A couple of officers, upon seeing the two men, stopped, wondering why the young man was cuffed.

Seeing Kroon across the room, Callahan called out "Lieutenant, gotta minute?"

Walking over, Kroon, seeing Danny, asked, "What's going on?"

Callahan spoke coldly "He killed that motorcycle cop on Long Island. I got a deathbed confession from the senator's man."

Kroon stared at Danny, incredulous. "You killed a cop?" turning, full of rage "Marty, book this piece of garbage, get him out of my sight, and put a suicide watch on him." The officer came over and took Danny away. The room was deathly quiet, as everyone watched him being taken away.

Kroon looked at Callahan, "In my office, Mike." He turned and Callahan followed him. He walked behind his desk and sat, Gesturing "Take a seat, Mike. Tell me what's been going on."

Callahan told him the story, giving him the pages to read.

Surprised, Kroon spoke "So, let me get this straight, the senator was shot by somebody, probably on the beach?"

"Yeah, I don't know what happened, honestly, Jack."

Kroon held up a hand, dismissing any argument "I believe you."

Pointing at the pages, Kroon gave his painful smile "Good stuff. I'd have liked to have seen the entire diary."

"Yeah, me too."

Kroon held out his hand, back to basics "Give me his weapon, I'll log it in as evidence and arrange for a ballistics test. If they match, I've no doubt the D.A. will push for the death penalty."

Callahan handed him the weapon.

"Mike, something else came up, while you were out. We got a call from your friend Claire. Charles Maitland passed away last night looks like a heart attack. Why don't you go see Ginny? You can do your paperwork later."

Callahan stood, appreciative "Thanks, Jack." He quickly walked out.

Commandeering a police car, Callahan had them run the siren to clear traffic. Arriving, he thanked the officers, and ran into the lobby of the townhouse. The butler who had answered the door recognized Callahan, and asked him to follow as they walked into Ginny's home. Callahan, as always, was impressed with the décor, thinking it was elegant and tastefully done, as he would have expected from his friend.

They walked towards a large set of double doors. The butler paused to knock and then slowly opened the door, "Michael Callahan is here, ma'am."

From inside, "Thank you, Fairchild, please show him in."

The butler ushered Mike into the room. Ginny was seated on a couch, looking as elegant as ever. She rose slowly as Mike walked over to her. They embraced.

"I'm glad you're finally here, Michael. It's been an absolutely horrid day."

They sat on the couch.

"I know; I heard that Charles suffered a heart attack."

Nodding, her eyes sad "That's the preliminary autopsy finding. I should know more later."

Mike gave her a small smile; changing the subject "You're not going to believe what happened with the case."

Ginny cocked her head slightly, raising an eyebrow she fixed him with a beautiful quizzical look.

Mike relayed the events of the last twenty-four hours the finding of the pages, the drive out to the estate, the trip out on the boat and the surprising death of Senator Thomas Shaw.

Ginny rose, asking with a degree of affection "Would you care for a drink?"

Nodding, Callahan spoke slowly "Please."

Gazing at his friend, he felt he had to ask "Ginny, you didn't have anything to do with the senator's demise, did you?"

She turned, holding out his drink, then sat, taking a sip of hers. Looking into his eyes, her face took on a hard, cold look. "Do you think for a moment I would allow you to investigate Eileen's murder with that little shit and not have your back?"

Callahan slowly shook his head, answering gratefully "No, I suppose not. Thank you, he was in a rage, he might have shot me."

She smiled warmly at him, dismissing the conversation "You're welcome. Let's not speak of this again."

Callahan smiling nodded, adding "You're not going to believe what else happened." He told her the story of the German's deathbed confession regarding the murder of the police officer.

Surprised, she asked "That's incredible. Why would Danny kill a police officer?"

"I don't know. He died before he could say more. Also, it seems that Shaw didn't order Eileen killed. The German admitted that he killed Eileen, without orders from Shaw. He wanted to free him from her influence."

"Incredible."

Shaking her head, "So let me get this straight, the German started to mention another killing and he died before he could tell you. I don't suppose we'll ever know who the other person Danny was supposed to have killed."

On the coffee table in front of them was a local paper with the headline stating that Judge Joseph Crater was missing.

Ginny glanced at her wristwatch. "Michael, would you stay for dinner?"

"Of course."

"Good, there's much I'd like to discuss with you."

Contact Stephen Larkin at:

Facebook.com/StephenBLarkin

www.stephenblarkin.com

Murder on Dog Island takes up where **The Kiss Off ends.** The sequel is available now on Amazon.

54292670R00175

Made in the USA
Middletown, DE
13 July 2019